Carbon-14
The Shroud of Turin

An Amari Johnston novel, volume 1

By R.A. WILLIAMS

D1713902

Printed in the United States of America
First Printing: September 2017
Amazon

ISBN: 978-1-522-03185-7

The characters and events in this novel are fictitious. Whereas some members of the Shroud of Turin Research Project are mentioned by name, any other similarity to real persons, living or dead, is coincidental and unintentional. In no way does the author imply that the AMS laboratory at the University of Arizona, nor the team that participated in the sampling process in Italy, were involved in any conspiracy to report misleading results from the carbon date performed on the Shroud of Turin in 1988.

Although this is a work of fiction, it was, however, inspired by a discovery that M. Sue Benford made in 2000. To learn more about her story, you can view the Discovery Channel documentary called *Unwrapping the Shroud.* For more detailed information, read *Wrapped Up in The Shroud*, written by her husband, Joseph. G. Marino.

Every fact mentioned about the Shroud of Turin in this novel is scientifically verifiable truth. The following books and documentaries were used for research:

Antonacci, Mark. *Test the Shroud: At the Atomic and Molecular Levels.* LE Press, LLC, 2016. Print.

Garza-Valdes, Leoncio A. *The DNA of God?* New York: Berkley, 2001. Print.

Grant, Jeffrey R., Dr. *Jesus: The Great Debate.* Toronto: Frontier Research Publications, 1999. Print.

Heller, John H. *Report on the Shroud of Turin.* Boston: Houghton Mifflin, 1984. Print.

Marino, Joseph G. *Wrapped up in the Shroud: Chronicle of a Passion: A Former Monk's Life-changing Odyssey into the Enigma of Christianity's Most Revered Relic.* St. Louis, MO: Cradle, 2011. Print.

The Real Face of Jesus. Dir. Trey Nelson. A & E Television Networks, 2011. DVD.

Unwrapping the Shroud. Prod. Michael Epstein. Discovery Channel, 2008. DVD.

Mr. Antonacci's book, *Test the Shroud: At the Atomic and Molecular Levels,* is in this author's opinion the most comprehensive reference available about the Shroud of Turin. It is highly recommended for anyone who wants detailed scientific and historical information about the Shroud.

http://testtheshroud.org

To my editor, Carla Rossi. If there is the thinnest of a romantic thread in this novel, it's thanks to you. http://carlarossi.com/

Thanks to Candace Sorondo for all your encouragement over the years and for giving this novel a final proofread.

Thanks also to my dad, Ted Williams, a former NASA engineer with attention to detail. His input was invaluable, and without his encouragement to write, this book would never have been written.

A very special thanks to my wife and daughter for their love, patience, and encouragement.

And most of all, thanks to God, through whom all things were made.

So Joseph bought some linen cloth, took down the body, wrapped it in the linen, and placed it in a tomb cut out of rock. Then he rolled a stone against the entrance of the tomb. (Mark 15:46)

He bent over and looked in at the strips of linen lying there but did not go in. Then Simon Peter came along behind him and went straight into the tomb. He saw the strips of linen lying there, as well as the cloth that had been wrapped around Jesus' head. The cloth was still lying in its place, separate from the linen. Finally the other disciple, who had reached the tomb first, also went inside. He saw and believed. (John 20:5-8)

Chapter 1

Tucson, Arizona, August 17, 1988

Father Hinton hurried to the old chapel, buttoning his shirt and adjusting his collar as he went. A man had an urgent confession. It could not wait until morning. The priest feared the penitent was suicidal. It wouldn't be the first time he'd talked a parishioner down from the ledge late at night.

The priest reached the thick wooden door of the chapel, jingled keys as he worked the lock, and pushed through the heavy doors and into the foyer. He stepped over to the ornate wooden confessional booth to the right side of the foyer. He pulled back the curtain, lowered himself to the wooden bench, closed the curtain, and waited. Moments later, the foyer doors whined open.

"I'm in the booth already," Father Hinton said. "Come through the curtain on your right and I will hear your confession."

The doors clapped shut and a quiet stillness returned to the foyer. The silence endured. Father Hinton sensed a presence, but there were no words. No movement. Only the faint, rhythmic whistle of air pressed through congested nostrils.

"I'm over here, in the confessional booth," Father Hinton repeated. "You may enter the confessional by the curtain, the one on your right."

Father Hinton suffered another several seconds of eerie silence. Finally, boot steps approached. The curtain snapped open. A figure of a man entered the booth. A mesh screen separated priest from penitent. Father Hinton could see a silhouette of a man, but the face was obscured. Finally, the man lowered himself to the bench, releasing a distinctive clunk of a metal can with the slosh of fluid inside.

"Are you Father Timothy Hinton?" the man asked.

"Yes, I am Father Hinton. I told you that on the phone."

"I needed to be certain."

"You also said you had an urgent confession."

"I have not come to seek forgiveness."

"Then why are you here?"

"I have no need for a savior."

"We all need God's saving grace."

The man's voice rose in anger. "*I* . . . am the savior."

Father Hinton shifted nervously in his seat. This was a mistake. He needed to learn to say no. No normal person calls a priest out of his pajamas for something like this. "Listen, sir, it's getting late. I have to say eight o'clock mass in the morning. You said on the phone you had an urgent confession."

"I do have a confession."

"Yes, I'm listening."

"I have committed murder."

Father Hinton tensed. Something in the man's voice said he wasn't joking. He slid his hand into his pant pocket and rubbed his thumb over the rosary beads, a nervous reflex. "I'm sorry, did you say you murdered somebody?"

"Yes, I killed a man."

"I see. Can you tell me who you murdered?"

"Religion is a virus. It invades the minds of the naïve. It multiplies and destroys. My fire is a sterilizing fire."

Father Hinton let the menacing words sink. He fumbled for a reply. Finally, he settled on a rehearsed response he often used to defend the faith. "Sir, you are mistaken. Religion isn't a virus. It is a seed. It grows like a flower. It gives hope to the hopeless, meaning for those who crave it. It provides a moral compass so society can flourish. If you don't believe that, then why are you here? This is a Catholic confessional."

"You see, your kind cannot be reasoned with."

Father Hinton was losing patience. Apprehension turned to anger. "Is this some kind of prank? Did you really commit murder?"

"You cannot tell anybody."

"Everything said in this booth is confidential. I am bound by oath not to tell."

"Your oath is not the reason you can't tell."

"I really need to get back inside."

"You cannot tell because you are the victim."

"What's that?" Through the mesh, he thought he saw the silver glint of something metal. He heard a click—like the cocking of a revolver.

A menacing voice boiled from the man's throat. "If thine eye offends thee . . . *pluck it out.*"

****

Detective Pete Johnston parked his department issued, unmarked, white Ford LTD at the curb and walked with the slightest limp toward the crime scene. The limp came from a 7-Eleven shootout back in '83. He stood on the wet sidewalk, next to a muddy puddle of fire hose water. Headlights from two police cruisers illuminated the scene, casting white beams through smoke that seeped from within the charred doors. It was a small, Spanish-style chapel that once served as the main sanctuary before Holy Ghost Catholic Church built a larger sanctuary a few years back. The building looked mostly intact. Firefighters had found a body in the church and there was a report of gunfire. That's why Pete got called out of bed at two in the morning.

Patrolman Chadwick held a clipboard against his black uniform shirt. Anyone who got close to a crime scene showed ID first and then signed the clipboard. When Chadwick noticed Pete, he straightened his posture, gave his head a quick shake, and flashed his eyes wide.

"Wake up, Chadwick," Pete said with a grin. "Don't you know night shift is for rookies?"

"One of those rookies called out sick," Chadwick said.

"It happens. So what we got here?"

Chadwick gestured to a priest leaning against a squad car with his arms folded over his chest. "Father Harris over there claims his roommate got a call about an urgent confession. The next thing he knows, he hears what he thinks is a shot. Then he sees the fire. Fire fighters say there's a body on the floor. It's burned up so we can't make an ID. Plus the fire chief says it's not safe. Says the roof may fall in."

"When can we get in there?" Pete asked.

"Once they make sure the trusses will hold. He says maybe 10:00 in the morning."

"All right, but keep this place secure. I want two patrolmen here until we can sweep the scene."

"Yes, sir," Chadwick said and yawned. "Nobody gets in."

Pete thumbed over at the priest by the squad car. "He the only witness?"

"Just the priest so far."

"We'll comb the streets in the morning and see if anybody else saw something."

The priest came off the car when Pete approached.

"Hi, Father, I'm detective Johnston." He pulled his sports coat back to reveal the gold detective badge hooked to his belt. "I understand you can shed some light on what we've got here."

"I can try," he said. Blue lights flashed on his troubled face.

"It's okay, Father. I know you're shaken up. Just give me what you can."

"Well . . .Father Hinton was already in his pajamas," he said, his voice strained. "The phone rang and he answered. I was already in bed, but I heard everything. After he hung up, he came to my room and said he was heading down to the chapel to take a confession. I asked him why this couldn't wait till morning, and he said it was urgent. He was afraid this man could be suicidal. You'd be surprised how often people come to us when they have suicidal thoughts. Father Hinton had to go. So he got dressed and I heard the door shut."

"And that's it?" Pete asked. "That's all you know?"

"Well, I was just about to fade off when I heard a muffled thump. I think it was a gunshot, but I couldn't swear to it. I got up and looked out the window, but I couldn't see anything. The next thing I know I hear a motorcycle rev its engine and fly down the street. Now I'm concerned, so I threw my clothes back on and came down to check on Father Hinton. The door was already on fire so I couldn't get in. That's when I called 911."

Detective Johnston pulled a spiral note pad and pen from his pocket and jotted a couple of notes. He glanced back to the priest. "So that's it? That's all you know? Try to think of anything. Is there someone who might want to hurt Father Hinton? Anything unusual happen lately?"

"No, not that I can think of."

"Okay, so what about this motorcycle. Can you describe the sound? Was it deep, like one of those chopper bikes or was it more like a chain saw?"

Father Harris bit his lower lip and considered the question. "It was sort of in between."

Pete jotted that down. "Are you sure there's nothing else? Anything exciting happen in his life? Good or bad?"

Father Harris forced a smile as he remembered something. "He was very proud of an article he got printed in the *Tucson Times*."

Pete hiked his brows. "You don't say. What was it about?"

"Have you heard of the Shroud of Turin?"

"It rings a bell. Enlighten me."

"It is the burial cloth of Jesus Christ. It bears his blood and crucified image. The miracle of the resurrection caused the image."

"Yeah, yeah, I know what you're talking about. Some think it's a hoax."

"Some say it is, but Father Hinton didn't think so."

"Okay, so..." Pete held his pen to paper, coaxing the priest for more words.

"You see, Father Hinton wrote an article for the paper. He said no matter what the carbon date showed, all the other evidence suggests that the Shroud is authentic. He said there's more than enough evidence to prove the point. Any carbon date result that says otherwise would be erroneous. Some say the carbon date will invalidate the other evidence, but Father Hinton insisted the other evidence will invalidate the carbon date."

"Okay, so, why does the *Tucson Times* think this is worthy of their paper? I mean, it's just his opinion, right?"

"The reason they're interested is because the University of Arizona did a carbon date on the Shroud this summer. There were two other labs involved. They haven't released the results yet, but it should be soon."

"So this is a big deal. The eyes of the world are on Tucson."

"That's right."

"And Father Hinton just wanted to put the word out ahead of time so nobody would believe the results."

"He didn't want the faithful to be discouraged."

"And that's all you've got? Just the article?"

"At this moment, it's all I can think of."

"Listen, I know you're shaken up by all this. Please accept my condolences. I'll do all I can to find who did this." He reached into his coat pocket and flipped a business card to the priest. "If you think of anything else, give me a call."

"Absolutely, Detective. I will."

Detective Johnston strolled back to Officer Chadwick. "Remember, keep this scene secure until the fire chief gives us the go-ahead." He slid his watch out from under his sleeve. It read 3:05 a.m. "I'm going to try to get some more shut eye."

Pete ambled toward his car but froze his advance when he spotted something scrawled on the ground. It was some kind of gibberish with the numbers 1035 in front. "Hey, Chadwick, how old you think this graffiti is?"

Chadwick stepped over. "I go up and down this street all the time. First time I've seen it."

"Could be our killer wrote this," Pete said. "Some kind of clue?"

"Could be," Chadwick said.

"I can read the numbers, but what do you think that scribble next to it says?"

"I have no idea, Detective Johnston. None whatsoever."

Chapter 2

Pete pulled his car up to the curb next to the crime scene at 10:15 the next morning. His partner, Detective Jorge Sanchez, sat next to him in the passenger seat. Jorge was thirty-seven, sixteen years younger than Pete, with two young kids and a wife at home. His face was acne pitted and he wore a thick mustache on his lip like *Magnum P.I.* Jorge was a Puerto Rican from New York—a Nuyorican—who had moved to Tucson a few years ago. This was only his first year working homicide. Most Anglos called him George because they didn't realize the J and G are pronounced like H in Spanish. Pete knew the difference but called him George anyway.

Pete and George got out of the car and went to the edge of the yellow crime tape. The fire chief had given the all clear. The debris had cooled and the structure was stable. Two different day shift officers stood sentry with their clipboard.

"Morning officers," Pete said and held out his ID. "We clear to head in?"

"Sure, go ahead." The patrolman jotted Pete and George down on the clipboard. He then lifted the yellow tape and let them through.

Inside the chapel foyer, a flood light mixed with sunlight to give a better view. Only a slight haze of smoke hung in the air, but it still managed to burn Pete's eyes. It stank of burnt wood and charbroiled human flesh—an acrid, metallic odor from iron-rich blood, a smell you'd never forget but only wished you could.

A doored entryway separated the foyer from the sanctuary and appeared to spare the rest of the chapel from the fire. Only the ceiling of the inner chapel had slight fire damage. Fire fighters must have put it out quickly.

Crime scene techs snapped photos of a human sized mound of ash and burnt flesh lying face down on the red tile floor. The victim's arms were splayed overhead. Skull and bone could be seen between gaps of charred meat. Forensics would need to make a positive ID, but since Father Hinton never returned to the rectory, it was safe to say this was the priest.

To the right of the foyer was a burnt out confessional booth. A crime scene tech dug into the wall of the confessional with tweezers, just about where a priest's head might have been. He plucked a slug out of the wall and dropped it into a clear, plastic evidence bag.

"Hey, Andy, bring that over here a second," Pete said.

Andy carefully stepped out of the booth's remains and handed Pete the bag.

"What do you think, George?" Pete asked.

"I think there's a hot place in hell for anybody who'd kill a priest. Even hotter for those who'd burn down a church."

"You got that right. But I'm talking about this slug," Pete said as he held the bag overhead, inspecting the smashed chunk of lead. "Looks like a .38 to me."

"That'd be my guess," George said.

"Hey, Andy, you find any shell casings?" Pete asked.

"Not yet."

"Probably won't," George said. "If it's a .38 Special, it doesn't spit out the shells. Looks like he offed the priest in the confessional and then dragged him out here. Or he could have crawled out."

"That .38-sized hole in his head says otherwise," Pete said as he pointed to the victim's skull.

"Thanks for pointing that out. I just ate, you know."

Pete grimaced. "Give it a few years, George. You been doing this as long as me and you'll drop crumbs on the body while you're eating a sausage biscuit."

"Man, you're gross. Anyone ever tell you that?"

"I've been called worse than that."

A man in navy coveralls stepped over to Pete. "Are you Detective Johnston, from homicide?"

"That's right, Pete Johnston. This is my partner, George Sanchez. Are you from Arson? I think we met already. A few months back. An apartment fire up in Vista Del Monte."

"That's right, but you had a different partner. My name's Jack Hedges."

"So, Jack, what's your take on all this?" Pete asked.

"Cut and dried. An accelerant was used. Lighter fluid."

"Dang, you're good," George said. "You can tell it was lighter fluid just by looking?"

"It's not rocket science. The can is sitting over by the door. You can still read the label if you look close. I'd say he hosed down the confessional, the body, the shoes, the wall over there, and then the front door. He must have thrown a match in on the way out."

"Hold on a sec," Pete said. "You said *shoes*?"

"That's right. About three yards from the body." He pointed to a small double mound of burned mush.

George stroked his bushy mustache as he pondered the shoes. "What do you make of that, Pete?"

"Heck if I know."

"That's not all," Jack said. "You notice something strange about the corpse?"

"Other than it being dead and burned, no," Pete said.

"There's not enough ashes around the body. It looks like the clothes were removed—except for his socks, T-shirt, and boxers."

"So you're saying this psycho killed the priest in the confessional, dragged his body out here, and took off the shoes so he could get the pants off," Pete said.

"And that's why his arms are over his head," George said. "His arms are up because his shirt was pulled off over his head."

"I'll type up my report and have it on your desk by tomorrow," Jack said.

"Thanks. It's good to see you again." Pete motioned for George to follow him. "Let's step outside. There's some graffiti on the sidewalk we need to look at."

They stepped outside and Pete searched the ground around the two bushes that flanked the door.

"I thought you said graffiti," George said as he polished his sunglass lenses with his shirt.

"It is. I'm just looking for a paint can, something else useful." A bottle cap and a weathered Burger King cup were all he found. Nothing fresh.

"I don't see anything recent," George said. "So where's the graffiti?"

"Over on the sidewalk, next to the street."

الجهاد 1035 was spray-painted in black on the dirty, chewing-gum-spotted sidewalk.

"I noticed that when we drove up," George said. "Graffiti's like weeds. You sure this wasn't here before?"

Pete stooped down and fingered the black paint. He found a thick drop and dug into it with his fingernail. "This is new paint. It's still rubbery. It's too clean to have been here long."

"You think 1035 is the time of the murder?" George asked. "Maybe he signed his name. It's too messy, can't make it out. Like most signatures."

"It's a little early unless the time on his watch was wrong. And there's no last name."

"Maybe this is his last name and he left off the first."

"If he wanted us to catch him, he would have hung around," Pete said, annoyed at the silly assumption. "Why would he sign his name?"

"It's Arabic, in case you're wondering," came a voice from behind.

Pete and George turned to see the medical examiner holding his bag. He wore thick glasses with even thicker half circle lenses near the bottom on his bifocals.

"Oh, hey, Doc," Pete said and came to his feet. "You speak Arabic?"

"My name is Qureshi, isn't it? My father was from Saudi Arabia."

"Well, I didn't want to assume," Pete said.

"Of course not. But that scribble you see on the sidewalk is most certainly Arabic. It is a very common word. It says jihad."

George raised his sunglasses and squinted at the doctor. "Jihad? You mean like war against the infidels, jihad?"

"That is what it says."

"What about the numbers?" Pete asked. "Any idea what that's about?"

"I couldn't begin to tell you. I'm just here for the corpse," Dr. Qureshi said as he pointed at the blackened doorway. "That body doesn't leave until I determine the cause of death."

"I know the routine," Pete said. "It's just inside that door."

Pete looked back at the jihad painted on the sidewalk and scratched the back of his head.

"Guess we should canvas the street and see if we can find witnesses," George said.

Pete frowned. He suddenly recognized that scribble. "You remember that homeless guy we found dead a few weeks ago?"

"The street preacher? Brimstone Ben is what they called him. Always carried a sign in one hand and a Bible in the other. The sign said 'Repent'."

"That's the one. The one we found stabbed to death. Something was scrawled across his forehead in black marker. It was smudged so it was hard to read. But don't it remind you of this? The jihad?"

"Now that you mention it."

"I got a bad feeling about this, George. A real bad feeling."

Chapter 3

August 22, 1988

Amari Johnston's mother was a full-blooded Navajo. She had succumbed to breast cancer a year ago. Haseya was her mother's name. It meant, 'she rises,' and Amari knew her mother would rise again. Though her mother was reared on the Navajo reservation just north of Winslow, Arizona, she had been devout in her Christian faith.

Haseya had been a master at weaving most anything, from rugs, to dresses, to baskets, to that chief blanket that hung on the wall. She was especially gifted on the vertical loom. Several of her rugs and chief's blankets had sold at auction for over a thousand dollars.

Amari sat on the floor in the den as she worked to finish the rug her mother had started before cancer took her. Haseya had learned the skill on the reservation from her mother and had passed on what she knew to Amari, her only daughter. For Amari, working her mother's loom was bittersweet. Finishing this rug her mother had started was like keeping her mother alive, but at the same time, her relative lack of skill served as a reminder that her mother was gone. Her mother's lines were straighter, her yarn more taut. Even the colors seemed more vivid on her mother's bottom half—at least Amari thought so. Still, she was determined to finish the rug. Working the loom taught perseverance. She envisioned her goal, the pattern she imagined in her head, and she labored toward the goal until completion. Never give up, her mother would tell her. Never give up until the job was finished, until you gazed upon the fruit of your labor with satisfaction—and then sold it at auction to the highest bid.

The loom sat vertically against the den wall of the house her mother once owned. It was a simple loom, just parallel strings called the warp, pulled tight by two wooden dowels at the top and bottom. The yarn was made of wool from the churro sheep, an animal unique to the Navajo Nation. The soft fleece under the overcoat was carded by hand, then spun in a spindle into yarn and dyed vibrant colors. This three by five rug was the typical teec-nos-pos pattern with horizontal stripes of black, white, and two shades of blue. Red and blue triangles were at the four corners and a diamond shape was dead center.

She had been working this session for more than three hours non-stop. Her back ached from the strain, but she persisted. Over and over, she used her left-hand fingers to lift the warp into a triangular shed. Her right fingers wove over and under in a simple tabby pattern, over the odd strings, under the even strings. When she reached the outer edge, she started back across the loom again, this time over the evens and under the odds.

"Crap!" She pelted the couch with the wooden comb. Two rows down, she noticed a mistake. Two warp strings skipped instead of one. "I can't believe this." She closed her eyes and took a deep breath to quell her anger. Mother had lectured her about her temper. 'Quick to listen, slow to speak, and slow to anger' her mother had repeatedly reminded her.

She gave a hard sigh and started to unwind the yarn. Her mother was right. She had to learn to control her temper. But the loom could be cruel, unforgiving. No matter how hard she tried, she couldn't match her mother's skill. To her mother, this was a labor of love. Amari enjoyed it enough, but sometimes it was just hard labor—no love to it. There was a tug of war within her, between the artist and the warrior. Her mother had told her she inherited her aggressive side from her grandfather—a descendant of a Native American war chief of the Dine' people. His real name was Bít'aa'níí, but he was known as 'Manuelito' to the Spanish. Manuelito was her great, great grandfather. Manuelito had courageously led attacks against the US Army in the Navajo Wars of 1863-1866.

Manuelito's grandson—Amari's grandfather—had stubbornly refused to allow Haseya to marry a white man, the reason Amari's parents had to elope against tribal wishes. And it was the reason she seldom visited the reservation and knew shamefully little about the culture that was her other half.

The doorbell rang and startled her from her thoughts. "Just a minute," she yelled.

She went to the door and pressed an eye to the peephole. Some short girl with puffed up blond hair and heavy eye shadow stood out front holding a flyer in her hand. She must have been there about the room.

The doorbell rang again. She straightened her posture, shoulders back. Look them straight in the eye, firm handshake. Show no weakness. First impressions were crucial. Establish control early, set the tone, and respect would follow. It was her typical pep talk before meeting anyone new. She wasn't sure why she did that. Maybe it was the warrior within her. Or maybe she was just an insecure girl trying to act tough. Either way, it seemed to work. Nobody liked to mess with her.

She opened the door and made immediate eye contact.

"Are you still looking for a roommate?" the girl asked.

"Oh, you're here for the room?" Amari played dumb as she sized her up. She seemed nice enough. Clothes were the latest fashion so she could afford rent. She looked like she had some brains behind that eye shadow. Maybe she was a student.

"If the room's still available," the girl said and stretched out her free hand. "I'm Jenny, by the way. Jenny Brenner."

Amari gave a firm handshake. "Amari Johnston," she said in a deeper than natural tone of voice.

Jenny cringed. "Ouch, that's quite a grip you got there."

"I work out," Amari said.

"I can tell."

The police scanner squawked from the kitchen counter. "Hold on a sec," Amari said. She stepped into the kitchen and silenced the radio. "Burglary in progress. Sorry about that. Come on in."

Jenny stepped into the den. "You're in law enforcement?"

"No, why would you say that?"

"The radio."

"Oh, that's my dad's radio."

"I see. So what's all of this?" Jenny asked as she looked around the den.

"Sorry, I'm kind of a slob." Magazines were randomly scattered on the coffee table and couch. A Rubik's Cube sat atop the TV, and her older brother's Atari and game cartridges sat in the corner collecting dust. The house plants were half dead and she hadn't vacuumed in a few days either. "I hope you don't mind. If someone else was living with me, I'd clean up more."

"No, not the mess. I'm used to that. You should see my cousin's apartment. I'm having to stay with him until I find my own place. I'm talking about what you're working on. Is that a rug?"

"You like it?" Amari asked.

Jenny went over to the loom and fingered the fabric. "I love it. It's beautiful."

"Thanks, but my mother did most of it. I'm trying to finish it. I did that basket over there. There's a dress in my room. I've sold some stuff too."

"Seriously?"

"Seriously. My mother was a Navajo Indian. They're known for their weaving skills."

"You're a Navajo Indian? How exciting. I've never met one before."

"Sorry to burst your bubble, but I'm only half Navajo. My dad's not, obviously," she said, pointing to her face. "He's Scottish. I mean, he's from New Hampshire, but Scottish heritage."

"I can see the Navajo. The long black hair. Love the braid, by the way. Your skin's sort of tan, and those cheek bones. All Indian in those cheeks. And that's a compliment. I'm jealous. You're very attractive."

"You think so?"

"Definitely."

"Well, thanks, but I'm nothing compared to my mother. She was beautiful. Unfortunately, I look too much like my dad." She narrowed her eyes at the mere thought of her dad. Just before her mother died, it came out that he was having an affair with another woman, a detective he worked with. She could almost understand the affair. He and Mother hadn't gotten along for years. But what hurt was the fact that he lied about it. For that, there was no forgiveness.

"You okay?" Jenny asked. "Did I say something to upset you?"

"I'm sorry, my dad's a sore subject."

"I see. Would you like to talk about it? One of my double majors was psychology. Maybe I can help."

"Double major?"

"Psychology and pre-med. One degree, two majors. That's why I moved to Tucson. I want to be a psychiatrist. I've got to get through medical school first. Go on, let me practice on you."

"Well, you're not licensed yet, so..."

"Oh, come on, humor me. Tell me more about your dad."

"I thought you were here to talk about the room."

"I'm sorry, you're right. What did you say your name was again?"

"Amari. Amari Johnston. Johnston with a T, not John*son*."

"*Amari.* Sounds like the planet mars. I like that. Is that a Navajo name?"

"Not really. It's kind of a dumb story, actually."

"I like dumb stories."

Amari laughed and relaxed her posture. This girl was harmless. She could drop the tough girl act. "You want something to drink? I've got lemonade, or I can make coffee."

"No, thank you, I'm fine. Now tell me this dumb story."

"When I was born my mother wanted to give me a Navajo name. But my dad didn't like anything she came up with. So he asked some Indian guy he worked with for some ideas. Now, this guy is from India, over in Asia, but my dad being my dad asked him anyway. This Indian man suggested Amari because it means *never gives up* in the Indian language. When my mother heard the name, she liked it too. She said it fit because my dad wouldn't stop pestering her until she married him."

"That's not a dumb story. I think it's a beautiful name. And your mom taught you to do all of this?"

Amari put her hands on her hips and tilted her head toward a book shelf. "And books. I've done a lot of reading."

"I see that." Jenny stepped over to the bookshelf and scanned the titles.

"You know," Amari said with a shoulder shrug, "some people play an instrument, some people paint, others write poetry. I'm into this. It's uh . . . it's sort of a way to keep my mother with me, you know? It's part of who she was. So I keep it part of who I am."

"I totally get that. And you're good at it too," Jenny said. "But I don't see any books on textiles. I see a lot of Sherlock Holmes, Agatha Christie, and Nancy Drew."

"No, there's three," Amari said. "Bottom shelf, to the left."

"Oh, I see. *Seven Thousand Years of Textiles. A Concise History.*"

"There's two others."

"So the skill came from your mother?"

"Mostly."

"If you don't mind my asking, how did your mother die?"

"Breast cancer. A year ago last week."

"I'm so sorry to hear that. It must be very difficult for you. What about your dad?"

"After the affair, they divorced in April of '87."

"He had an affair?"

"Yeah, that's why he's a sore subject. Don't get me started. Anyway, she was in remission, had been for almost a year. We thought she'd beat it, but I guess with the stress of the divorce and everything, you know . . ."

"That's terrible."

"To sum it up, she got the house and then she left it to me. And a little life insurance too. But that's gone." Amari pointed to the flyer still in Jenny's hand. "That's why you're here. I'm a student too and only work part time. I need help paying the bills."

Jenny folded the flyer in two and set it on the coffee table. "So what's your major?"

"Art."

"You're an art major?"

"Last semester I was. Before that I was in criminal justice."

"Wow, that's a big change."

"Shift in priorities, I guess. You know, after Mother died. Art seemed like a good choice at the time."

"A way to keep her alive a little longer."

"Something like that."

"So do you speak Navajo?"

"A few words. Mother spoke perfect English. It's all we talked at home, and I went to high school here, so, you know how it goes. I've only been out to the reservation maybe three or four times in my whole life."

"Yeah, I know how it goes. I've got cousins in Kentucky I never see either. It's just three hours away, but we hardly ever made it up there."

"I hear the accent."

"Do you really? I didn't think it was that bad. "

"It's subtle, but it's there."

"That's because I'm from Tennessee. Knoxville. Well, Farragut, actually. It's about twenty miles west of Knoxville."

"A hillbilly in the desert, huh?"

"Oh, come on, Amari, it's not that bad."

"I'm just teasing. It's hardly noticeable," Amari said and rolled her eyes.

"Oh, stop it. If you think mine's bad, you should hear my cousin Kevin's accent. He's from Oak Ridge. I grew up with a lot of transplants. My best friend was from right here in Arizona. But Kevin grew up with locals. And it shows."

"You said you were staying at your cousin's for now. So is that why you came out here? Because of your cousin?"

"Partly. That and the fact that the University of Arizona has a great medical school. Kevin pulled some strings for me here. He's a genius, did I mention that? He's ten times smarter than me. He works at the university. At the WMS laboratory. *Weiss Mass Spectrometry lab*," Jenny said slowly so she wouldn't fumble the words.

"So why don't you just stay with him?"

"His couch is killing my back. It's one of those fold-out beds. There's this steel rod that digs into my spine. Besides, I need my own bedroom, my own bathroom. You're a girl. I'm sure you can appreciate that."

"I most certainly can."

"Plus, he's got, well, *issues*."

"Issues?"

"I think he's borderline obsessive-compulsive."

"Really?"

"He's very functional, don't get me wrong. But he tends to obsess over things."

"Hey, I do that too. Once I set my teeth into something, my jaw will break before I let go. So what's he so obsessed over?"

"The Shroud of Turin. His lab is one of the first labs to run a carbon date on it."

"The shroud of what?"

"The Shroud of Turin. Jesus was supposed to be buried in it? His face and blood are on it?"

"That's right, I think I have heard of that. When I was a kid, I read something about it in *National Geographic*. Can't remember much."

"You're going to hear a lot more about it soon. I'm not sure this in common knowledge, but they tested a piece of it in my cousin's lab to see how old it is. They want to see if it's old enough to really belong to Jesus. And Kevin's right in the middle of it. He keeps mumbling about inconsistencies, sampling issues, and, quote, 'those idiots in Italy.' Apparently, his reputation is at stake. He's afraid if he gets this wrong, he'll never work again."

Amari gazed out the window, pondering the subject. "The Shroud of Turin, huh? A forgery?"

"It showed up during the medieval period. I overheard Kevin say it dated to the 1300s. So it must be a forgery."

"Huh. Interesting," Amari said. "And your cousin's right in the middle of this?"

"His name's all over it."

"That's pretty cool. He'll be, like, sort of famous or something. At least with the other science nerds he will be."

"Or *infamous*, if he screws this up."

"You said he was super-smart. He'll be fine. So when do you want to move in?"

"Tomorrow works for me."

"Then I'll see you tomorrow."

Chapter 4

The next day, Amari led Jenny through the den and into the bedroom on the right. She set a suitcase down on the floor. "I hope this is okay," Amari said. "I'm in my parents' old room, so you can have this one. It was mine when I was a kid."

"This is great. The mattress looks a lot better than Kevin's couch."

"The bathroom's across the hall. I use the one in my parents' old room, so it's all yours."

"This is perfect."

"There's a desk in my brother's old room if you want to use it for school."

"You've got a brother?"

"An older one. He's actually a Catholic priest. He's awesome. He let me keep everything when Mother died. He had no use for it. He was doing missionary work in Guatemala, but he just got transferred to Spain. Some town called Oviedo."

"Really? So then you must be Catholic."

"Me? No, I was raised non-denominational. I haven't been much of anything for the last year. Hey, listen, tell me more about this Shroud of Turin."

Jenny set her suitcase on the bed. "I'm all Southern Baptist, in case you're wondering." She pulled out clothes and folded them into stacks on the dresser. "How does your brother become a Catholic priest when he was raised protestant?"

"My mother wanted us to keep an open mind about Christianity, so we chose not to commit. That's why we were non-denominational."

"And your brother?"

"He got a scholarship to Notre Dame. It's one of the best Catholic universities. I guess he decided to commit. So tell me more about this Shroud of Turin."

"Your brother must be very smart."

"He is very smart. Now tell me more about the Shroud."

"You got extra hangers in the closet?"

"I think there's some. If not, I've got some in my room. So tell me more about this. You've got my curiosity going. I told you I was an art major, right? If this thing is a forgery, then it was painted. I've never heard of the Shroud being a piece of art. Who says it's a forgery?"

Jenny kept unpacking her case.

"Jenny?"

She draped a blouse over her forearm and turned to face Amari. "I wish I hadn't mentioned that. I wasn't supposed to say anything. I think Kevin may have some kind of confidentiality agreement, and he's not supposed to talk about the results until the big announcement in October. I just know about it because I've heard him talk on the phone."

"I promise, I won't tell anybody. I'm a cop's kid. You can trust me."

"Well . . . I guess I've already spilled some of the beans. Might as well empty the whole can."

"Might as well."

"Like I told you yesterday, his lab carbon dated the Shroud. And if I remember right, his lab dated the Shroud to around 1300 give or take a few years. They tested it three times, actually, and got three different numbers, but they were close enough."

"If it dates from 1300, then it's definitely a forgery. Jesus was crucified around 30 A.D."

"Maybe."

"What do you mean, maybe? If it dates at 1300, then it's a medieval forgery."

"By maybe I mean Kevin isn't sure if his results will match up with the two other labs they sent pieces too. One lab was in England, Oxford, I think. I can't remember the other one." Jenny pulled two cans of hairspray out of her bag and placed them on the dresser. "That's why he's so worried. He's afraid the other labs will get different results, and it'll make him look bad. And I mean bad in front of the whole world. He could lose his job over this. He might have trouble finding another one if he gets the blame."

"If he's the genius you said he is, then I'm sure he'll be all right."

"I think so. There's other scientists working there too. I'm sure they check each other's work. It's not like he's doing all the work himself."

"So it's medieval, huh?"

"Seems that way."

"Then it's perfect. I'm taking an art history class this semester. I got the syllabus yesterday. I've got a report due in November and it has to be on medieval art. And since this just so happens to be a piece of art on a woven fabric—and you know I like weaving—this is perfect."

Chapter 5

As one of Tucson Police Department's senior detectives, Pete had earned his own office. It had an L-shaped desk. Crime scene photos and notes filled every inch of a bulletin board that hung on the wall over the desk. Stacks of papers laid scattered over the other arm of the desk that faced the door.

"I think I'd know if it was here," Pete said into the receiver. He held the phone with one hand and sifted through papers with the other. "When did you send it?"

George stepped into the office and tossed a manila folder onto Pete's desk. "This what you're looking for?"

"Never mind. George has it. Thanks anyway, Harry," Pete said and hung up.

Pete's reading glasses rested in the nest of his army-issue flattop haircut. He slid the glasses down to the bridge of his nose, opened the envelope, pulled out the papers, and read silently to himself.

"What's it say?" George asked.

"It's like I thought. Dental reports confirmed it. The deceased is Father Hinton. Coroner said the priest died from a gunshot wound to the head. In the front and out the back. That slug did come from a .38. He also confirms that no clothes were on the corpse, except for T-shirt, underwear, and socks." Pete flipped to the second page and read some more. "Accelerant analysis confirms charcoal lighter fluid. There were no discernible prints on the door. If there was, the fire ate them off."

"So that's it?"

"Hold on, there's more. The trajectory of the bullet says the killer was between 5 foot 3 and 5 foot 7, assuming he was sitting on the bench when he pulled the trigger. And they confirmed what the medical examiner told us. The writing did say jihad in Arabic. The handwriting guy says it matches what we found on the street preacher's head."

"Looks like we got us a serial killer. Should we bring in the FBI?"

"I guess we should. I'll leave that up to the chief."

"I went back to that street last night and found a couple more witnesses," George said. "They were at work when we first checked, so I went back when I knew they'd be home. Three said they heard a motorcycle race down the street. Nobody heard the gun shot and nobody saw anything."

Pete tossed the papers onto his desk. "We're still where we were the other day then."

"This case is going cold. There's got to be something else."

"There is, I just can't find it," Pete said and shuffled through his inbox file. "Ah, here it is." He pulled out another sheet and scanned the page. "Bingo. Phone records say a call came into the church rectory at 11:15 at night. Call came from a payphone on Speedway."

"Let me see that."

Pete pointed to the right line. "Right there."

"I know that address. It's right across the street from the mosque. You know, that white one with the guard tower looking thing."

"And it's just a few streets over from Holy Ghost. He could have made the call and been at the church in less than five minutes. Let's head over there and nose around, see if anybody saw something. Maybe one of their members has been acting a little crazy lately."

"Let's go," George said. "There's another mosque on Bellevue. We can check that one out too."

****

Bishop McClure, from the St. Augustine Cathedral, had been the one who'd finally convinced Amari's brother to become a priest. He had been very accommodating when she showed up in his office looking for help with the Shroud of Turin. He had a library full of books on Catholic stuff, and several were about the Shroud of Turin, which, as she had learned, was the most studied artifact on the planet. When she explained her project to the bishop, he kindly allowed her to take some books and reports home with her. She got copies of twenty-six research papers and two of them were written this year. He even gave her enlarged pictures of the Shroud. After that, she got more books from the university library, and then more from the city library.

When she got home, she scooped the books and folders out of the passenger seat of her white, 1976 Camaro. It was fast and paid for, but the transmission job last month had put her eight hundred dollars in the hole. She'd thought her dad was exaggerating about changing the oil every three thousand miles, but apparently not.

She pulled the books closer to her chest and kicked the car door closed. She came out from under the carport and squinted as the punishing desert sun shined down on her. She came to the front door and kicked it twice. "Jenny, it's me," she yelled. "Can you open the door?"

A moment later, Jenny came to the door. "Let me help you," she said and grabbed half the books.

"Just put them on the kitchen table."

They set the books, papers, and photos in the kitchen. Jenny eyed some of the titles. "These don't look like textbooks to me.

What about school? Don't you need textbooks for your art classes?"

Amari sat at the table, let out a deep breath, and wiped sweat from her brow with the back of her hand. "I'll buy it tomorrow."

"It? What about your other classes?"

"I couldn't afford full tuition, so I'm just taking this one class. It's okay. I'll be able to work a lot more this semester and save money for next year."

"You do what you gotta do, I guess." Jenny sorted through the books and folders on the table. "Where in the world did you find all this?"

"The university library had this book on ancient textiles. It's by a Swiss textile expert named Mechthild Flury-Lemberg. It came out this year. I'm surprised the library had it. And I found these two other books on medieval art. I want to see if there was anything else like the Shroud from that period."

"Looks boring," Jenny said.

"It gets better. I found these two books about the Shroud of Turin at the university library, these other two at the city library, and my brother, Jason—you know, the priest. He knows the bishop at the cathedral, so Bishop McClure loaned me these three other books and some research papers."

Jenny started picking up books and reading their spines. "*Report on the Shroud of Turin*, by John H. Heller."

"That guy was on STURP."

"You say that like I should know what that is."

"Bishop McClure told me all about it. It's the Shroud of Turin Research Project. Back in 1978, a team of forty scientists were allowed to study the Shroud. They did a bunch of scientific tests. That book talks about what they did over in Turin."

"I see," Jenny said and picked up another book. "*The Holy Shroud*, by Monsignor Giulio Ricci."

"That's a Catholic priest in Italy."

Jenny lifted a manila envelope and pulled out a thin stack of papers that were stapled together. "*Quantitative Photography of the Shroud of Turin*," she said and then pulled out another stapled group of papers. "*Examination of the Turin Shroud for Image Distortions*. Where did you get these?"

"That's the best part. The bishop had twenty-six research papers published by STURP. He let me photocopy them. He even gave me these four enlarged photos of the Shroud. Two of them are negative photos, one from the front and one of the back. That's the part Jesus was lying on."

"Was *supposed* to be lying on," Jenny said. "Remember, this is a forgery."

"Well, anyway, he also gave me two front and back regular pictures so you can see what it really looks like, not the black and white negative version."

"He just gave you those?"

"He said he had others. He's the one who convinced my brother to become a priest. That's the only reason he was so nice to me. He's like a friend of the family."

"It's good to have friends in high places."

"I guess so."

"So you've got ten books and twenty-six research papers to study. This sounds more like a master's thesis than an art report."

"I like to be thorough. I'm going to be pretty busy."

Jenny stared at Amari with a doubtful smirk on her face, nodding her head in disbelief.

"What? Why are you looking at me that way?"

Jenny tapped on the stack of books with her middle finger for audible effect. "You're not an artist, Amari. I've seen your sketches. They're awful."

"Hey, my water colors aren't half bad."

"I don't see them on display like I do your rugs or baskets. You're not that proud of them."

"It takes practice. You don't get good at something overnight."

"You see, you're not even offended when I say that. Get mad or something. I insult your painting and I get nothing from you. Just a puny 'hey.' Look at you. Look at all these books and papers." Jenny picked up one of the research papers and tossed it back on the table. "You're not an artist. You're a detective. Just like your father. And a darn good one."

Amari ignored the comments and started sorting the research papers.

Jenny pulled out a chair and sat.

"You know I'm studying to be a psychiatrist, right?"

Amari glanced up at her, wondering where this was going. "Of course, it's all you talk about."

"Then can I make an observation?"

"I guess."

"I don't think you're really interested in the Shroud of Turin because you think it's a piece of art."

"Then why would I research it for an art class?"

"I'm sorry, but you just don't seem like the artist type to me. You have an authoritarian personality. I mean, it's all over you. It's in the way you hold your posture, the way you dress, the way you shake hands. You don't belong behind a canvas with a paint brush in your hand. You belong behind a badge with handcuffs hooked to your belt."

"So, does that mean I can't like art?"

"No, but if the Shroud was made in 1300, then it must be a forgery. And that's what really intrigues you. Because forgery is a crime. This case has gone cold and now you've got the bug to restart a seven-hundred-year-old investigation."

"Okay, I admit. It does sound interesting. I'd love to crack this one wide open. You think it was Leonardo da Vinci? No, two hundred years too old. I don't know. I'd have to do some research."

"And I have no doubt you will. And you may even figure this seven-hundred-year-old mystery out. Because that's who you are. That's what you're driven to do. You ever consider going back to criminal justice?"

"What's wrong with art?"

"I don't think your heart's really in it."

Amari stared at her for a long moment, mulling her response, trying to say something in her defense that wasn't a lie—because she hated lies.

"You see what I mean? You know I'm right."

"I really like art. Why is that so hard to believe?"

"Maybe you do. So keep it as a hobby. But you *love* criminal justice."

"And you love psychiatry."

"Yes, I do."

"So don't you have some studying to do?"

"Fine, I can take a hint," Jenny said and went back into the den.

Chapter 6

Little Robby sat at his desk, leaned forward, elbows against the wood, palms mashed against his cheeks. He stared down at his history book. A watery drop fell from his nose and onto the page. He wiped the mucus away with the back of his hand. His legs stung from the red marks on his shins and thighs. Father had just spanked him because he saw his report card. He was a bad boy. Not deserving of God's grace. Father insisted on all A's, even in math. He had to try harder. Much harder.

A pounding came from the door.

It was Father! Without closing the book and losing his place, Robby quickly placed it into the top desk drawer and slid it closed, careful not to make noise.

"Yes, Father, I'm coming!" Robby rushed to the door. He unlocked it and stood back, waiting, hoping Father wouldn't discover his secret.

The door flung open. Father looked like Moses with his long, messy beard, only the really mad Moses, like when he found out about the golden calf and broke the stone tablets. Robby's little heart thumped hard in his chest and he wanted to cry, but that would only make it worse. Father would give him something to cry about.

"I told you never to lock this door again!" Father screamed.

"But I was changing," Robby lied. "I didn't want anyone to see my nakedness."

Father grabbed him by the hair. "Lying lips are an abomination to the Lord!" Father's open hand clapped hard against the boy's cheek.

He wailed from the pain.

"Where is it? Is it here?" Father went to the desk and snatched the top drawer open. He found the book and dropped it onto the desk. The page was still open to seventy-eight.

"That was from yesterday!"

Father dabbed his fingertip into the wet drop of booger-snot. He rubbed the wetness between his finger and thumb. "Lies! Take the position," he said and pointed at the bed.

"Father, *please. . .*"

"'Six days shall work be done, but on the seventh day there shall be to you a holy day, a sabbath of rest to the Lord.'"

"But they said in school that the Sabbath was Saturday. I promise, Father, I didn't study yesterday. I didn't."

Father didn't like that answer. He got even madder. "You just told me that book was open from yesterday!" He unbuckled his belt and yanked it out of the loops of his pants. "Take off your shirt."

Tears and snot mixed in Robby's nose and dripped down onto his lips. He didn't want to, but he had no choice. It would only get worse the longer he waited. Not minding only made the spankings longer. Robby pulled off his shirt and fell face down on the bed. He held his face in his hands to catch the tears. And he waited.

"'Honour thy father and thy mother: that thy days may be long upon the land which the Lord thy God giveth thee!'"

Pain bit into the boy's bare back.

"Tell me the verse!" Father demanded.

"Exodus 20:12."

Another crack on his back. "And what does it mean?"

"It means to never disobey you."

The belt bit again.

Chapter 7

A few days later, Jenny sat on the couch studying infectious diseases. Amari was at the kitchen table again, digging through her research. She had used Scotch tape to affix the images of the Shroud to a larger, firmer poster board for support. The ghostly, white photo-negative image of what was supposed to be Jesus seemed to watch her with knowing eyes, encouraging her to keep searching. *Seek and you shall find, knock and the door will be opened* kept ringing in her thoughts.

"I don't know about this," she called from the kitchen. "This is supposed to be a medieval forgery, but the history of this thing goes back way before medieval times."

"What are you mumbling about over there?"

Amari flipped a page on her spiral notebook and followed her finger down to the entry she was looking for. "Here it is. It wasn't called the Shroud of *Turin* until it actually came to Turin in 1578. But before that, it was in France, a town called Chambery. A fire broke out there. The box it was stored in had a silver lining. The silver melted and burned the Shroud. That's why you see these four big burn marks on it. It's like that because it was folded." She held up a poster board for Jenny to see. On the front was an enlarged photo of the Shroud taken with normal photography. On the back was the photographic negative of the Shroud. "Can you see this?"

Jenny got up from the couch and came to the table. "I'm listening."

"See," she said and pointed. "These are the burn holes I'm talking about. It's a miracle it wasn't destroyed. Before that, it was in Lirey, France, in the mid-1350s. This is when the Shroud becomes well documented by the church. A knight named Geoffrey de Charny displayed it at a Catholic church and then, when he died in battle, his wife showed it later in 1389."

"Did you know that viruses can live dormant in the nerves for years? Antibodies can't penetrate the blood-brain barrier. So when the immune system weakens, viruses like the chickenpox can come back as shingles."

"I'm sorry, Jenny, I know you have a test tomorrow. Just hold on a second and I'll be done. So before that, there were reports of a cloth bearing the image of Christ in Constantinople. It was probably folded in a frame to show only the face. But there are two other references that claim there was a full-length image of a dead and naked Jesus in Constantinople at the same time. But during the Fourth Crusades, this image disappeared from Constantinople and suddenly the full-sized image shows up in Europe. They think maybe the Knights Templar were involved. Which could explain why the *knight* Geoffrey de Charny got ahold of it. But that's just speculation."

"Purulent pustules caused by the herpes virus are not speculation," Jenny said. "I'm going to your brother's room to use his desk." She got up and patted Amari on the arm. "You're doing an amazing job with this, Detective Johnston. But I'll never be a psychiatrist if I don't get through medical school first."

"Not a licensed one, anyway."

"Funny," Jenny called back before she shut the door.

Amari went over her notes in her head. If this was a forgery, all the evidence suggested it was done much earlier than 1350. The year 944 was when the cloth first showed up in Constantinople, only back then they referred to it as the *Mandylion*. Before that, around the year 600, paintings of Jesus started showing up that were symmetrically identical to the image on the Shroud, along with the beard and long hair. Before 600, all images of Christ were clean shaven with short hair. But all of the sudden, people believed Jesus had long hair, with a long nose, and big, owlish eyes. They must have known the image on the Shroud was of Jesus, so they were using the Shroud as a template for their paintings. A Justinian II coin was minted in 695 A.D. There was a face on the coin that looked like the face on the Shroud.

And in 325, historian Eusebius recounted a story about a King Abgar that reigned in Edessa from A.D. 13 to 50. Abgar had been ill and had sent a messenger to Jesus himself, asking if Jesus would personally come up to Edessa and heal him. But Jesus said he would send one of his disciples there after his earthly mission was complete. After Jesus' death, Thaddaeus, one of the disciples, brought the king a cloth bearing the image of Jesus' face. Miraculously, the king was healed of leprosy and paralysis. The image was then referred to as the *Image of Edessa*. The image of Jesus stayed in Edessa until the Christian community there left.

Amari folded her notebook, tossed it on the table, and leaned back in her chair. She hadn't bargained for this. If it was a forgery, then she had to pin down the time of the forgery before she could begin to research any possible culprit or even the means of making such a realistic depiction. What if it wasn't a forgery at all? What if it was the Shroud that held the crucified body of the historical Jesus?

Her eyes burned with fatigue. Her back and neck ached from leaning over that table all evening. She was too tired to think. It was after midnight. Jenny could stay up all night if she wanted, but Amari had had enough. She got up and cracked open Jenny's door. "I'm going to bed. My brain's fried."

Jenny swiveled her chair around to face her. "You're starting to remind me of my cousin, Kevin."

"How's that?"

"Your determination. Kevin's the same way."

"And look where it got him."

"He's very successful. I'll give him that."

"Jenny, you've heard Kevin talk about this a lot. Is he sure this carbon date is right? From what I've found, history doesn't agree with him."

"He never told me he doubts the numbers, but his body language and the concerned look on his face says otherwise."

"Are you serious?"

"I could be wrong. Like you said, I'm not licensed yet, but my gut tells me he's worried."

"Now that's interesting."

"You want to interrogate him, Detective Johnston?"

"I thought you said he had some sort of confidentiality agreement."

"I asked him about that and he said it was more of an expectation than a rule. He never signed any papers. Once they make the official announcement, it'll be public knowledge. You can talk to him then."

"You think he'd talk to me?"

"I'm sure he would. As long as you don't make any trouble for him."

"I don't know, Jenny. I've got a lot more reading to do. Let me think about it."

Chapter 8

The next afternoon, Amari sat at the couch reading. She wanted to finish Monsignor Ricci's book before her evening shift at Pizza Hut. She knew now her obsession with the Shroud wasn't just because she thought it was a forgery, and that she was simply trying to crack the case. Now she was obsessed because there's no way it could be a forgery. And if it wasn't a forgery, then it was real. She had always imagined what Jesus must look like. Sometimes she doubted he was real at all. The Shroud answered both questions. Yes, he was real, and this is what he looked like. Why wasn't the whole world in on this? Why was it that the only thing she could remember about the Shroud was some article she saw in *National Geographic*? Everybody on the planet should be obsessed with the Shroud.

Whether you believed Jesus was the Son of God wasn't even the point. Jesus was the most influential man in history. Every historian knew that. The world needed to pay more attention to the Shroud. And if she could have her way, that's exactly what would happen. Somehow, she needed to find a way to open the eyes of the world. Unfortunately, she had no clue how a twenty-two-year-old college student was supposed to pull that off.

Jenny walked in and sat on the couch beside her. "Still at it, I see."

"Still at it," Amari said.

"Good. This is what you need to be doing, not finger painting."

Amari rolled her eyes and turned to face Jenny. "It's my time. Why do you care what I do with it? If I want to be an out of work artist, then just let me do it."

"I know you're grieving your mother's loss, but it's time to move on. You need to forgive your dad and go back to the world you love."

"My dad hasn't asked for forgiveness."

"He's probably too ashamed to mention it. Men are like that. They avoid emotional exchanges. Especially macho men like your dad. You'll probably have to initiate the talk. It would take a load off his conscience if you did."

"Didn't we agree you wouldn't practice psychology on me anymore?"

"And didn't you tell me your name meant, 'never gives up?'"

Amari refused to look at her.

"But you gave up. You spent three years and a half in college pursuing your dream, and then you just tossed it in the garbage. You gave up. Just like that."

"Mother didn't want me in law enforcement. She thought it was dangerous."

"That's because she couldn't bear to see you get hurt. She won't see it now."

"I think she does see me."

"So if something does happen to you, then you'll join her in heaven. Don't you believe in heaven, Amari?"

"I hope so. What about you?"

"Of course, I do. But this isn't about me. It's about you."

"You remind me of Lucy from Charlie Brown. You know, when she offered psychiatric advice from a booth for five cents."

"Oh, I love that episode. The Christmas one?"

"The point is, *Lucy*, I'm not paying you for advice."

"I'm just following my dream, Amari. Everyone should do that. It's why it breaks my heart to see you give up on yours. Especially when you're so good at it," she said and pointed at her book sitting next to her on the couch. "If I had a missing child, I would want you on the case. There's a lot of kids out there. There's a lot of criminals. The world will suffer if you gave up. Your mother wouldn't want that."

****

Robby wrapped the two ends of Father's worn, brown belt around his fists, leaving about a foot gap of leather in between. This time, it was Father who would be spanked. He was one of those hypocrites Jesus talked about in Matthew 23:13. He deserved to be punished.

Father had made Robby read the Bible every day. Only Father seemed not to know what the Bible really said. The Bible said not to get drunk. Colossians said to love your wife and not abuse her. First Peter said to honor your wife as the weaker vessel. Father preached the Bible, but he was terrible at obeying it.

Father slept in his recliner. The sound of his snores mixed with Johnny Carson's monologue on *The Tonight Show*. Smoke from a cigarette rose from the ashtray next to the recliner and filled the room with a smelly blue fog, illuminated only by the light from the TV. An empty bottle of whiskey sat next to the ashtray. Father never started a bottle he didn't finish.

The truth was, Father wasn't his real father at all—only his *step*father. Mother had revealed that just yesterday. She'd said a teenager was old enough to know the truth. She'd showed him a picture of his real father—a picture she'd hidden away all these years from her current husband. She let him keep it if he promised to hide it away from his not-real father—his *fake*-father—whose real name was Daniel.

He clenched his fists tighter around the belt and slowly moved toward Daniel. The beatings had gotten worse, and lately Daniel seemed to prefer Mother since Robby was almost his size. Something had to be done before it was too late. Either they had to leave or Daniel had to leave. And Daniel wouldn't leave on his own. He would have to be forced. And then he would only come back—maybe at night or maybe during broad daylight. They would never be safe while he was alive.

Mother was in the hospital. She had told the doctors she had *fallen* down the stairs, but Robby knew the truth. He hadn't hidden the picture of his true father good enough. Daniel found it and got furious. He had warned her never to tell Robby the truth. He *pushed* her down the stairs. Daniel would eventually kill her. It was only a matter of time.

Daniel had started to use his cigarette lighter on Robby's bare skin when the bite of the belt wouldn't make him cry anymore. Daniel said he did that so Robby would get a taste of what hell felt like, so he would learn to behave and go to heaven instead. It was the least of evils, Daniel had explained to him. It was done for his own good. But Daniel was the real sinner, not Robby. It was time Daniel paid for his sin, to get his own taste of what hell felt like.

Robby snuck through the dark and carefully moved into position behind Daniel's recliner. Daniel snored even louder. Thunder couldn't wake Daniel after he finished the whiskey bottle. The flames of hell would surely wake him. If God designed hell for sinners, then sending Daniel there was the will of God. Robby was an instrument of that will. Daniel was right about one thing. Sometimes in life, one had to choose the least of evils.

Robby snapped the leather belt taut between his fists. Blue veins bulged from the top of his now strong hands, hands that were merely an instrument, he reminded himself. He slowly reached the belt over Daniel's head, careful not to wake him. He gently slid the belt under his long, tangled beard, and pulled it under the chin, resting the leather strap against Daniel's throat. He clenched the belt so hard his fists trembled. He did this for Mother. He did this for the good of the world.

The least of evils...

****

Steam and aroma rose from the skillet as Jenny grilled chicken for a salad. "Why don't you chop the cucumbers?"

Amari was at the kitchen table, but she barely heard Jenny. She was too engrossed in her investigation.

"Or do you even like cucumbers in your salad?"

"Okay, why would you go through all the trouble to forge what's supposed to be the burial shroud of Christ, yet do it in a way that you barely see the image? You can't even see it up close. You have to be several feet away before it comes into view. And you can't really see it as a lifelike picture until you look at the photographic negative. That's when the image really pops. So why would anybody go to all the trouble?"

"So I guess we're eating on the coffee table again."

"And they didn't even have photographs back then. How could a forger know to make a picture that could only be seen clearly by a photographic negative? It doesn't make sense. This thing would cost a fortune to make, even if they had the technology. How could a poor knight who didn't have enough money to buy his way out of getting killed in battle pay for such a thing?"

Jenny turned the burner off and put the lid on the skillet. "You see how engrossed you are? You would make such a good detective. You're like a beagle tracking a rabbit."

"I know, you're right. It's like a drug I get hooked on. One time when I was in Junior Detectives, I shadowed my dad at work. We were on a case. We were getting so close. It was intoxicating. And we got the guy!"

Jenny pulled out the kitchen chair and sat across from Amari. "It's the thrill of the kill, isn't it? It's the hunt that excites you."

"Yes, I think that's it."

"So are you going to change your major back to criminal justice or what?"

"I don't know, Jenny. I don't want to talk about that right now. Right now I need to focus on the Shroud. There's so much evidence that says the carbon date is wrong. I mean, just look at this. That knight they claimed first displayed the Shroud couldn't have been the forger because Nicholas Mesarites—this guy was the custodian of the treasury at the Grand Palace in Constantinople—he cataloged having the Shroud in 1201. That's 150 years before Geoffrey de Charny got a hold of it. And besides, they have no idea how the image was formed. There's not a fleck of paint on it. It's like the fibers have microscopic burns." She flipped through her notes. "Denatured cellulose is what they think caused the image. The linen is made from cellulose, and some kind of energy caused it to denature. They say light or even radiation coming from the body could have caused it. Now tell me how a forger could have done that?"

Jenny picked up the photographic negative of the Shroud and studied it, an intrigued look on her face. "You think this could be real?"

"All I know is that when I look at his face, it's like something comes over me. It's like he's speaking to me. I think God is calling me to prove this isn't a forgery."

"To me it's just sad. If this really is Jesus, then seeing his bloodied, tortured dead body is very disturbing, don't you think? And even worse, it's on the table I'm trying to eat a salad on."

"Fine, Jenny, I'll move it to my bedroom. I'll put it on a card table or something."

"The kitchen table isn't the point. I don't see how you can read all the gory details about how much Christ suffered without being just a little sad. You don't seem to be fazed about the pain he must have gone through. And this is the price he paid for your sin. It makes me want to cry when I look at it."

Amari gazed upon the face of Jesus on the shroud. "But that's not the way I see this. That picture is the moment Jesus came alive. The energy that caused this image was God's power bringing him *back* from the dead. This is victory over death. It means that someday I'll overcome death too. Someday I'll be in heaven."

Jenny gasped. "Why didn't I see this before? This is about your mother. You're still grieving for your mother," she said and pointed to the table. "This is how you can feel assured you'll see your mother again. It's a psychological protection mechanism against the harsh realities of death."

Amari stared at the setting sun streaking into the kitchen, as a beam of light illuminated her research. "Maybe you're right. But it's not the whole reason I'm doing this. The Shroud is hope I feel for a lot of people out there. Millions of people." She outstretched her hand and blocked the sun, causing a shadow to fall on the face of Jesus. "For a lot of people out there, that carbon date will cast a shadow on their only hope. For some other people, it might remove hope completely. If that hope is going to be taken away, then it better be because of something that's true. It can't be because of a lie." She pulled her hand away and let the sun beam fall on the face of Jesus. "The world deserves to know the truth."

"Yes, Amari, they do. That's what a detective does. She exposes the truth. An artist can't do that. Listen, if this thing is real, then the carbon date is wrong. Something went wrong somewhere. Use your detective skills to find out what happened."

"I can't prove anything. I'm just a novice."

"But your dad isn't. Call him. See what he says about all of this."

Amari rubbed at her eyes. "Jenny, *please.* Stop bringing up my dad."

"I don't want to be a psychiatrist for the money. I want to help people. And right now, you need my help."

"And how do you plan on helping me?"

"You said the world deserves to know the truth, right?"

"It does."

"Well, so do you. You have to confront your feelings. I think you changed your major to art because of repressed hostility toward your dad."

That statement caught Amari off guard. "It's not repressed. I'm very vocal about that."

"Yes, but there's more going on behind your words. Unconscious impulses you aren't even aware of. I think you changed your major as a way of lashing out at your dad while attempting to extend your mother's life through art. You preferred to carry on her legacy rather than his."

"Jenny, this is none of your business. I don't want to confront my feelings. I just want to move on."

"You won't find peace until you confront the truth."

"If you're trying to make me cry this out, it's not going to work. I've done that already. There's nothing left for me to *let out*, if that's your therapy angle."

Jenny crimped her lips. "Hmmm. I was going for that, actually. Seems like a good cry helps most people."

"It's not going to work on me. You're just going to make me mad."

"My job as a therapist isn't to cause any particular emotion, but to discover what emotions you're feeling and go from there."

Was she ever going to shut up? Every day, it was the same thing. She was driving her nuts. "I told you I didn't want to talk about this. If you don't shut up, I'm going to raise your rent."

Jenny just stared back, her lips pursed, an indignant look on her face.

"You want to know why I'm still mad? It's because my mother didn't die from breast cancer."

"You said she did."

"No," Amari snapped. "She died from a broken heart. She was doing better. She was in remission until this came out. And then he lied to us both. Always, always, *always*, he told me. Always tell the truth! And then he lied, and then my mother died." She slumped back into her chair and cupped her hands over her face.

"I'm sorry, I didn't mean to make you m—,"

"Don't interrupt me. I'm counting to ten." She took deep breaths as she continued to count. When she finished, her hands fell from her face and she heaved a heavy sigh. "All better now. Mother said I had anger issues. She said count to ten."

"And did it work?"

"A little."

"Good, then we're making progress."

"If you say so."

"Amari, I know he did a terrible thing. Maybe he did it because your mother's illness made him feel vulnerable. Your mother couldn't provide comfort, so he found it any way he could. Who knows why he did it, but it doesn't matter. We're all flawed." Jenny picked up the picture of the Shroud. "That's why Jesus had to die for us. It's because we do things like your dad did. Listen, I don't want to preach, I really don't. But you know what Jesus said about all this. Unless you forgive others, you can't be forgiven." She set the photo back on the table and pointed to Jesus' wrist. "He paid a terrible price for our sin. If you don't find forgiveness, then you can't have it either. Don't let him die in vain."

"I thought you were a psychiatry student. Now you're in seminary?"

"How long has it been since you've gone to church?"

"Not since before mother died. Let's just say God and I haven't been on the best of terms since then."

Jenny pointed at her research. "Then maybe he's using the Shroud to bring you back."

"I don't know. Maybe."

"This Sunday, you need to go back to your church."

"Not back to my old church."

"Why not? You grew up there."

"Because it's too embarrassing. Everybody there knows about my dad. Everybody knows I quit going to church. I'm just a backslider to them, the daughter of a man who committed adultery."

"Don't be silly. Nobody thinks that. They probably haven't stopped praying for you this whole time. Listen, I'll go with you if it helps."

"But you told me you were Southern Baptist. This church is nondenominational."

"It's the same God, isn't it? Besides, I haven't found a church in Tucson yet. Maybe this will be it. I'll go back to Southern Baptist when I go back to the south."

"You'd really do that for me?"

"And for me. We both need to get back to church."

Amari massaged her tense jaw muscles as she pondered Jenny's statement. "I don't know, let me think about it."

"Raise my rent if you want to, but I'm not going to stop pestering you until you say yes."

Amari let out a heavy sigh. "All right, I'll go. But I like the ten o'clock service."

"I'll start doing my hair at eight."

Chapter 9

It was ten at night when Pete and George drove out of the Catalina foothills on East River Road. There had been a suspicious drowning in one of the Spanish tile-roofed mansions that overlooked Tucson. It looked like the fifty-something man may have had a heart attack while swimming alone. His wife found him floating when she'd gotten home. Nothing looked out of place, but they'd have to see the toxicology report to be sure.

A call came over the radio from dispatch. A burglar alarm reported, 3928 North Alvarez.

"Hey, Pete, that's just two streets over," George said. "You want to check it out or let patrol handle it?"

"It's probably the wind," Pete said. He was bushed. It had been a long day already. Why make it any longer? "May be a short circuit. It's late."

"Suit yourself. You're the boss."

Then again, Pete knew it would bug him all night if they weren't first on the scene and something was going down. "You say it's just two streets over?"

"It's near that big Jewish Center."

"Jewish center, huh?" Pete merged left on East River. He had a hunch. "What are the odds that another place of worship gets an alarm this time of night?"

"Punch it then."

Pete mashed the accelerator and sped down East River, past the compound of the Jewish Community Center, through the sparsely housed Jewish quarter of north Tucson. He cut left. The car slid sideways on the dirt-caked road. Back wheels sent dust flying as he corrected and pushed toward the target.

"Slow down, it's right here on the left," George said.

Pete swerved into the parking lot and skidded to a stop while he got his bearings. Bushy green mesquite trees in the parking lot medians obscured the synagogue. He flipped off the headlights and eased the car forward. A full moon lit the way and threatened to blow their cover. The place looked empty. No cars in the lot.

He parked and scanned the scene. It brought back memories of a murder he'd worked in a synagogue a few years before. Up front on the stage were expensive Torah scrolls that could be the object of a theft. "Let's check the perimeter. See if all the doors are locked."

They got out of the car and stood under flood lights that illuminated the building. A pack of coyotes cackled and yelped in the distance, an eerie noise that sounded more like kids playing on a playground than a pack of wild canines.

George looked over to his left. "You hear that, Pete?"

"The coyotes?"

"No, that hum over by the corner of the building."

"I hear it. Probably a noisy air unit."

George gave two quick sniffs. "Smells like spray paint."

"That's because you're standing on it," Pete said and pointed at George's feet. "It's graffiti."

The light was too low to read it, so George stepped over to the car and got the flashlight. Pete heard a noise from within the church, like a door slamming shut. He drew his gun and moved toward the door. He reached for the knob—the door flung open and bashed him in the head. He fell back into a cactus and hit the ground. A man wearing a motorcycle helmet dashed down the sidewalk. "George, he's coming your way!"

"Hey, man, you better stop!" George yelled as he ran after him.

Seconds later, the revving engine of a motorcycle roared. Before Pete could react, he smelled it. Smoke. He clamored to his feet and yanked open the door. A piece of the broken lock clanged as it fell onto the concrete.

He heard the motorcycle scream off down the parking lot, followed by two gunshots from George's pistol.

He rushed into the foyer and a jab of pain shot from his hip. He winced as he searched for the flame. A table with flyers and prayer hats was on one side of the sanctuary door. White prayer shawls with blue stripes hung on a rack on the other side. He saw no fire but sure smelled the smoke. Then he noticed the smoke curling from the top of the wooden sanctuary doors.

Pete limped over to the doors and threw them open. Orange flame glowed from the altar and lit the large open room. Smoke rose to the high ceilings and gathered around darkened skylights. He spotted the fire pull station in the corner, rushed to it, pulled the fire alarm, and hefted the fired extinguisher from its hook.

He limped into the sanctuary. The fire alarm clanged in his ears as he pushed forward to the front, hobbling past wooden pews, desperate to quench the flames before it got out of control. He pulled the pin and kept toward the stage. Flames on carpet inched toward mosaic walls and a tall case with heavy cloth curtains. A light beamed down on the curtains from small light bulbs. Behind those curtains, were the sacred scrolls of the Torah. He had no time to waste.

He climbed the stairs and aimed for the base of the fire. He squeezed the trigger. A jet of white powder spewed from the extinguisher. He swept the nozzle back and forth, following the trail of flame as it consumed carpet.

Finally, the fire was out. He dropped the extinguisher and stopped to catch his breath, wiping at his stinging eyes with the top of his wrist. He pulled his shirt over his mouth as a filter for the smoke and worked his way to the exit. He'd done a good thing. Maybe now God would forgive him for the affair. If only Amari would do the same.

"Pete, you okay?" The beam of George's flashlight made a white streak through the smoke.

"Yeah, you?" He limped over to George. "It's out."

"Your hip again?"

"Only when I fall on it. Or try to run."

"Good job on the fire, partner." George slapped him on the back.

Burning pain reminded him of the cactus. "Hold on, hold on."

George shined the light on his back and saw the thorns. "Sorry, boss. That looks painful."

"It is, thank you. Let's go outside so we can breathe."

Blue lights flashed onto the sidewalk when they stepped out of the synagogue. An officer walked up, shining a flash light in Pete's face. "Detective Johnston, is that you?"

"It's me," he said and sat on a bench.

"Take two ibuprofens and you'll be good in the morning," George said.

"And maybe an ice pack for my head," he said, fingering the knot rising on his forehead.

"Are you hurt?" the patrolman asked. "Do I need to call an ambulance?"

"I'll live. Thanks anyway," he said to the patrolman and then turned to George. "So what happened out here?"

"That hum I heard was his motorcycle. It was idling around the corner. He jumped on it before I could catch him. I squeezed off a couple of rounds, but he went behind those mesquite trees.

Couldn't get a clear shot. He went out the other entrance. I saw his lights head up into the foothills."

Pete reached around and winced as he pulled a thorn from his shoulder. "I told you I had a bad feeling about this."

"Jihad."

"What's that?"

George shined the beam of his flashlight on the sidewalk graffiti.

الجهاد 76

Chapter 10

Thursday, October 13, 1988

Amari was cooking dinner in the kitchen when Jenny came through the back door carrying a sack of groceries.

"Did you get milk?" Amari asked. "Cause we're almost out."

"Yep, I got it," Jenny said. She pulled a jar of peanut butter from the bag and placed it in the cupboard. "Hey, before I forget, make sure you watch the news tonight. I talked to Kevin a few minutes ago. He said the carbon date announcement is tonight on the evening news."

Amari's heart throttled up. Why was she so anxious? She knew what they'd found here in Tucson. But what about the other labs? Maybe they dated the cloth to the time of Jesus. "What channel?"

"All channels. ABC, CBS, and NBC. Kevin said this was headline news."

"So is he still worried about it? I mean, if his lab's results were way off from the other two labs, wouldn't that make him look like an idiot in front of the whole world?"

"I asked him about that. He said if the numbers were way off, they would be sweeping this under the rug rather than announcing it on the news. Scientists like to credit themselves, not discredit themselves. He said they typically only publish the stuff that agrees with their hypothesis."

"That seems a little dishonest, don't you think?"

"I think that's just the way the world works, Amari. Everyone's out for their own best interest."

Amari finished the casserole and put it in the oven. She went to the den, flipped on the television, and pushed the record button on her VCR. She went to the couch and hugged a throw pillow tight to her chest.

Jenny sat beside her.

"I'm taping over *China Beach*," Amari said. "I hope you don't mind."

"Like I have time for TV. I just hope they don't ramble on about Bush and Dukakis. I'm so tired of politics."

A short burst of violin music played as horizontal blue lines came together to form a world map. CBS EVENING NEWS WITH DAN RATHER flashed on the screen next. "This is the CBS evening news, Dan Rather reporting." Amari turned up the volume and made sure her VCR was recording.

Finally, Dan came to the Shroud. It was a press conference at the British Museum. Michael Tite of the British Museum stood with large round glasses next to the director of the Oxford University's carbon dating lab, Edward Hall. Edward stood there with a smug look on his face, arms folded across his chest. Behind them, numbers scrawled on a chalkboard said 1260-1390! The exclamation point felt like a slap. An arrogant insult. A blatant lie.

The screen shot switched to the Shroud of Turin as Dan Rather spoke. The camera panned down to the section that was sampled for the carbon date tests—the bottom left corner.

Amari's mouth fell open. She came off the couch and jutted an accusing finger at the screen. "*That's* where they did the test? On the bottom corner?"

"What's wrong with there?"

"That's the worst possible place to take it."

"Did you want them to take if from Jesus' face?"

"No, but anywhere else but there. Do you know how many times over the last two thousand years they must have handled the Shroud? They would stretch it out for everyone to see. And that corner is the place they would grab, over, and over again, maybe hundreds of times. In fact, one of those books has a painting of some guy holding it right there on the corner where they did the carbon date."

"Well, I'm sure they washed it off before they did the test."

"You don't get it. There's no way that corner couldn't have been damaged from all that handling. At some point, it would have started to tear, or at least unravel. At some point, somebody must have fixed it."

"Rewind that. I want to see that again."

"Me too," Amari said and set the TV to VCR mode. She rewound the tape and played the scene again.

"Well, it's kind of fuzzy, but I don't see any patch."

"And you wouldn't, either. It was probably done by French weavers. They were experts at weaving new cloth into old. They would dye the new fabric to match the old. Then they twisted the fibers together until you could hardly see a difference."

Amari gasped as a thought occurred.

"Are you okay?"

"I bet they did that on purpose. Because they *knew* it was a patch."

"You're being silly. Who would do such a thing?"

"I don't know. Maybe I'm wrong. Still, I'd love to get a better look."

"Are you ready for me to set you up with my cousin? I think he's got some close-up pictures."

"You think he'd talk to me?"

"I already asked him. He said anytime you're ready."

The warrior in Amari came to the surface. Any doubts she had about proceeding with her investigation had vanished when she saw where the sample was taken. God was forcing her hand now, his will made clear. "Okay, but let me get some notes together. I'll let you know when I'm ready."

Amari hit *rewind* and watched the press conference again.

Chapter 11

It was Pete's day off. He drove down East Harvey Street in his personal 82 Buick Regal. The road was so gray and sun-cracked it looked more like the skin of an elderly elephant than asphalt. To his right, the semi-barren Santa Catalina Mountains were partially obscured by power lines. To his left, tall, spindly palm trees were painted against a blue, cloudless sky. He continued past the Free Will Christian Church, with its red brick walls and A-frame roof. The little congregation of just over three hundred members had been home to his family for years.

That was before the affair. The shame of his sin—that despicable moment of weakness during a law enforcement conference up in Phoenix two years earlier—would forever haunt him. Sure, alcohol was a factor. He drank to numb the horror he witnessed daily at his job. It helped him ignore the guilt he felt for letting his marriage turn stale over the years, the broken promises he'd made to his young Navajo princess, promises he used to bribe her away from the reservation and a family she loved. The sight of her frail, emaciated body under the red bandana she used to cover her chemotherapy-ravaged-hair only fueled his guilt, especially on the days he couldn't bear to see her in that condition, those nights he volunteered for all night stakeouts that could have been done by rookies instead.

Detective Sikes knew about Haseya. She knew Pete had grown apart from his wife, had been deprived of marital benefits for some time. She used his deprivation as an excuse, a way to rationalize the behavior. Haseya would want this, she'd had the gall to suggest. Of course, she was drunk and so was he. Nothing clouds rational thought more than alcohol. It all came together to cause the biggest mistake of his life, much worse than the decision to take on a 7-eleven armed robber without backup, the one that put three slugs in his body and left chronic pain in his right hip. How was he to know Detective Sikes wouldn't keep her mouth shut? Why did she insist on making it more than it was, just a moment of weakness? Pete wanted nothing else to do with her. Just as he wanted nothing else to do with alcohol. But she wouldn't let it rest until she'd wrecked his marriage and ruined his relationship with his best friend, his spunky little girl named Amari.

He rounded the corner and drove past low-roofed, brick, ranch style homes with gravel front yards and cactus gardens. They were comfortable but nothing to brag about. It's all they could afford on the salary of a police detective whose wife had made money by weaving rugs and blankets in her den. Half of that money went to her parents on the reservation.

He parked his car along the curb of what used to be his house before the divorce. Now he lived in a single-room furnished efficiency apartment several blocks from the police station.

He and his Navajo princess, Haseya, had raised their two children in this home. Haseya had reluctantly agreed to become his wife in 1959, a time when mixed relationships between Indian and the white man were scandalous, at least amongst the Navajo people. But Haseya defied the will of her people and followed the man she loved.

If his Haseya had to die, he wished she could have died in his arms, the arms of a good and loyal husband. After the divorce, he'd tried to visit, but it never went well. He needed to hug her, to console her, but how could she benefit from the comfort of a man who'd promised her so much only to betray her at the time she needed him most? He'd meant to come more often, to somehow make amends, and then before he could muster the courage, she was gone. She was in heaven with a God he'd also disappointed, a God he'd begged for forgiveness every day since the affair. And maybe God did forgive him—just as promised after the sacrifice of his own son. If only Amari could see things the way God did.

He noticed another car in the driveway, parked partly on the brown, crushed stone yard to allow Amari's car to pull out from under the carport. It was a sensible car, a white VW Rabbit. The car a person drives speaks volumes about the driver.

Obviously, Amari had moved on. Was that a new boyfriend's car? She hadn't dated in so long. Not all men were like her last date. Not all men were scumbag rapists.

A smile crept onto his lips. "That's my girl," he said to himself. Nobody messes with Amari. Not unless they want a broken windpipe and a groin that would never be the same. That boy wanted to press charges against her for assault. The judge thought otherwise and sent him away for ten years when two other girls from the college came forward. Pete half suspected Amari was working undercover to expose this guy. He wouldn't put it past her, but she never admitted to it. But that was three years ago, and she'd been a little gun-shy ever since. If she'd dated since then, he didn't know anything about it. Of course, he knew next to nothing about what she had done since the divorce. Only that now she wanted to be an artist like her mother instead of a cop like her dad.

He grabbed the toolbox and a hand-held pipe snake from the passenger seat. When he rang the bell, a short, twenty-something girl answered the door. She had a pointy beak of a nose, her eyes were the color of blueberries, set under heavy eye shadow of a similar color, and her blonde hair was teased up like steel wool. He sensed this girl was sizing him up just as much as he was doing the same to her.

"Is Amari home?" he asked. "Her car's here, so I assume she is."

"May I ask who's inquiring?" The girl asked. She had a pitchy squeak of a voice, yet somehow intimidating at the same time, like the mean little school teacher he had in third grade.

"I'm her father, young lady. The guy who paid for the house. Can I come in?"

"It's okay, Jenny," Amari called from behind. "That's my dad. You can let him in." It saddened him when he heard the reluctance in her voice.

Magazines were neatly stacked on the coffee table, the floor was clean with fresh vacuum tracks, and there was a flowery smell in the air. "Place looks great," Pete said.

"I'm what some people would call a neat freak," Jenny said.

"I can see that."

There was Haseya's loom against the wall. It looked like Amari was trying to finish the rug Haseya had started before she died. Amari was good at weaving too. You could hardly tell the difference from where Haseya left off and Amari took over.

Amari came into the den and stood with her hands on her hips. She looked good. It had been weeks since he'd seen her. She had his square jaw and dark brown, wide crescent eyes, but she had her mother's Navajo skin, only a couple of shades lighter. Her deep brown hair was pulled into a braided ponytail and dropped down just above her hips. She was beautiful, yet bold. Just like her mother.

Pete set the heavy toolbox on the parquet floor landing in front of the door. "So how's it goin', kiddo?"

Amari looked at him with weary eyes. "Jason told you about the shower, didn't he?"

"He called collect from Spain. You should have told me. Nobody knows the pipes in this house better than your dad."

Amari folded her arms across her chest and averted her eyes to the kitchen.

"That good, huh?"

She brought her eyes back around and focused on his bruise. "So what happened to your head?"

He reached up and felt the knot. "Had a run-in with a synagogue door."

Amari perked up. "That was you?"

"In the flesh."

"The scanner radio went wild over that one. Are you the one who put out the fire?"

"It wasn't that big of a fire. But it was me." He picked up the toolbox and started down the hall. "So which bathroom is it?"

"It's the one in your old bedroom. You're limping again."

"Yeah, door knocked me over. It's better than it was."

She followed him to the bedroom. "Dad, you're fifty-four years old. You need to let the younger guys take care of things like that. You're going to get hurt."

"It hurt like. . . holy cow, Amari, what's all this?"

Two large photos of the Shroud of Turin were thumbtacked to the drywall, one a black and white photo negative, and the other one regular. Papers and sticky notes were stuck to the sliding glass door that led to the fenced back yard. Books and papers were spread all over a card table.

She moved between him and the pictures on the wall. "It's an art project. The bathroom's over here," she said as she pointed to the master bath.

"I know where the bathroom is. I showered in it for seventeen years."

"Well, I can't shower in it now. I've tried drain cleaner, but I can't get it unplugged."

"What kind of art class are you taking?"

"It's a paper for medieval art. Since the news said the Shroud is a forgery, then it must be a painting, right?" She folded her arms across her chest again. "That makes it medieval art."

"That's an awful lot of work for a class paper. It reminds me more of my desk at work. If I didn't know better, I'd say you were on a case."

She folded her arms even tighter. "I take my schoolwork seriously."

"I know that. You made straight A's in criminal justice. Why are you still doing this? I thought you'd take art one semester and get it out of your system."

"Well, I haven't."

"What are you supposed to do with an art degree?"

"Maybe I can teach art."

"But all you can do is weave."

"Then I'll teach underwater basket weaving. Are you going to fix the drain or do I need to call a plumber?"

"Doesn't look like you can afford a plumber. Otherwise, you wouldn't have a roommate."

"How do you know she's my roommate? I never told you that."

"You never kept the house this neat. I'm not blind, Amari. You've run through your mother's life insurance, haven't you?"

"It wasn't that much." She reached for her dad's tools. "Just give me that pipe snake and I'll fix the drain myself."

He rubbed at the knot on his head. Was this ever going to end? "Fine, fine, give me a second and I'll have it fixed." In the bathroom, he pulled a screwdriver out, popped the top to the drain, fed the snake in, and pulled out a big soapy chunk of her hair. He turned on the water to check his work. Satisfied, he packed his tools and went back into the bedroom. She sat at the card table with her nose in a book.

"The Shroud of Turin, huh?"

"You've heard of it," she said without looking up.

"It was in the news. Carbon date says it's a fake."

"Well, it's not."

"What do you mean, it's not? Science geeks don't lie. The carbon date says it's from 1390."

"That's because they're idiots," she said, never looking up from the book.

"What's gotten into you? Get your nose out of that book and talk to me."

She glanced up at him with a pout of mock sincerity. "Is this better?"

"You hear about that priest that was murdered?"

She sat up straight in her chair. Now she was listening. "I did. Are you on that case?"

"First on the scene. Well, after the uniformed guys. The perp offed him in the confessional."

"He shot a priest in the confessional? What kind of monster would do that?"

"The worst kind. That's why we've got to catch him. Anyone who would kill a man of the cloth the way he did is capable of anything."

"Well, tell me what you've got so far. Maybe I can help."

He saw her gears were turning now. These were the first civil words they'd had since the affair broke. He knew he'd better run with it. "Unfortunately, we don't have much. Trajectory of the bullet says he was fairly short. He started the fire with lighter fluid, then sped out of there like a bat out of hell on a motorcycle. I'd put money it's the same guy we ran into at the synagogue. M.O. is exactly the same. He had a black motorcycle helmet with a tinted face shield on the whole time, even when he came running out of the church. Couldn't make him but he wasn't tall and a little on the thin side."

"Any prints? Witnesses? What about tire tracks? Could you get anything on the bike?"

"They got some tracks at the synagogue. Pretty generic tire. Not much help. You know, the funny thing is, this Shroud of Turin thing you're working on may have something to do with this. There may be a link."

She stood and put the book on the card table. "Really? What kind of link?"

"This priest wrote an article for the newspaper. He was trying to say it didn't matter what the carbon date said about the Shroud. All the other evidence proved the Shroud was authentic. Of course, this was before the carbon date came out on the news. But apparently, he suspected what the results would be, so that's why he wrote the article."

She paced to the bedroom door, spun round, and paced back as she worked the details in her head. "So you think that's why he was targeted?"

"Who knows?"

"So why the synagogue? Surely Jews don't want the Shroud to be real."

"You're right. It's probably nothing," he said and lifted up one of the papers on the table. There was some science jargon on top he couldn't begin to pronounce. "Amari, this isn't an art project. Why is this so important to you?"

"It started out as an art project. But I'm telling you, Dad, that's not a painting. The Shroud of Turin is no forgery. I don't care what the carbon date said."

"How can you say that?"

Her cheeks flushed red like they always did when she was getting mad. "Because the evidence says that. Detectives go with the evidence and with their gut. Both say this is real. It's not a forgery."

He knew from experience he'd better diffuse the situation. Just go along. "Okay, so it's not then. I believe in Jesus. I got no problem with that. I mean, it looks like Jesus to me. So why not just let it go? It's a matter of faith, isn't it?"

"It's more than just that," she said, her voice rising in anger.

"What else is there? Why are you making such a—"

"Because it's a lie!" she yelled and slammed her fist into the table. Papers and books jumped from the shock. "And I hate lies!"

Pete held up his hands. "Hey, now, calm down."

"Why couldn't you just tell the truth?" Her eyes were wet over blazing cheeks and her lip quivered. "You always told me to tell the truth. And yet when we asked you about it, you looked us in the face and lied. And I believed you!"

He hunched his shoulders and dropped his chin to his chest. Bitter remorse clawed at him when he saw his baby's angry, accusing eyes. How could he ever get her to trust him again? "Amari, your mother was sick. It was just a one-time thing. You know your mother and I hadn't been getting along for years. We were just too different. I know that doesn't make what I did right, but I'm sorry. I was afraid if I told her the truth, it would just make her condition worse. The doctors told us we needed to keep her emotionally strong. The last thing she needed was to hear her husband cheated. I lied because I thought it was in her best interest."

"And look what happened," she shot back. "Was that in her best interest?"

"She got better. She went into remission."

"Better enough to kick you out of the house and serve you divorce papers."

"That she did. I had that coming. But why does that mean I have to lose my daughter too?"

"Because you lied to me," she said, her tone softening. "That's why. And I'm still mad at you."

She sat on the bed, elbows resting on her thighs. He sat next to her and started to put his arm around her, but thought better of it. "I know you are. I'm mad at myself too. I'll never forgive myself. I only hope you will."

That said, he picked up his tools and went to the doorway. "Next time you have a problem, with the house, or anything, call me, okay? I'm your dad. That's what I'm here for."

He waited for her to respond, but she didn't look up. He knew her well enough to know he could only make matters worse if he kept prodding her. He would just have to try again later.

"It's all fixed," he said to Jenny and walked out the front door.

"It doesn't sound fixed to me," she said as the door closed behind him.

Chapter 12

Friday, November 4, 1988

Amari sat on the floor and worked the thread into her mother's rug. Knowing this rug was her mother's last project frequently brought to mind her mother's last words.

The hospice service had provided a hospital bed for home use. They came and went on a daily basis, providing drugs and basic medical needs. The Catholic Church granted Jason leave so he could help Mother while Amari was in school. Her dad had come around occasionally, but it was always awkward and unnecessary, so he eventually got the hint and stopped trying to help.

She remembered walking into her mother's room with a fresh pitcher of water. The head of her bed was inclined because it was less painful that way. Mother's hair was black, streaked with gray. Much of it had returned from the last round of chemo, but it was still short and thin, and her chest was flat after the double mastectomy. When the cancer returned, it had invaded her liver and there was no point continuing the treatment, no point in prolonging her suffering.

Mother was gaunt and her eyes were glassy, glazed over by narcotics to numb the pain from the cancer pressing against her spine, brain, and now, liver. But her words were alive with hope and that's what Amari chose to relish.

Amari knelt by her bed, holding her cold, weakened fingers inside her own.

Mother startled awake. Her eyes probed the dim light until they found her daughter. "Amari. Is that you?"

"Yes, Shimi. I'm here." Amari gently caressed her mother's hand.

"Before I go to heaven, I want to know something."

"Yes, Mother. What is it?"

"Tell me your dreams, Shiyazhi," she said, which meant *my child* in the Navajo language. "I cannot be here to see them come true, but at least tell me what they are."

Amari forced an upbeat, happy reply. "I'm going to be an artist, just like you."

"An artist?" She strained to make a puzzled expression. "Shiyazhi, that was *my* dream for you. Your dream is to be like your father. Tell me, what do you really want to do?"

"I honestly don't know anymore, Shimi. I just don't want to be like him."

"Your father is not perfect, but he is a good man. Don't involve him in your decision. Tell me your dreams for *your* life?"

"I don't know, Shimi." Her voice cracked as she strained to hold back the tears. "I don't know anymore."

"When the time is right, you will know, Shiyazhi. Trust in God. He will show you his purpose. Be open to his will. That is all you have to do."

"But God doesn't listen anymore. If he did, you wouldn't be dying. Dad wouldn't have done this to you." She fell against her mother's hollow chest and she wept.

Her mother stroked her hair as she spoke, her voice strained, but alive with emotion. "Diyin Ayói Át'éii," Shiyazhi. Trust in the Great Spirit. Don't you give up on him. He will show you his will. One day, you will join me again and then you will tell me all about it. Jesus will bring us together again, Shiyazhi. Someday, you will tell me all about it." Then her mother faded into sleep. The next day, she ascended into heaven. Amari would not speak to her again.

She let go of the loom's yarn and returned to her feet. Moisture had built in her eyes as she remembered that day, but the hope of her mother's final words kept the tears in place. The day of mourning had passed, and now it was time for action, to build upon the story she would someday tell, the lives she'd changed for good. Someday in heaven, she would tell her mother all about it.

Chapter 13

Amari parked in the student garage and made her way towards University of Arizona's Weiss Mass Spectrometer Laboratory—WMS for short. She passed in front of the Old Main building, which was at the head of the university's long, green, palm tree-lined lawn. It was like a small version of the lawn in Washington DC, only with the library, gym, and classrooms instead of Smithsonian museums. She made her way past the College of Agriculture and approached the rectangular, red brick building that housed the WMS lab. It was four stories tall with four long rows of windows running down its side, windows with white shades jutting out from them to block the brutal Arizona sun. Date palms with their arched, hanging branches provided shade for bicycles chained to steel racks.

She found an entrance and paused before she pushed through the door. It wasn't too late to change her mind. She could just turn around and walk back to her car. But she thought of her mother again, about the stories she would tell in heaven. She knew she couldn't stop now. Besides, her name meant *never gives up.* She had to live up to that name.

She drew a deep breath and pushed through the door. In the corner of the foyer, an elderly woman sat at a desk reading a romance novel through reading glasses.

She stepped over to the desk. "My name's Amari Johnston. I have an appointment to meet with Dr. Brenner."

The receptionist picked up a clipboard, tilted her head back, and crinkled her nose as she read the names of daily appointments. "What was your name again?"

"Amari Johnston."

"How do you spell that? Oh, hold on, here it is. Johnston. You have an appointment with Dr. Brenner at 3:00 p.m."

"Yes, ma'am."

The lady lowered her glasses and peered up at a wall clock. "You're very punctual. Follow me. It's just down the hall."

Amari followed her down the long, painted cinder block hallway. The farther she went, the more the apprehension built. According to Jenny, Dr. Brenner had graduated high school at sixteen. He graduated college with a double major of physics and mechanical engineering at twenty. He finished a master's degree at twenty-one and a Ph.D. in physics at Boston's prestigious MIT at twenty-three. He was currently doing his post-doctoral work at the WMS laboratory. Along the way, he'd won several awards and accolades. He was an intellectual rock star. Could she match wits with a guy like this? The butterflies in her gut turned to hornets and she started to feel nauseated.

The receptionist stopped at the door and punched a code into a keypad. The door made a click and she pushed it open.

"That's him in that ugly orange cap," she said as she pointed.

"Thank you," Amari said and the door closed behind her, cutting off her escape.

A steady, pervasive hum saturated the air. Long, thick metal pipes were bolted together and snaked through the room, entering square mechanical modules, then exiting these same modules on the other end, only to enter another contraption. A fat pipe which looked more like a tank connected other pipes. Meters and gauges were fixed to the pipe's path in strategic places. Other gizmos and gadgets were scattered on tables and shelves throughout the lab.

Dr. Brenner pointed at one of the gizmos as he talked to another colleague dressed in a white lab coat. They continued to talk and point, saying something that looked important, so she waited her turn as she sized him up.

Snug on top of his head was a dirty, obnoxious orange baseball cap with a big white letter T on its front. His long brown hair fell a good two inches below the back collar of his shirt. Under the brim of the cap were friendly, brown eyes that left no hint of the genius brain behind them. He wasn't anything liked Jenny had described. Maybe it was her genetic blindness because they were cousins, but she thought he was really cute, not the dorky, bow-tie-wearing dweeb she'd expected.

Finally, Dr. Brenner patted his coworker on his back and glanced her way. He walked over and his coworker followed close behind. "You must be Amari. Jenny said you'd be coming by. I'm Kevin. This here's Jerry."

"It's Jeremy, actually," the colleague said. Jeremy was about Amari's height. Black bangs fell to his eyebrows, just over eyes that were blue like a swimming pool. His demeanor seemed that of a bullied kid, the kind Amari used to defend on the school bus.

She shook Dr. Brenner's hand. "Amari Johnston. Nice to meet you," she said, holding her grip for an awkwardly long moment. He wasn't like she'd imagined—not at all.

She let go and turned to shake Jeremy's hand, but they were jammed into his front pockets and he simply nodded his approval.

"Jerry's grandfather practically built this place," Dr. Brenner said. "It's why they named it after him. Ol' Jerry here's thinking of majoring in physics. Probably run the place himself someday."

Jeremy just stood there, expressionless.

"Hey, Jerry, keep working on that thing," Dr. Brenner said. "Miss Johnston just has a few questions. We'll be in my office if you need me."

She followed him to his office. He sure didn't look like a future Nobel Prize winner. He dressed more like a hobo. Didn't they have dress codes in places like this? He wore faded, stone-washed jeans, and a rustic, worn leather belt kept his baggy pants from falling to his ankles. His shirt was a plaid flannel button-up that looked like it had come from a thrift store.

He stopped at the door and opened it. "Sorry, ma'am, office is a mess," he said and ushered her in. His desk was cluttered with papers and manuals. More manuals and notebooks lined a shelf against the wall.

Dr. Brenner slid a fold-up chair beside his desk next to his chair. "Have a seat. Can I get you something? I've got Mountain Dew," he said and pointed to a small, brown refrigerator. He had a southern accent, a little stronger than Jenny's, but nothing like she had described. Apparently, Jenny had a knack for exaggeration.

Amari sat and smoothed out her skirt. "No, thank you, Dr. Brenner. I won't be long. You know, you're not the way Jenny described you."

"Oh, man, I'd hate to hear how she described me."

"She didn't say anything bad. She just described you in terms of, you know, accolades and achievements."

"You were expecting that guy from *Revenge of the Nerds.* The guy with tape on his glasses."

She threw out a laugh. "Something like that. So did you really get your Ph.D. from MIT when you were twenty-three? I'm twenty-two and haven't even finished my bachelor's yet. You must be really smart."

"Nahh, I'm not that smart. Just impatient. Norbert Weiner got his Ph.D. from Harvard in mathematical logic when he was seventeen. By that standard, I'm a real slacker."

She giggled and gazed at him for a moment. He was so easy going, humble, and self-deprecating. Any anxiety she had left seemed to dissipate. Suddenly, she'd forgotten why she came. She fumbled for words. "Uh, so, what was your degree in again?"

"Experimental physics. They hired me for that carbon date contraption you saw outside. I'm also tweaking the design a bit. I'm working on a new time of flight detector. Ion source needs some improvement too."

"That sounds impressive. So are you done with school or are you going to keep going?"

"I'm doing my post-doc work right now. I just want to settle down and work for a while, you know, live a little."

"I don't blame you."

"You know, Jenny thinks the world of you."

"Really? That's surprising. I figured she'd classify me as a non-compliant patient."

"Oh, no. She would never tell me that. It would be a breach of patient-client confidentiality," Dr. Brenner said with a smirk.

"That's Jenny, all right."

"Ain't it, though? Are you sure I can't get you a Coke or something?"

"No thank you, Dr. Benner. I know you're busy," she said and held up her notepad. She needed to stop wasting this poor guy's time and get on with it. "I just have a few questions for you."

"I'll do my best to answer them, under one condition."

"Okay."

"Stop calling me Dr. Brenner. Just call me Kevin. It's what my friends call me."

"Okay, Kevin. If you'll stop calling me ma'am. Just call me Amari."

"Well, then, Amari, what can I do for you?"

"It's about the Shroud of Turin."

"Then you've come to the right place. Jenny said this was for an art class?"

"It started out that way. I mean, if it is a forgery, then it must be a work of art, right? But from what I've found so far, I can't figure out how an artist could have pulled this off. Certainly not with medieval technology."

Kevin leaned back in his office chair. He laced his fingers and rested them on stomach. "I can't help you much with the art angle, it's not my thing," he said as he tapped the tips of his thumbs together. "But if you've got science questions, I'd be glad to try."

"Okay," she said and flipped a page in her notebook. "Carbon-14 dating. How does that work?"

"That's an easy one. It's like this. All plants and animals have about the same amount of carbon-14 in them when they're alive. Now, in the case of the Shroud of Turin, those linen fibers came from a flax plant. Linum usitatissimum, if you want the scientific term."

She jotted notes on her pad while he waited for her to catch up. She didn't bother writing that last tongue twister.

"Now, there's three naturally occurring isotopes of carbon. There's carbon-12, carbon-13, and carbon-14. Carbon-14 is a radioactive isotope. It forms in the upper atmosphere when cosmic rays knock a proton out of nitrogen-14. You follow me so far?"

"Sort of." She stopped writing and decided to listen and get the gist of it. "Keep going."

"Now, you know how when plants breathe in CO_2 and let off oxygen, right?"

"Right, I remember that from biology class."

"Okay, so the carbon from the CO_2 stays with the plant, and some of that carbon is the radioactive carbon-14. So all plants have about the same amount of carbon-14 when they die. But over time, carbon-14 begins to decay at a known rate. In other words, over time there is less and less carbon-14. What we do here is we turn the sample into graphite and shoot it through that big machine you saw out there. It's got these detectors that count the carbon-14 that passes through it. The less carbon-14 there is, the older the sample is."

"Okay, that makes sense. So you turned the piece of the Shroud into graphite."

"Pure carbon."

"That's right, and you shot it through this thing out there and you figured out that it dated to around 1300."

"1260-1390 if you take the average of all three labs." Something in his subtle facial expressions and the tone of his voice suggested he didn't believe the results either.

"You don't sound like you're completely convinced."

He shrugged. "We feed in the sample and the machine spits out the numbers. The Shroud dated as medieval from 1260-1390, using information averaged from all three labs. Here at our lab, we got 646 years old, plus or minus thirty-one years. Oxford got 750 years old, plus or minus thirty years, and Zurich got 676 years old, plus or minus twenty-four years old."

"So if the average date was between 1260-1390, then you're saying it had to be a forgery."

"That's what this particular piece of evidence suggests."

"Do you believe that?"

He puffed his cheeks and blew air. "I'm still pondering that one."

"Huh," she said and studied his face. She wasn't expecting that kind of answer. Scientists are supposed to be sure about things, not just pondering things. This seemed to be the perfect time to bring up her next question. She flipped to a dog-eared page in her notebook. "Some archeologists say carbon dating can be wildly inaccurate, even contradictory. I've read that some scientists say the fire in 1532 produced carbon that could easily skew the carbon date."

"It's all true. But that's not our job at this lab. We just spit out the numbers. What other scientists do with that information is none of our business."

"Fair enough," she said and turned to another page. "Around the time of Christ, the herringbone twill of the Shroud was common in ancient Syria, but there's no evidence it existed in Europe during the medieval period."

"Like I said, what we put out is just one piece of evidence," he said and pointed to her notebook. "But there's obviously other evidence."

She read another page. "The wounds on the head suggest it was more like a rounded *cap* rather than a *crown* that we see in paintings. The wounds from the nails are on the wrists, not the hands. The Bible says it was a *crown* of thorns and the nails were in the hands. Most paintings of the period show it this way. So why would a forger make a mistake like this? Or was the Bible maybe a few words off from what actually happened? My dad's a cop, and he'll tell you that every witness tells something a little differently. It's how we know the event really happened. If they all said the same exact thing, then we know they're in collusion with each other. The gospels are an eyewitness account, so we can expect a few discrepancies. But any forger who wanted to pass this off as the real shroud of Jesus wouldn't have known that. He would have made it look like the gospels, like the other paintings of the age."

He shrugged and scratched the back of his head, right under his obnoxious orange cap. "We just put out the numbers. Like I said, science is my wheelhouse. What you're talking about is for historians and Bible scholars."

She could see this was leading nowhere. He was clueless about anything regarding the Shroud that wasn't related to physics. Baiting him to make statements that discredited his work wasn't going to work. And she felt a little ashamed for trying. It was time to move on. "Okay, fair enough," she said and flipped another page. "Let's stick with the science then. I'm sure you're familiar with STURP."

"The Shroud of Turin Research Project. Of course. I've met some of those guys. Top of their field."

"Impressive. You get around."

"You know, conferences, things like that."

"So tell me about the VP8 camera. This camera says the Shroud is a 3-D image. Can you explain that one to me?"

"The VP8 was used by NASA to map out the terrain of the moon. It plots light and dark areas into a 3-D grid using a computer. The computer interprets the brighter areas as being closer to the camera and the darker areas as being farther away."

"Oh, okay. It makes much more sense when you explain it. Interesting. Thank you."

"My pleasure. You've done your research here. I'm impressed."

"I like to be thorough." She wasn't sure if he meant that, or if he was just being polite. "So according to my thorough research . . . are you really impressed? Coming from someone like you, that's a big compliment."

"Heck, yeah, I'm impressed. It must have taken you months to get all of that together."

"Not months. Weeks, maybe."

"Then I'm even more impressed. Jenny said you were determined. Said she'd never seen anyone like you before. I see what she means now."

"She really said that about me? I figured she thought I was crazy."

"Was Einstein crazy? Was Thomas Edison? They were determined, just like you."

"That's very sweet of you. Thank you for saying that."

"I call it like I see it."

Amari returned his smile for an awkward moment. She broke eye contact and went back to her notes. "I'm sorry, where were we?"

"You were talking about STURP."

"That's right," she said, moving finger down the page to find the right spot. "When Dr. Jackson and Dr. Jumper analyzed the Shroud with the VP8 camera, they found a 3-D image. But when they did the same thing with any other paintings or photographs, all they got was electronic noise. Apparently, no other image like the Shroud exists."

"Not that we know of."

"Right, not that we know of. So how could a forger know to encode a 3-D image that could only be interpreted by a VP8 analyzer? And while we're on the subject, how could a forger make an image that is only clearly revealed with a photographic negative, when they didn't even have cameras back then? Not to mention the fact that there are no pigments, dyes, or binding agents that we see with paint. So if it wasn't painted or drawn, then can you tell me how this could have been forged?"

"Well, isn't it obvious?"

Was he a believer? Jenny certainly never mentioned he was a Christian. She had assumed all these science types were either atheist or agnostic at best. "It's obvious to me. But what do you think?"

"Aliens, obviously," he said emphatically. "They're the only ones with the technology to pull this off. It's got to be aliens."

Chapter 14

Amari cracked a curious grin. Was she supposed to laugh at that? Was he for real? But Kevin wasn't smiling. He just leaned back in his chair with his fingers laced behind his head with a serious look on his face.

"Aliens," Amari said. "Like from Mars?"

"Oh, not from Mars," he replied. "Way farther out."

"Little green men made the Shroud of Turin?"

His expression remained firm and he gave a slow nod of his head. "Aliens. It's the only way."

The door suddenly came open and startled her. Kevin quickly sat up in his chair. A fifty-something man with Arab features stood under the door frame. His black hair was streaked with gray and his eyes seemed slightly misaligned so she couldn't tell if he was looking at her or Kevin.

"Dr. Rahal," Kevin said. "I didn't think you'd be back until tomorrow." He sifted through papers on his desk. "I've got that report for you somewhere."

"I just had a question or two." He folded his arms across his chest. "Who is your guest?"

She stood and straightened her skirt. "Amari Johnston," she said and offered her hand. A firm handshake, look him straight in, well, one of his eyes.

Dr. Rahal refused her hand. He eyed her suspiciously and gave a small nod. "What business do you have with the lab? Are you a vendor? A radiocarbon client? From a museum?"

"No, nothing like that," she replied. "I'm his cousin's roommate. I was just asking him a few questions."

"Questions? Questions about what?"

"She's just curious about how carbon dating works," Kevin broke in.

"Then go to the library. Dr. Brenner is not being paid to answer your questions. He has work to do."

"I'm sorry," she said. "I didn't mean to cause any trouble."

"Just finish up quickly. Dr. Brenner, when you are finished you can see me in my office," he said and closed the door behind him.

She cringed. "Sorry, I didn't mean to get you in trouble."

"That's Dr. Rahal," Kevin said. "He's the director here. My boss. Stickler for the rules. I've never seen him smile. I think maybe it's a cultural thing. He's from the middle east."

"So he's Muslim?"

"Not sure, didn't ask. He signs my check and that's good enough for me. I wouldn't worry about him, though. All bark, no bite. Besides, I'm in good with Dr. Weiss, the emeritus professor here."

"So Dr. Weiss is who your lab is named after?"

"He's the one who started this place. Gotta name it something. He's got a lot of clout with the university. If Dr. Weiss wanted Rahal gone, I bet he could manage it."

"So what exactly does an emeritus professor do?"

"It's a professor that's sort of retired. Only they're still involved. They offer advice and serve on university boards. Stuff like that."

"So they still have power, but don't actually have to put in a nine to five day."

"Something like that. Dr. Weiss likes me. Jerry, out there in the lab, the guy that I was talking to? That's his grandson."

"You mean Jeremy."

"I like to call him Jerry. He doesn't mind. We're pretty good buds. He's thinking about changing his major to physics so Dr. Weiss got him this gig so he can try it on for size."

"That was nice of him."

"He's a really nice man. Jerry thinks the world of him. Worships the ground he walks on."

Suddenly, Jeremy pushed the door open using a handkerchief.

"Speak of the devil," Kevin said. "What's up, Jerry? I was just telling Amari here how great your granddad is."

"Sorry to bug you, Dr. Brenner, but we have another problem. We're still losing pressure in the number three carbon extraction line."

"We tightened all the valves, didn't we?"

"I did so personally."

"Well, crap, only thing I know to do is get new seals. Hey, tell you what. Dilute out a little dish soap and put some on all the seals. If you see bubbles, there's the problem. At least we can narrow down which seals we need to replace."

Jeremy didn't look impressed.

"Hey, don't knock it. Back in Tennessee, that's how I found inner tube leaks on my ATV. Soap bubbles show you where to put the patch."

Jeremy hiked his brows over those blue eyes of his. "Simple yet effective. I'll let you know how it works. Sorry for the intrusion." He used the handkerchief to close the door behind him.

Kevin waited for a few seconds before speaking. Then he leaned closer and said, "He's a germaphobe. That's why he uses the handkerchief."

"I can see that."

"He claims he has problems with his immune system. Personally," he said in a whisper. "I think he's just a hypochondriac."

"That must be why he wouldn't shake my hand."

"Girl germs, *ick*," he said and crinkled his nose in disgust.

"You're funny, Kevin. Listen, I better let you go before Dr. Rahal comes back and catches me. Hey, do you like pizza?"

"Who doesn't?"

"I work at the Pizza Hut down the street. Come by for a freebie. I get free pizza on dinner break. I'd like to ask some more questions." She hoped that didn't sound like she was asking him out. But obviously they couldn't talk at the lab and she had a whole lot more questions.

"I'd like that. But I'm going to be here kind of late this evening. Got things to do, you know."

"That's okay. I'll be there kind of late. No pressure, come by if you're hungry. Or maybe I can just call you with more questions if you'd prefer it that way."

"I'll see what time I can get out of here," he said and slid his desk drawer open. "Just in case, here's my card if you want to call me later."

"Thank you, Dr. Brenner."

"Kevin."

"Thank you, Kevin. You've been a big help."

****

"So do you want pan or original crust?" Amari asked the family of four, pencil pressed against note pad.

"We'll take the pan," the dad said. "Hey, ask them if they can burn the cheese a little."

"Burn cheese, got it."

Amari took the order back to the kitchen. She slumped over the prep station and made the pizza herself since the main cook was doing dishes. It was after 8:30 and the dinner rush had died down, so it was cleanup time. She might as well be useful since it didn't look like Kevin would show. Apparently, he had better things to do. She would just have to get the information she needed by phone call, or maybe relay information through Jenny.

She made a couple more pizzas and then went back to check on her tables. A grown man played Mrs. Pac Man over by the front door. She widened her eyes and did a double take. The bright orange rim of a baseball cap jutted out of his front pocket.

Wakawakawakawakewaka the game sounded. "Dang! Ah, come on!" The machine twirped and whined, signifying game over.

"Dr. Benner," she said. "You made it."

He stood up and thumbed over to the machine. "I rock on regular Pac Man, but this lady Pac Man, just can't beat it."

"Must be rigged," she said with a big grin.

"Must be."

"So you hungry?"

"Starved. Just got off work. Me and Jerry had a time with those valves. More than one was leaking."

"Let me get you a seat. You want a booth or a table?"

"Booth is fine."

She led him to a booth by the window. The red curtains matched the red seats which also matched the red and white checkered table cloth, which was made of vinyl instead of fabric so it could be easily wiped down with a wet rag.

"What do you want to drink?"

"Mountain Dew if you got it."

"We only carry Coke products."

"Then make it a Coke. I'm not choosy."

"What do you want on your pizza?"

"Anything but anchovies. Who eats those things anyway?"

"Pepperoni and mushrooms?"

"My favorite."

She turned in her order and clocked out for the day since the dinner rush was over. She ran to her car, got her notebook, and came back. She tucked the notebook under her armpit, carried the drinks to the table, and slid into the booth across from him.

"Okay," she said and exhaled. "Where were we?"

"Before Dr. *Nay-All* interrupted. That's what we all call him. Nay, nay, nay, is all he says. Won't agree to anything."

She stared blankly into those easy-going brown eyes under his wavy, feather-cut, parted in the middle brown hair. She hoped her face wasn't too greasy. She didn't wear much makeup, but the little she did, she'd touched up before he came.

"Nay-All rhymes with Rahal, get it?"

She broke from her trance. "Oh, I get it. You're so funny."

"It's funnier if you knew the guy."

"I guess so. Hey, listen, thank you for coming, Dr. Benner. I was beginning to think you couldn't make it."

"Kevin, remember. Just call me Kevin."

"Thank you, Kevin."

"Hey, it's no problem. It's on my way home anyway. I live in Rio Vista."

"In the foothills, nice."

"Right under them. And they're okay. Lot cheaper and better than anything close to campus. I'd of been here sooner, but we got to get up and going before next week. Hey, ever heard of the Dead Sea scrolls?"

"Of course."

"We're supposed to carbon date some of those in January."

"That's amazing. The Dead Sea scrolls."

"Yep. So what else did you need to talk about?"

"That's right," she said and flipped open her notebook. She had to focus, just stick to business. He was just doing his cousin a favor, nothing more. "Well, aside from your *alien* theory," she said and hiked a brow, "I've got my own idea as to how the carbon date might appear medieval."

"You got a more *down to earth* theory?"

"Yeah, mine has nothing to do with little green men, I promise."

"I'd like to hear your theory then."

She took a deep breath and dove in. "Okay, I'm sort of an expert in weaving."

"An expert, huh?"

"Okay, not an expert. Not the way my mother was. But it's a skill my mother passed down to me. I've read some books on the subject and I'm pretty knowledgeable about ancient weave techniques. I also know that before modern factories, it took a lot of hours to produce something as simple as a cloak. If you got a tear, you fixed it. You didn't throw it out and go down to the mall and buy a new one made in China. It was much easier and less expensive to make a repair, and in the past, they were experts at the craft."

He dug his straw into the crushed ice. "I'm listening. Go ahead."

"Now that corner they took the carbon date from might as well have been called a handle because every time they displayed the Shroud, they would have to grab it at one of the four corners. In fact, I've got a picture of an old painting at home that shows them holding the Shroud on that same corner. They must have done this hundreds, even thousands of times over the last two thousand years. There's no way that corner couldn't have been damaged. And for that matter, there's a good chance someone could have snipped off a piece of the corner to sell or even keep as a souvenir."

He hit the bottom of his drink and made slurping noises like an eight-year old kid. For some reason that didn't bother her. It made her feel even more connected to him, like he was really down to earth with his own flaws, just like her. His laid-back, relaxed manner was contagious and she felt at ease just being close to him, like she'd known him all her life, like they were somehow connected.

"You want some more Coke?" she asked.

"Sorry, just trying to get more glucose to my brain. You really got the wheels turning. Go ahead, this is interesting."

"I'm sure you're aware of the fire that broke out in 1532 at the Sainte Chapelle church in Chambery. Silver from the box that held the Shroud melted and caused the burn marks that are so noticeable."

"That's right. The marks look so much alike because it was folded."

"Right. So in April of 1534, Chambery's Poor Clare nuns repaired the Shroud. They sewed a backing into the cloth for support and then they patched the holes from the fire. I think it's very possible that they also repaired the corners. And if not in 1534, then another time. The French weavers in the Court of Margaret in Austria could have easily done this. Just because there is no history of another repair, doesn't mean there wasn't one. So what I think happened is fibers from the sixteenth century got mixed in with fibers from the first century and that's why we come up with a date somewhere in between."

Rebecca, the other waitress, stopped at the table. "Sir, would you like another Coke?"

"That would be awesome," he said and returned his focus on Amari. "That's an interesting theory. Actually, it explains something unusual I found."

She scooted forward. "Unusual? What do you mean?"

"Statistically unlikely. Not impossible, not by a long shot. But still not the most probable outcome. Not random enough."

"So I might be onto something?"

The waitress set a new Coke in front of him and he immediately plopped his old straw into the new one and started sucking down more carbonated sugar.

"Well, don't just sit there, Kevin. Tell me what you found."

"Sorry, I was just trying to remember all the exact figures. These aren't the published numbers, so I'm having to rack my brain. Hand me that pencil you got in the spine of your notebook."

"Here, write on this," she said and flipped to an empty page of her notebook.

He wrote down four numbers in order: 1430, 1376, 1246, and 1238. "It's like this. When they cut the piece of the Shroud off that corner, they divided it into four pieces. We got the two outer pieces and Oxford and Zurich got the two middle pieces. Our outer edge, the edge closest to the outer edge of the Shroud, dates the youngest at 1430. Zurich is the next piece over and it dates at 1376, then the one from Oxford dates at 1246, and then the other edge that was sent to us, the one closer to the center of the Shroud, dates at 1238. See a pattern here?"

"They're in descending order."

"Exactly. It could be because the outer edge has more new fibers than the inner edges."

"I knew it," she said, clenching her fists in victory. "They gradually wove the thread in to make it look more even. The outer edges would be almost completely new. The inside pieces would have more original cloth."

"Now don't get too excited, not just yet. There's one problem. How did they get the color to match? Linen yellows over time. The new linen they wove in would look a lot lighter."

"They wouldn't have used linen. They used cotton because cotton takes up dye better than linen. And all they had to do was dye the cotton to match the color. Then they would unravel the ends of each piece, the old and the new, and carefully wind the fibers together. It was tedious work, but they did it all the time back then."

"Hmmm," he said.

"Hmmm? What does that mean?"

"You know they took over 5,000 photos when STURP studied the Shroud in 1978, photos from all kinds of wavelengths. I remember seeing an ultraviolet photo that looked funny around that corner. I can't remember why it looked funny, but for some reason you reminded me of it."

"I'd love to see those photos. Do you know how I could get a hold of some?"

"Come back by my office and I'll show them to you. I've got some of them on floppy disc. The one I'm referring to is on one of those."

"Oh, my gosh, Kevin, I can't believe this. Are you serious? How did you get those?"

He shrugged. "I know people. A friend of mine named Jeffery works as a physicist at Los Alamos National Scientific Laboratories. He works with Ray Rogers, and Ray was a member of STURP. Jeffery got them from Ray and he copied them for me.

Why don't you come by and I'll show you. But come by on my lunch hour so Rahal can't say I'm helping you on company time."

"I'd love too."

"Come Monday if you want. You know, you're quite the detective. And you say you're an art major?"

"Actually, I started out in criminal justice. My dad's a cop so he turned me onto that. Guess I had a change of heart."

"Art? Boy, that's a big shift in priorities."

"Big time. Now, I'm not really sure what I want to do. Maybe I'll go back into criminal justice. I think that's where my heart really is."

"You're just like Bono."

"Bono? From U2?"

"Still haven't found what you're looking for," he said with a satisfied grin.

"I love U2. I saw them up at Red Rocks outside Denver in 83."

"No way. When they recorded the live album in the rain?"

"That's the one. I got soaked, but it was worth it. Hey, *Rattle and Hum* opens tonight. You should go with me." She couldn't believe that came out of her mouth. She hardly knew this guy.

"Gosh, I'm bushed tonight. Might be too late to get tickets anyway."

"You're right. I'm sorry, I didn't mean to be forward." Naturally, he made an excuse. He was just being polite.

"How 'bout tomorrow? I hate going to movies alone and I sure ain't missing this one. What do you say?"

"I'd love to. I work the afternoon shift, but I'm off the evening. I can just meet you there if you want."

"Seven o'clock show sound good?"

"Perfect. Maybe we can stop by Chili's after."

"It's a date."

Chapter 15

Amari walked toward the ticket office of the Miramonte Cinema 8. She wore her colorful long Benneton sweater that stretched down to her thighs. She hoped it didn't make her hips look too big. Then again, Kevin was a genius, not superficial like most guys. That's why she chose to stick with only a dab of makeup. If he was going to like her, he'd like her for what she was, not for the mask she put on her face like Jenny did.

She spotted him in front of the box office. He wore jeans and a knit pink Polo Shirt, not the worn flannel shirt he'd worn at work. He looked a little 1983, but at least he tried to look nice for their date—which wasn't a real date. They both liked U2. Nothing more.

She walked up behind him and tugged on his shirt.

He spun around to face her. "Hey, Amari."

"Where's your hat?"

"Oh, that? That's my thinking cap. University of Tennessee. Go Vols."

"That's where Jenny went too, isn't it?"

"Orange blood flows in our family."

"You should see a doctor about that. Could be serious."

"Could be."

"Hey, you know who you look like without the hat?"

"Who?"

"MacGyver. You know, it's cut up over your ears, parted in the middle and wavy on top, long in the back."

"Sweet," he said with delight shining in his eyes. "It's like the only show I watch—that and Star Trek. You think I should go for a Jean-Luc Picard look next?"

"And shave your head? Don't you dare," she said and ran her fingers through his hair like a comb. She snatched her hand back when she realized how forward she was being. Seriously, they just met.

"Hey, let's go get some good seats toward the back," he said like he didn't even notice. "I got tickets already."

****

After the movie, Amari followed Kevin's Honda Accord to Chili's. *Rattle and Hum* rocked, of course. U2 was amazing, as always. And Kevin was so non-threatening, it was easy to let her guard down, which wasn't usually easy for her to do since her last date with that guy from the wrestling team. It seemed like the only guys that were interested in her were jocks, the testosterone reeking man's man type that only wanted to control her—which was the last thing she was looking for from a guy. In the past, her brief relationships would start with a cheesy pickup line and end the first time they put their uninvited hands on her. Sometimes it got ugly. But this date happened differently. It had started out of mutual interests, a working relationship between two people who were interested in the Shroud and just so happened to love U2. And Kevin was way different from other guys. He wasn't pushy and his intentions were totally innocent. If he saw anything in her, he'd be interested in her thoughts, not just her looks. At least that's the impression she got from him.

Unfortunately, the Chili's waitress sat them right next to the smoking section, but once the Awesome Blossom arrived, neither of them seemed to notice the smoke drifting to their side.

"What do you think about Bono's voice?" she asked. "It's gotten raspier since *The Unforgettable Fire*."

"Man, he can wail, though, can't he?"

"I hope he doesn't trash his voice. He keeps that up, and he's going to," she said and dipped an onion slice into the sauce. Good thing she had cinnamon gum in her purse. The onion was his idea.

He took a bite and there was a moment of silence while they both chewed and just kind of looked at each other.

He finally spoke. "So you're half Indian, huh?"

"My mother was a full-blooded Navajo."

"Yeah, Jenny told me about your mom. I'm sorry to hear that."

"That's breast cancer for you."

"That must have been hard."

"It's still hard." She quickly changed the subject. "So what about your mom?"

"Still living in Tennessee. She loves it there. It's the change of seasons she likes the most. The dogwoods—wow. You ought to see it during the Dogwood Arts Festival. It's amazing."

"I'm sure it is. Hey, you should come with me to see the saguaro cactuses bloom in spring. They may not be pretty as dogwoods, but it's a closer drive, that's for sure. Saguaro National Park is maybe fifteen miles from here."

"It's a date," he said.

She just realized she'd asked him out again. She'd better back off before she chased him away. "Well, they don't start blooming until April, so we have a little time."

"I'll mark it on my calendar."

Well, he didn't seem to mind. Maybe he was interested in being more than friends. Still, he had some odd beliefs. She'd better go into detective mode and find out more about this guy before she got involved. "So, Kevin, does everybody in Tennessee believe in space aliens?"

"Most people out there don't read as much as I do. You ever read *The Bible and Flying Saucers* by Barry Downing? He's a Presbyterian minister up in New York. He thinks a big UFO is what led the Israelites out of Egypt."

"I think you've been watching too much Star Trek."

"What about Ezekiel's wheel within a wheel? Elijah taken to heaven by a chariot of fire? Or was it a glowing space craft? Think about it, Amari, Jesus was beamed up into a *cloud*? More like the mother ship. Angels and all these unidentified lights people keep seeing? They're one in the same. Well, I think so anyway."

"That's not how I was taught in church," she said with a wry smile. "Is that what they teach where you went to church?"

"I wouldn't know. I'm not really into church."

That response took the wind out of her, but she tried not to react. She was afraid he wasn't a Christian. Most science types weren't. "Well, I am into church and I don't remember the Sunday school teacher saying anything about little green men carving the Ten Commandments. That's pretty weird, don't you think? Like crazy *cult* weird. You are just kidding about all this, right? Please tell me you're just messing with me."

"Hey, I didn't come up with this stuff. It's in the books. I just read them. I don't write them."

"You've never had a girlfriend, have you?"

"Why would you say that?"

"Because girlfriends are very needy. They're time-consuming. You wouldn't have time to read all those crazy books if you had a girlfriend."

"No serious girlfriends. I've been pretty busy the last few years. What about you?"

"I've had a couple, nothing too serious either."

"You've had a couple of girlfriends?"

Amari wadded her napkin and playfully flung it at him. "No, Kevin, I meant *boy*friends."

Kevin snickered and handed her napkin back. "I'm just messing with you."

"You like doing that, don't you? Like the alien thing?"

He simply grinned for a moment and then changed the subject. "So what were you saying about your boyfriends?"

"Oh, that. Let's just say it's been a while. I lost interested after the last guy I dated."

"Really, was he a jerk?"

"He tried to rape me."

His eyes narrowed in anger. "I'm sorry, Amari."

"Not as sorry as he was. When you're a cop's kid, you take self-defense classes. Guess I should have warned him." She held up her arm and flexed her bicep. "You don't have to be big or strong to defend yourself. You just have to know the moves and hit the right spots. Memorize them. Practice them. You have to be smart, quick, and have good aim."

"That muscle in your arm's bigger than mine. Let me feel that thing."

She pulled back her sleeve and flexed her muscle for him. He reached over and squeezed. His hand lingered on her arm for a second and then he pulled away.

"Feels pretty firm to me. I wouldn't want to mess with you. So what did you do to him?"

"I kicked him in the groin and crushed his Adam's apple. He'll think twice about trying that on another girl—when he gets out of prison."

"Ohh," he said and cringed. "That hurts. But good, that's where he belongs."

"I wasn't his first victim, so he went away for a while."

"You don't have to worry about me."

"I know, I don't. That's why I'm with you now. You're harmless, I can tell."

"That I am," he said and dipped another onion piece into the sauce.

Amari was sick of reliving that date in her mind, so she changed the subject. "So tell me about Tennessee. I've never been there."

"I grew up in a valley, between the Smoky Mountains and the Cumberland Plateau. It's not too hot, not too cold, and we don't get many tornadoes. Fall and spring are pretty."

"So how did you end up there?"

"World War II. My grandfather was a physicist. He helped develop the atomic bomb. He actually worked with Einstein, you know."

"Albert Einstein?"

"That's the one. So when we started to make the bomb, the government sent my grandfather to Oak Ridge to help with the nuclear fuel enrichment."

"The Manhattan Project?"

"That's what they called it. After the war, he stayed there and worked for the Oak Ridge National Lab. Then my dad followed in his footsteps and worked for ORNL too."

"I hate to tell you this, but when I think of Tennessee, I usually think of *The Beverly Hillbillies*."

"I love that show. But that's just Hollywood. Some of the smartest people in the world live where I come from."

"So I guess you were valedictorian?"

"When I was sixteen. Oak Ridge High School. I skipped a couple of grades. Then I got my undergrad and masters at UT.

That hat I wear is the one I wore in Knoxville. It's my good luck hat. So then I went to MIT for my Ph.D."

"So how'd you get so smart?"

"Genes, I guess. My buddies in school seemed to struggle, but it came easy to me. Plus, my dad helped me a lot, pointed me to the right books. He was pretty strict about TV. He only had it for watching the news. So what about you?"

"Not much to tell. What you see is who I am. I was born in Winslow but moved to Tucson when I was three. All I remember is this. I never spent much time on the reservation. My dad and Mother's parents didn't get along."

"You know, Amari, the two of us have a lot in common."

"You think so?"

"Sure, we both like U2, we're both interested in the Shroud of Turin, and I'm part Indian myself."

"Really? You don't look it."

"Seriously. My grandfather's grandmother was a full-blooded Cherokee."

She counted generations on her fingers. "So that makes you one sixteenth?"

"Yep, isn't that weird how we got that in common?"

She threw out a laugh. "The only thing weird here is you."

Chapter 16

It was the following Monday afternoon, and Kevin let Amari into the lab. They went to his office and closed the door behind them. She sat a white bag from McDonald's on his desk. He had cleaned the place. His papers were neatly stacked and all the books and manuals were shelved.

"Big Mac with extra-large fries?" he asked.

"You said not to bring drinks."

"Got my own little fridge. Fully stocked. What are you drinking?"

"Water if you have it."

He pulled out a plastic bottle with a pink and blue label. "Try this. It's mineral water from France."

"Evian mineral water. Fancy."

He ate his Big Mac and she had her McDLT as he talked about the eleven other employees of the lab.

When they'd finished eating, he wadded up the white bag and tossed it into the garbage can. "We better get this show on the road before my lunch hour is up. Rahal might be on the prowl."

"So show me these pictures you talked about."

He snapped up a floppy disc and displayed it proudly between his index finger and thumb. "It took me a while to find the right one, but this is it. It has regular close-up photos of that corner of the Shroud. Ultraviolet photos too. Let me whip this baby into my spiffy new Compaq Deskpro 386 with 4 kilobytes of memory. It's capable of 4 million operations per second, you know."

"Impressive."

He inserted the disc. The drive clicked rhythmically as it loaded its information into the computer. "It's got a 32-bit chip with 275,000 transistors," he said as he typed away at the keyboard. After a few seconds, an image popped up on the screen. "Here's the one. This is a close-up shot of the spot they sampled for the carbon date. This picture was taken about ten years ago. Lean in so you can see it better."

She leaned close and squinted as she examined the herringbone twill of the fabric. "Okay, you can clearly see this is woven in a three-to-one herringbone twill pattern and spun with a Z-twist. This weave pattern was common in the Middle East during the time of Christ."

"You know your twills."

"I try." Her eyes flashed wide. "I knew it! Look, I can see it."

"See what?"

"I can see the repair!"

"Looks all the same to me."

"No, seriously, look here." She pressed her fingernail to the glass of the computer monitor. "See, the weave patterns are misaligned. They're off axis."

He leaned closer and followed her fingernail across the screen as she pointed out the subtle differences. "Yeah, you're right. I can see it now."

"When you work a loom, everything is in a straight line, up and down, left to right. You would have to go out of your way to cause this sort of misalignment. But it might be the best you could do if you were making a repair."

"Wonder why nobody noticed?"

"Nobody would notice this unless they knew what they were looking for. I can see how they missed it." She narrowed her eyes. "Unless, of course, they chose this spot on purpose," she said in a suspicious tone. "Let me see that other picture, the ultraviolet one you told me about."

"Yes ma'am," he said and typed in a few commands. The floppy drive did a rhythmic click, click, click, until the photo appeared. "This one isn't so subtle. I'm surprised nobody noticed."

On the computer screen, an image of the lower left quadrant of the Shroud glowed brightly in varying shades of yellow, orange, and green. Some pinkish color could be seen toward the top.

"This is called a blue quad mosaic," he said. "Now, look here, down next to where they took the carbon date sample. Just to the left is a known repair. You can clearly see the stitching. Notice how it's a bluish green color?"

"So the newer cloth fluoresces differently in ultraviolet."

"Exactly. Now look just to the right, at the spot they took the carbon-14 sample from. See anything funny?"

"It's fuzzy green and blue. The edge is the greenest and it gradually turns orange. Kevin, you're a genius! That proves my point. The newest fibers are on the outer edge, and they gradually get older. That's because the newer fibers are woven into the old fibers."

"Well, now hold on, Amari. This is evidence, but it doesn't prove anything. Not by scientific standards. You would need to look at it under a microscope and actually see the cotton fibers. Otherwise, we just have a photographic anomaly. It doesn't prove anything."

She sank back into her seat. "You said they had to burn the piece of the Shroud to do the carbon date. That's too bad. Otherwise, I could look at it myself. They've got this great scope over in the biology lab. You can even take Polaroid pictures with it. I don't guess you know where we can find another piece of the Shroud?"

He pointed down the hall. "Locked up in Rahal's office, that's where."

She sprang to her feet. "Are you serious?"

"We didn't burn it all up. We kept a little just in case we needed to repeat something."

"Then let me see it."

"You'll have to ask Dr. Rahal."

She sat back down. "You mean Dr. *Nay-all.*"

The door suddenly swished open. Rahal stood in the doorway. "Dr. Brenner, did I not make myself clear. I told you this woman wasn't allowed in this lab anymore."

"Actually, you sort of said she couldn't be here on company time. This is my lunch break. Still got fifteen minutes left," he said and pointed at his watch.

Dr. Rahal's misaligned eyes flashed with rage. "You know well what I meant, Dr. Brenner. This is a secure facility. There is a reason we have a keypad on the door. It is to keep unauthorized visitors out." Rahal noticed the computer screen. "What is this? What are you showing her?"

"Oh, it's just . . ."

Dr. Rahal didn't wait for an answer. He moved closer to the computer screen and peered down at a little black box in the lower left of the picture and read what it said. "Shroud of Turin Research Project, blue quad mosaic. Where did you get this?"

"Oh, that just came from a friend of mine."

"Then why is it on a computer that belongs to the university? The Shroud of Turin project is over, Dr. Brenner. You have a new assignment. I don't want to see anything in your office that doesn't involve the work ahead, do you understand me? The university isn't paying you to show souvenir photos to nosey undergrads. If I had my way they would never have hired you. I saw no need for an inexperienced post-doc but somebody else thought otherwise."

Amari clinched her jaw and she felt the burn of blood rushing to her cheeks. How dare he talk that way to him? This wasn't Kevin's fault. He was just trying to help her. She hadn't felt that way since she was a kid on the school bus, when she'd stood up for the kids who were harassed by the neighborhood bully. She jumped to her feet and locked her gaze on what she assumed was Dr. Rahal's good eye. "Dr. Brenner is helping me with a school project, and that *is* university business."

Rahal gasped in surprise. "What was your name again?"

"Amari Johnston."

"And what is your major?"

"I'm an art major. He's helping me with a project."

"Miss Johnston, what sort of art project would require input from a physicist? The two subjects are totally unrelated."

Stay calm, she told herself. It wasn't the school bus. "Are they? According to your lab, the Shroud of Turin is a forgery. That means it's a work of art. That puts it into my territory, don't you think?"

Jeremy appeared in the doorway with an older gentleman. The elderly man's hair was swept over in a vain attempt to cover his bald head. He wore square bifocal glasses and an amused smirk on his face. "I'm sorry to intrude," the elderly man said, "but I couldn't help overhearing. Is there a problem? Maybe I can help."

"Amari, this is Professor Weiss," Kevin said. "Remember, I told you about him. Hey, Jerry."

"Hey, Dr. Brenner," Jeremy replied.

"Professor Weiss, this is a friend of mine," Kevin said without the slightest apologetic tone to his voice.

"Amari Johnston," she said and extended her hand. Firm handshake, look him in the eye.

The professor took her hand with an equally firm grip. "A pleasure to meet you. There seems to be a disagreement? Is there anything I can do to help resolve this?"

"Actually, there is," she said. "I have good reason to believe the carbon date you ran on the Shroud was actually done on a repair. I think it was a patch. And if that's the case, then the work you've done here doesn't count."

Rahal looked like he'd been punched in the stomach. "That's preposterous! We utilize only the highest of scientific standards. How dare you accuse us of such carelessness?"

"I'm not accusing anyone," she said. "Unless you know what you're looking for, this could be an honest mistake."

"Dr. Rahal, if I may," Professor Weiss said. "Miss Johnston, you seem very convinced of what you are saying. Do you care to elaborate? Tell us why you believe this could be true."

"Because that corner the sample was taken from is the worst possible place. For two thousand years, they used that corner to stretch out the Shroud for everyone to see. It had to have damaged the corner, so it had to have been repaired."

"No, they handled it for around six hundred years," Dr. Weiss corrected. "According to the results of the carbon date."

"Then your carbon date is wrong."

"Dr. Brenner," Professor Weiss said. "What do you know about all this?"

"She has a valid theory. We looked at some photos. Looks like it could have been repaired at some point."

"You are not being paid to call the results of this lab into question," Dr. Rahal said. "Now I want this young lady out of here immediately."

Dr. Weiss placed his hand on Rahal's shoulder. "Oh, calm down, Dr. Rahal. Don't be such a stick in the mud. Just listen to what she has to say. It sounds very interesting to me."

"She claims to be an art major," Dr. Rahal said. "She told me her interest in the Shroud is because it was a forgery. If it was a forgery, then it must be art. Now she is saying something completely different."

Dr. Weiss looked like he wanted an explanation.

Amari offered one. "Okay, at first I wanted to figure out how it was forged. For artistic reasons. But I did my research, and I honestly don't see how it could be a forgery. I think it's real."

"Then that is a matter of faith," Dr. Weiss said. "I assume you are a Christian?"

She stalled for a second, wondering what he was driving at. "Yes, I am a Christian. But that doesn't change the facts."

"That explains it," Dr. Rahal said. "She's a fanatic. She's just trying to stir up controversy. The carbon date damaged the credibility of her faith and now she's striking back."

"Just because I'm a Christian doesn't mean I'm wrong," she said. "The truth is the truth and that is all I'm trying to prove."

"I agree, the truth is very important," Professor Weiss said. "Tell me, Miss Johnston, what do you want from us? How can we help you see the truth?"

"I understand you still have a piece of the Shroud. I want to look at it under a microscope and see if I can find cotton fibers. The Shroud was made of linen. If cotton fibers are there, then I can assume it was repaired. If it was repaired, then the new cloth is mixed with old. Then the carbon date is invalid."

Every eye turned to Dr. Rahal as if asking permission.

"Absolutely not," Rahal replied. "I will not have this pushy undergrad march in here and accuse us of incompetence."

"Oh, come now, Dr. Rahal, what would be the harm?" Dr. Weiss said. "She won't find anything. Then her curiosity will be satisfied. I admire her determination."

"She is not as determined as me. No, I will not allow it."

"No wonder they call you Dr. *Nay-all* behind your back," Professor Weiss said with a grin. Jeremy snickered and quickly caught himself before Dr. Rahal saw him.

Amari bit her lip and tried not to laugh.

Anger raged all the more in Rahal's face. "I'm going to call security," Dr. Rahal said and rushed down the hall.

"Don't worry about him," Professor Weiss said. "He can't do anything the board of directors won't allow him to do, and I happen to sit on the board. Dr. Brenner, I do suggest, however, that you walk your friend to the door. Dr. Rahal is, after all, in the right. Miss Johnston is not supposed to be back here."

Amari's anger subsided and she measured her words carefully. Professor Weiss was a man of reason and perhaps he could be reasoned with. "Thank you, Professor Weiss. I really didn't mean to cause any trouble, but getting to the truth is sort of in my blood. My dad is a detective. His job is finding the truth. And to be honest, I was only a full-time art major for a semester. Before that I was in criminal justice. I'm changing my major back to criminal justice."

"Yes, I can see you as a detective. But if your concern is for the rule of law, then you should know that if you are not an employee of the lab, nor have official business with the lab, then you really must go. And you wouldn't want to get Dr. Brenner in trouble, would you?"

"Hey, I'm sorry, Dr. Weiss," Kevin said. "I didn't see this coming. I promise I won't let her back here again."

"I know you won't. Even a brilliant physicist has an occasional miscalculation."

Just then, a campus police officer walked over to the door. Professor Weiss gripped the young officer on the shoulder. "That won't be necessary. She was just leaving."

Chapter 17

Amari had learned that sometimes you attract more flies with honey than vinegar. She tended to let her anger get the better of her. It got her in trouble at school all the time. But she was an adult now. It was time she took her mother's advice: quick to listen, slow to speak, and slow to anger. She needed to take a gentler approach with Dr. Rahal. She should flatter him rather than anger him. Perhaps that would change his mind. It was worth a try.

On Friday afternoon Amari stepped up to the receptionist desk. The elderly woman put a bookmark in her romance novel and met her gaze. "Back for more, I see? I have been instructed not to let you in under any circumstances."

"I may have gotten off on the wrong foot," Amari said apologetically and extended an envelope. "I wanted to give this to Dr. Rahal. It's an apology letter and a gift certificate to Applebee's. Just to show I'm sorry."

The woman glanced down the hall and lowered her head to see over her reading glasses. "There comes Dr. Rahal now. You can tell him yourself."

"What is this?" Rahal huffed. "I told you not to come near this lab again."

"Dr. Rahal, I just came to apologize. I know sometimes I cross the line. I wanted to tell you I'm sorry and give you this." She handed him the envelope.

He promptly handed it back. Jeremy stepped into the hall and hesitated, looking awkward, not sure what to do.

"I don't want your apologies," Rahal continued. "I want you off this property."

"Dr. Rahal, all I want to do is look at your piece of shroud under a microscope. I promise, you can have it right back."

"Absolutely not! I told you that already."

She fought to push down her anger, but he wasn't helping. More honey, less vinegar. Get on his good side. "Please, Dr. Rahal, I know you're a very intelligent man. You have to see that something doesn't feel right about this. I think somebody in Italy made a mistake. It may be an honest mistake, but it needs to be investigated."

The security guard walked into the foyer. "Is there a problem?"

"Steven, get this woman out of here," Rahal demanded.

Steven moved toward her.

"Steven, I'll leave in just a minute."

He reached for her arm. "You have to leave now."

Amari held up her finger as a warning. "Don't you touch me."

"Please, don't make me do this the hard way."

"All right! But this isn't over. I promise you that." She stuffed the envelope in her pocket and slammed through the double doors. She went out into the sun and tried to stay calm, to steady her breath as she pressed toward her car. That wasn't just some territorial jerk in there. He was hiding something, she could feel it. He was up to something illegal. That lab was a crime scene— and she was determined to prove it.

****

Amari walked into her home, wet from perspiration. She went to the bathroom, splashed cold water on her face, and looked up into the mirror to meet her own gaze. She could see her mother in her cheeks, but her dad's eyes stared back at her. She splashed more cold water on her face and dried it with a towel. There was no way she was going to crack this case on her own. She stared at herself in the mirror for several seconds and made the hard decision. Even her great, great grandfather Manuelito eventually surrendered. Maybe it was time to call a truce.

She went to her bed, sat on the corner, her eyes fixed on Jesus' crucified image on the Shroud hanging on her wall. What agonizing pain he must have suffered so willingly for her—and for her dad. Yet, somehow, there was serenity on his face, and it seemed to radiate to her. Anger melted into an odd sense of peace. She felt an urge to forgive, to let go, to surrender. Her dad had repented of his sin. He had apologized to her the best way he knew how. It was a sincere apology. Nobody had suffered more than him. The guilt clung like a film over his eyes. But she knew he wouldn't grovel. If she lost him forever, it was her own fault.

She cupped her hands over her face. She was so tired of being mad, so tired of pushing her dad away, pretending she wanted nothing to do with him. She missed the old days. They were so close back then. She wanted so badly to have that back again. And now that things had changed, she didn't just want him back, she needed him back. But she didn't kid herself. She was still mad at him, still had not completely forgiven him, but she was getting closer.

She pulled her hands away and looked back at the peaceful face of Jesus. She knew what she had to do. If things were ever going to be right with her dad again, she had to take the first step. She would use the case with Dr. Rahal as an excuse, just so he wouldn't think she'd forgotten what he did. But it was an important first step. She went to the phone before she changed her mind.

Chapter 18

It was Sunday and Amari stepped into the rapidly filling church and scanned for an empty pew. Jenny hadn't come with her. Instead, she'd gone to church with a guy she met at Campus Crusade for Christ.

Amari moved closer to the front. Should she squeeze by old Mr. Haun with his bad knee or move up a little more? Then she smelled it—that cologne. Memories flooded her mind. Good memories.

"You always liked sitting up front as a kid."

She turned to see her dad in the aisle, standing in the same Sunday suit he always wore and smelling of Old Spice, the same aftershave she would give him every Christmas. "It's about time you came back to church."

He raised his thick eyebrows, deepening the worry lines on his forehead, just under his gray-streaked Army crew cut. "It's been too long. It's time I got right with God."

"Well, come on, it's about to start."

They sat in the front row just like they used to. She sat next to him in silence, not sure what to say around the scrutiny of congregational ears. As the preacher preached, and the choir sang, she felt her defenses wane. She was so tired of being angry, pretending she didn't love her dad anymore. Nothing could be further from the truth.

Toward the end of the service, the congregation always joined hands in prayer. When Reverend Davis signaled the prayer, her dad hesitated, testing the water, and then opened his hand to her. She hesitated too, but finally took it and held it firm. She looked up into his regretful eyes and her heart played out its final beat of anger. Then forgiveness came, like a cool rain from the hot desert sky.

After the service, she walked her dad to his car and looked him square in the eye. She felt emotion's tug and wanted to hug him, but he was a man's man who typically shied away from public displays of affection.

"Amari," he said, "I'm so sorry about what I did to you and your mother. If there was any way I could take it all back, I would, you know that, don't you?"

"I know, Dad." She held out her hand to shake. He took it and she squeezed it firmly, just like he had taught her. She held his gaze and said with a tone of finality, "We're square."

His shoulders went limp and he pulled her in for a hug. "I owe you more than a hand shake, baby. Thank you."

"It's okay, Daddy, we all make mistakes."

He let go and met her eyes. "Daddy? You haven't called me that since you were a little kid."

"You'll always be my daddy. Nothing will ever change that."

"And I pray to God nothing ever will." He then pulled the sunglasses from his shirt pocket and cleaned smudges off the lenses with his shirt. "So what's this you say about the Shroud of Turin?" He inspected the lenses and slid the glasses over his eyes. "You said you had a case for me?"

"Back at the house," she said. "I've got it all set up for you."

****

They went to Roslyn's Diner after church, just like they used to, and talked about the good times, avoiding talk of Mother's cancer or the affair. They talked about her brother, Jason, and how surprised they were he'd become a Catholic priest. Then they talked about adventures in Girl Scouts, the hikes at Ventana Canyon and Finger Rock trail, the trips to Disneyland, and Amari's favorite, the Junior Detective program in which kids shadowed detectives in a sanitized version of the profession.

When they finished eating, they went to the house, and she showed him the kitchen table. Post-It notes covered in blue ink dotted the boundary of the poster-board she had made with the positive and negative images of the Shroud affixed to the front and back. There were also hand-written notes on the poster board with arrows pointing to the areas of interest.

"I see you finished your research," Dad said. "I'm impressed. You're such a good investigator. Are you sure you won't reconsider and change your major?"

"It's done already. I turned in my change of major form to admissions last Thursday. I start back where I left off in January."

"That's my girl. I knew you'd come around. This is in your blood."

"I didn't have a choice. Have you seen my paintings?"

"I'm sure they weren't that bad."

She pointed at a watercolor painting hung on the refrigerator with a magnet.

"Oh, well, hey it looks like modern art."

"It's supposed to be a self-portrait."

"You're right. God wants you to be a detective."

"Apparently so. And I think this is my first big case."

"So let's see what you've got."

"Okay, like I told you on the phone, at first I thought this was a forgery. That's what the carbon date said, so that's what I believed. When I started the investigation, it was a six-hundred-year-old crime. So I'm reading all these books and I realize there's no way this could be a forgery. And if it's not a forgery, then it must be the authentic burial cloth of Christ."

"How do you know it belonged to Jesus? Maybe it covered someone else who was crucified."

"Okay, good question. First of all, this is by far the most studied relic in history. We know a lot about it so you might want to sit down."

The chair scuffed against the floor as her dad pulled out the chair and sat.

She pointed at the feet of the image, near the bottom of the poster. "I'll start with the feet and work my way up. The blood on the feet is consistent with being nailed on a cross." She pointed to the image of the underside of the body. "Every rocky soil has a unique mineral fingerprint. The dirt on the heel of this image matches the mineral fingerprint of Jerusalem. Whoever this man was, he walked those streets barefoot, just as Jesus would have if he walked to Golgotha."

Her dad scooted the chair closer. "Somebody could have planted that dirt on the feet."

"Okay, but back then they didn't have a microscope or knowledge of mineral fingerprints. Why bother? It wouldn't make it more realistic to the eye."

"You have a point. Go, on. I'm listening."

She pointed to the back of the image. "There's over a hundred scourge marks, on the back and on the legs. Mostly on the back. These are clearly from the Roman flagellum. Lead pellets and sometimes bone are stuck on the end of leather straps to make a whip. The pattern of injuries match exactly to historical records of what the flagellum looked like. In fact, I even have a picture of one in this book. Want to see it?"

"I believe you, go on."

"The gospels say that the hands were pierced by the nails. All old paintings show the nails through the hands. But the Shroud has the blood flowing from the wrists. Medical professionals have proven that the palms could not withstand the weight during crucifixion because the flesh would tear. Also, when you drive a nail into the wrist the thumb contracts inward because of injury to the medial nerve. This is seen in the Shroud. Notice you don't see the thumb? And the blood flows down the arms, which shows that the arms were elevated at an angle consistent with crucifixion."

"It's possible a forger could know about the wrists. I'm sure they tortured each other all the time back then. They may have known the hands wouldn't hold."

"Did they have X-rays back then?"

"Now what kind of crazy question is that?"

She pointed at one of the hands. "Notice anything funny?"

"He's got awfully long fingers."

"That is an X-ray of the bones on the hand. What you see is the bones in the top of the hands merging into the finger bones, so it just looks like he has long fingers."

"That makes no sense."

"It doesn't if it's a forgery. But you have to think about how the image was formed. There are no pigments or dyes, not a single stroke mark on the whole Shroud. The image you see is caused by *oxidized, dehydrated cellulose*." She said the words carefully just as she had rehearsed. "Cellulose is a natural material found in all plants and fibers. Linen will yellow or darken when exposed to radiation. There are tiny radiation burns, or darkened areas, that are only on the topmost fibers. It's a very faint image. So why would a forger go to the trouble of making a forgery you could barely see?"

"I don't know, Amari. You're making my head spin. What about the bones? You were going to explain why we see bones."

"That's easy. The bones are visible because radiation came from *within* the body. As the radiation came out, it happened to make an imprint of the bones. Special scanning of the Shroud also shows other bones. The teeth are visible if you look closely and so are the bones of the skull. It's hard to see with the eye, but hi-tech scanners picked it up. Radiation coming from the body would cause that. It would also explain the negative image I'm showing you now. Before 1898, all anybody knew about was the positive image, the one visible to the naked eye. But in that year, a man named Secondo Pia took the first photograph of the Shroud and discovered that the negative image clearly revealed much more detail than the positive image, which is opposite of the way it should be. The positive image looks fuzzy, you can't make out many details, but the negative image shows everything. How does a medieval forger know to make the image visible with a negative image if they didn't even have cameras back then? And *why* would he do it?"

"I need some water."

She got a glass and filled it from the sink.

He took a long gulp. "Are we finished?"

"Not even close." She pointed to the next Post-It note, midway up the image. "On the right side of the chest there is a large pool of blood that coincides with the gospel account that Jesus was pierced by a spear to make sure he was dead. The size of the wound is consistent with the Roman lancet of the period. Medical professions also have proven this blood was post-mortem because there is no swelling in the area and it pooled rather than being pumped by a heart. Also, there's evidence of a watery fluid which would have come from the pleural cavity in the chest. The Gospel of John said there was a sudden flow of blood and water."

She then pointed at the shoulders. "Abrasions from a rough object such as a beam of wood are seen on the shoulders. This is consistent with the Gospel account that Jesus carried his own cross beam. The knees show signs of injury like you would expect if someone fell carrying such a heavy beam, a fall mentioned in the Gospels. He wouldn't be able to break his fall if he was carrying that beam."

"It's like reading the Gospel account play by play," Dad said. "All the forensic evidence is right here."

"There's more."

"I'm sure there is. Let's hear it then."

"The hair and beard are consistent with Jewish traditions of the period. The cheeks appear swollen as if he was beaten." She pointed to the eyes. "Now this is very interesting. Archaeologists now know that there was a tradition around the time of Christ to put coins over the eyes during burial. In fact, they've found skulls from the period with coins still inside them. And if you look very closely—you really can only see it well if the picture is enlarged and you use a microscope. But anyway, there is an imprint of a coin over the eye. You know what the imprint says?"

"Now how would I know that?"

"It has the Greek letters UCAI, the inscription for Tiberius Caesar. This is consistent with the Pontius Pilate lepton minted between 27 and 32 AD. This not only nails down the time but the geographic region."

"Then case closed," Dad said. "No judge in his right mind would rule this a forgery."

"Oh, but I'm not done yet."

"I'm sure you're not. How many hours did you spend digging all of this up?"

"I lost count. But let me finish."

"I've got all afternoon."

"Okay, there are pollen grains all over the Shroud, pollen from plants that only grow around Israel. If this was forged in Europe, then how did the pollen get there? But the really interesting thing is the pollen found around the head. It was . . ." She snatched up the sticky note she had by the head so she could read it. "Gundelia tournefortii," she said with satisfaction.

"I'm no botanist. What does that mean?"

"It's pollen from a thorn bush—a bush that grows in the hills around Jerusalem. They used that bush to make the crown of thorns. And if there is pollen, that means the plant was in bloom. Do you know when that bush blooms?"

"No, but I'm sure you do."

"Between March and May. Easter. That plant only blooms during Easter, the time of the crucifixion. So now tell me. Do you still think this is a forgery?"

Dad sat, eyes transfixed on the image of the Shroud. "You know I always wondered what Jesus looked like. And now I know. It's like looking at a primitive photograph. It's like he left this on purpose, for everyone to see long after he was gone. For everyone to see the proof that he existed and the gospel account was true."

"So you don't think it's a forgery either."

"I never said it was a forgery. Heck, I had hardly heard of the thing until the other day."

Amari sat down at the table and folded her hands into each other.

Her dad had that scowl on his face that signified he was pondering a case. "Remember we were talking about the priest that was burned up at Holy Ghost the other day?"

"Of course. You said it was your case."

"It is."

"So what does it have to do with the Shroud of Turin?"

"I don't know that it does have anything to do with the Shroud. It may just be a coincidence. See, the only thing unusual that happened in the priest's life lately was that he had an article published in the newspaper. It said that no matter what the carbon date showed, the vast amount of the evidence that proves the Shroud is real would be enough to prove the carbon date was invalid—assuming the carbon date didn't agree with the time of Jesus. He wrote this article before the news broke about the date."

"So you think he knew something? Do you think someone was trying to shut him up?"

"There's no way for us to tell. We searched what few possessions he had, questioned friends, family, and coworkers, but there's no evidence anyone was out to get him. The case went cold after a week."

"Maybe there's some sort of cover-up."

"I wouldn't jump to conclusions."

"Dad, one of the reasons I called you here is to tell you about what happened at the university the other day."

"You seemed pretty mad on the phone. What gives?"

"You know Jenny, my roommate?"

"Yeah, I know her. She's a sharp kid. You think it's an accident I showed up at church today? She called and made the suggestion."

"I can't believe she did that. No, wait, yes, I can believe it."

"I'm glad she did."

"I am too, Dad."

"So what about Jenny?"

"Her cousin is a genius. He's only twenty-five years old and he's already got a Ph.D. in physics. He's doing post-doc work at the WMS lab. That's where they did the carbon date. It's at the university."

"I'm familiar with it."

"So I have this theory that the corner they did the carbon date on was repaired at some point, and the repair fibers were mixed in with the old fibers. And that's what gave a young carbon date age."

"You came up with that?"

"I know a little about weaving."

"Your mother saw to that. She was amazing with a piece of string."

"The point is, I went over to the lab and talked to Jenny's cousin. His name is Dr. Kevin Brenner. He likes to be called Kevin. So Kevin showed me these pictures that clearly show there was a repair done. At least to me, it was clear. He said that in order to prove this case scientifically we would have to look at it under a microscope first. And it turns out they still have a piece of the Shroud left."

"So why don't you ask to look at it?"

"I did. I begged, but Dr. Rahal wouldn't let me."

"You got ugly with him, didn't you?"

"Maybe a little."

"I warned you about that temper of yours. It's going to get you in trouble someday."

"The point is he refused to let me see it. Even the Emirate Professor, the guy who started the lab, asked Dr. Rahal to show it to me and he refused. He kicked me out of the lab. I tried to apologize and he called security on me."

"Why is he being so stubborn?"

"I don't know. I think he's hiding something. I was hoping you could, you know, apply some leverage. Maybe you could get him to show it to me."

"No can do, Amari. He hasn't committed a crime. I can't just march down there and tell him to show it to my daughter because she thinks he's hiding something."

"I guess you're right. Any suggestions then? He won't listen to reason."

"Why don't you talk to the dean? Maybe they can force him into letting you see it."

"That's a good idea."

"But then again, if I can somehow tie this to the case with the priest."

"Then we could tie it to a crime."

"It's a long shot, but maybe so. I still need more information. I know what happened after the Shroud piece got here. But what about before? If there is some kind of cover-up, then they're covering up something that happened before it got here."

"You need to talk to Kevin. I bet he knows everything you would want to know about how the sample was collected and how it got here."

"Can you set something up?"

"I bet I can. Let me talk to him and I'll get back to you."

Chapter 19

Pete and George pulled into the parking lot of the mosque on Speedway Blvd. After the murder of the priest, they had interviewed the imam of the two mosques in town. They had hoped someone knew something. Maybe they knew a member that was acting funny lately, maybe a member that might want to kill a priest, burn the place down, and write jihad on the sidewalk. Or a member who would want to burn a synagogue down. Maybe someone was new in town they didn't know so well. Anything they had was useful. Unfortunately, they came up empty, but Pete had told them to call if anything odd should occur. He got the call that morning. It was their first lead in three months.

Pete parked the car and they went to the front door. It was a small, white building with a domed peak and a thin Arabian-looking prayer tower. It didn't feel appropriate to barge into another faith's house of prayer, so he knocked at the door.

A moment later, the imam answered. He had a short black beard, a black cloak that fit snuggly around his neck, and a white cylindrical cap on his head. "Good afternoon, Detective Johnston," the imam said.

"Good to see you again, Mr. Sadiq," Pete said. "I understand you have some information for me."

"I am not certain you will find it useful, but I did notice something peculiar Friday, during our congregational prayer."

"So one of your members said something? They act strange?"

"No, it was not a member of our congregation. Not a Muslim at all. It was a Catholic priest."

"A priest? At a Muslim church?"

"He did not come inside. He stood across the street, on that sidewalk. He watched as our members left."

"He just stood there. Watching?"

"Until he noticed that I was watching him. Then he walked away."

"Which way did he go?"

"He went that way, toward Helen Street."

"So you called us out here because a priest stopped to watch your congregation and then kept on his evening walk?"

"I called you because I don't believe he was really a priest. Do you notice how snuggly my collar is around my neck? Clergy have their clothing specially tailored. It is no different in the Catholic faith. But this priest's clothes did not seem to fit. They were too loose. The pants almost dragged against the ground."

Alarms went off. He started to speak, but George beat him to it.

"Pete, that's our guy! I bet he was casing the joint. That's why he stole the uniform. So he could pose as a priest."

"Could be," Pete said and focused on the imam. "Can you tell me what he looked like? Do you think you could identify him?"

"He was wearing dark glasses. He had a black hat as well. It had a circular rim as protection from the sun. I could not see his face well."

"Anything you got would help. Any distinguishing features? Was he white or black, heavy or thin?"

"He was Caucasian. Thin. He had a black beard. It was long. It fell to his chest. And he was not very tall."

"That's something," Pete said. "I'm going to need you to come downtown and describe what you saw to our sketch artist. And by the way, do you have a burglar alarm? A sprinkler system?"

"No, we do not."

"You might want to look into that. In the meantime, double up on the locks. Keep plenty of light on the place. I'll see what I can do to get a patrolman out here at night. Just until we catch the guy."

****

Amari watched the class through a window in the door. Pink pig fetuses were splayed open on black countertops as students picked through the formalin soaked guts to learn the pig's anatomy, which was supposed to be similar to that of a human. She remembered doing this dissection during her freshman year of college. She also remembered using a dissecting microscope to see the tissue up close and that there was a camera attached to it as well. There was no point in getting access to Dr. Rahal's piece of the Shroud if she couldn't examine it under a scope, and there was no point in making the examination if she couldn't capture proof of her discovery on a photograph.

At 12:50 she heard the muffled voice of Professor Kelley instructing the students. When the students had wrapped their pigs with cellophane so they could continue their examination later, they filed out the door and left Professor Kelley to tidy up the lab before the next class.

She stepped in and waited for the professor to look up. "Can I help you?" he asked. Although Dr. Kelley was pushing sixty, he had a muscular build with bulging pecs and biceps.

"I don't know if you remember me, but I took your class three years ago. My name is Amari Johnston."

"Of course, I remember you. You were going to be a detective. I remember you telling me how you looked forward to going to autopsies with the coroner. It was when we were studying the human cadaver."

"You remember that?"

"Most students are repulsed by the idea, but I remember that zeal in your eyes. It made an impression. So what can I do for you?"

"I'm on a case. I was hoping you could help."

"A case? Have you graduated already?"

"Not exactly, but I'm still investigating something."

"I'll do what I can. You'll need to make it fast because my next class starts at one."

She walked over to the microscope. "I'd like to use your scope to examine something."

"That shouldn't be a problem. Forensic evidence?"

"Exactly. I'm sure you've heard about the Shroud of Turin."

"Of course, I have. They did the carbon date right here on campus."

"I know. And they still have a piece of the Shroud over at the WMS lab. If I can talk Dr. Rahal into letting me see it, I'd like to look at it under your scope. You used to be able to hook up a Polaroid camera and take pictures. Can you still do that?"

"Yes, I can still rig it that way. What do you hope to find?"

"I'll cut to the chase. I think the carbon date is wrong. That corner they took the sample from had been handled for nearly 2,000 years. It had to have been damaged at some point, so at some point, there had to have been a repair."

"You're telling me you think they carbon dated a patch?"

"Exactly."

Dr. Kelley lowered himself to his desk chair and laced his fingers, making a steeple out of his index fingers as he thought.

"Is this something you read, or is this something you dreamed up yourself?"

She shrugged apologetically. "I have an active imagination. But I think I may be onto something. The only problem is, Dr. Rahal refuses to let me see it. He's hiding something. I think he knows it's been repaired. That's why he won't let me see it."

Dr. Kelley rubbed at his chin. "That's a serious accusation."

"It's a serious issue. If I'm right, the whole world is being misled. No matter what you believe about Jesus, you need to know the truth about this."

Dr. Kelley bit his lower lip and thought about it. "Well, it's just a scope. It's for the students. I don't have any problem with you using it. In fact, I know someone else who would like a look at the Shroud while you have it in here."

"*If* I get it in here. So far he won't budge."

"Well, if you get to look at it, I know Dr. Eastman from microbiology would like to look at it too. He has his own theory as to how the carbon date could be invalid."

"Oh really? What's his take?"

"He told me he thinks bacteria can create a bioplastic coating. He says bacteria can deposit new layers of younger material that can cause a carbon date to read younger. In fact, this has been shown to be the case with mummies from Mayan artifacts."

She thought about the prospect. "Makes sense. Maybe it was a patch with bioplastic coating. That's two reasons the carbon date is wrong. You think Dr. Eastman can reason with Rahal?"

"I tell you what, if you can hang around till my next class is over, we'll discuss this with Dr. Eastman together."

****

Two days later, Amari sat in Dr. Judith Schmidt's office. She was the Dean of the College of Science. Dr. Eastman had been intrigued by the prospect of examining the Shroud. He'd placed a phone call to Dr. Rahal and asked to see it. Unfortunately, Dr. Rahal wouldn't budge, not even at the request of a microbiology professor. He left Amari no choice. She had to go over his head.

It didn't take a detective to surmise that Dr. Schmidt was not impressed. Puffy, crescent shaped bags were under her eyes. She glared at Amari with weary disdain. "The only reason you are in my office now is because my secretary is a devout Catholic. She didn't ask me if I would see you, she simply put you on my appointment list. I would reprimand her, but I'm afraid she would quit and I'd be lost without her. So I've seen you now, I've heard your pitch, and now you may leave."

Amari arched her back and her mouth fell open. "So I take that as a no."

"Yes, that is a no. You need to learn your limits, young lady. Students don't barge into the dean's office and demand to see anything."

"I didn't demand, Dr. Schmidt, I stated my case and asked you nicely."

"*Your* case?" she said with a mix of anger and amusement. "What do you think, you're in the FBI? You're just a silly undergrad with delusions of grandeur. You're not a scientist. You're not a historian. You're just an arrogant young woman who thinks she can bully this university into handing over a priceless relic of medieval history. That sample of the Shroud will stay locked in Dr. Rahal's office, do you understand me? Now, if you don't mind, I really am a busy woman."

Amari stood and folded her arms defiantly.

"I said you can leave now," Dr. Schmidt said and pointed at the door.

"Ooookay, then," Amari said and paced toward the door. "Thank you for your time." Before she left, she turned back to Dr. Schmidt. "This isn't over, just so you know."

Chapter 20

In 1891, class began for the first time at the University of Arizona with thirty-two students in the Old Main building, a two-story red brick structure with a covered porch encircling the entire building on the second floor. It had an old west, historic feel to it. Old Main stood in the heart of campus with a fountain on the west side and a palm tree-lined grass mall on the east. It was the perfect place for Amari to post her first petition.

The petition read:

> Nearly all scientific evidence gathered to date suggests that the Shroud of Turin came from the period and location of the crucifixion of Christ in A.D. 33, and all evidence on the Shroud corresponds with the events recorded in the New Testament. The only evidence that suggests otherwise is the carbon date performed at the WMS laboratory here on campus and two additional laboratories in Europe. Please sign this petition to allow further study of the remaining piece of the Shroud that is kept locked away at the WMS laboratory. There is reason to believe that the portion used for dating the Shroud of Turin in all three locations was repaired during the 16th century and is contaminated with newer fibers, making the carbon date invalid. Please encourage Dr. Rahal to release this section of the Shroud for further study. Sign this petition so the world can know the truth.

She placed the second copy of the petition on the front door of the Administration Building, the third was stuck to the main library's bulletin board, the fourth copy was on the bulletin board at the student union memorial center, and the fifth copy of the petition went on the front door of the WMS laboratory.

****

Amari had just left her art history class and walked down the sidewalk toward the WMS laboratory. No, she wasn't going inside. Kevin was coming out to meet her instead. It was his lunch hour and he wanted to spend it with her. That's right, this time he had asked her out.

As she approached the lab's entrance, Jeremy came out. His bright blue eyes flashed surprise.

"Hey, Jeremy," she said. "I promise, I'm not going in."

"No," Jeremy said, clearly alarmed at Amari's presence. "I don't think I would do that."

"Hey, tell your grandfather thanks for standing up for me. He seems very nice. You're lucky to have him."

"He's a great man," Jeremy said.

Amari smiled playfully. "So did you sign my petition?"

Jeremy wasn't laughing. "Can I give you some advice?"

"Sure, I like advice. Can't promise I'll take it, but I'll listen."

"You need to be careful with Dr. Rahal. I don't trust him."

"I don't either. He seriously needs to take a chill-pill."

"Amari, I'm not kidding. And neither should you. Rahal can be dangerous."

"What do you mean by *dangerous*? You mean he might get Kevin fired?"

"No, worse than that."

"What's he going to do? Kill me?"

"He's changed, Amari. Ever since we tested the Shroud, he seems to have gotten worse."

"What do you mean, worse?"

"Much angrier. More defensive. Like this is personal to him." Jeremy stepped a little closer and looked over his shoulder to be certain nobody was listening. "Did you notice how he accused you of being a fanatic?"

"I've been called worse."

"Well, it takes one to know one. He's a Muslim, you know. *He's* the fanatic, not you. You're a threat to his faith. That's why he got so mad. I mean, think about it. If the Shroud is authentic, then where does that leave him? There is no way he is going to let you examine his piece of the Shroud. I wouldn't be surprised if he hasn't destroyed it, just in case you're right."

"He doesn't seem like a very religious man to me. Just a jerk."

"Just be careful," Jeremy said in a fearful voice. "Don't push him too far."

"Wow, thanks for the heads up. I'll keep that in mind."

"You should," Jeremy said and walked away without another word.

Amari stood there stunned, pondering what just happened. He seemed really concerned for her. Was Rahal that dangerous? A man in his position? Maybe there was a link between Rahal and the murder of that priest after all. Maybe her dad should investigate him. She'd have to remember and tell him about Jeremy's warning.

Just then, Kevin came out and met her. "Hey, Amari. So where we going today?"

"That was weird."

"What was weird?"

"Jeremy just warned me to be careful with Dr. Rahal. He said he could be dangerous."

"I don't know, Amari. He has been acting kind of weird lately. Maybe it's just midlife crisis."

"He's kind of old for midlife crisis, don't you think?"

"Not if he lives to be a hundred. Come on, let's try that new deli down the street. I'll drive."

****

Two days later, when Amari had gotten out of her eleven o'clock art history class, she found herself waiting outside Kevin's lab again. Only this time she was buying lunch. Friends usually go Dutch, or in this case, maybe they could just alternate who pays.

Kevin rushed out of the lab. "Rahal's wigging out. We better book-it before he sees us," he said with a mischievous grin.

"What's he mad about this time?" she asked as she walked briskly beside him.

"Who knows? He was just yelling at someone on the phone when I went by his office. I didn't stick around to find out."

When they crossed the street, he slowed his pace. "I think we're safe now."

"That guy is such a spaz," she said.

"Big time. Lately, he wigs out over the smallest thing."

"It's actually kind of funny."

"I know," he said with that cute little smirk of his. "He's like a hornet's nest you just can't help but poke."

They kept walking, kept talking, kept joking about Rahal as they made their way toward the café inside the student center. They always had such fun together. If he had any intimate feelings for her, he didn't show it. Still, she hadn't known him very long.

Love wasn't something that happened overnight. Then again, she was a Christian and his odd beliefs would only cause problems in the future. Logic said they should stay friends. Her faith came first. But what if God had drawn them together for some reason? Maybe she was supposed to lead him to Christ. She just needed to be patient and see where the Lord was leading her.

They strolled easily on the sidewalk between the Old Main building and the long, palm tree-lined lawn. Amari dodged a student who wasn't watching where he was going. Her hand brushed against Kevin's. She held it there for a second to see what he would do. He used that hand to scratch an itch on his stomach and moved a step away. Nope, nothing there. Not yet, anyway.

They bought lunch from a sandwich shop named Ray's and sat outside in the shade, enjoying the cool, dry air of a city that stayed a sunny sixty-five during November. "What did Rahal say when he found the petition?" she asked.

"He didn't find it, Jerry did."

"Ah, so Rahal never saw it?"

"Not that I know of. Jerry gave it to me and said that wasn't a good idea. He's afraid Rahal will try to get me fired."

"You're right, Kevin, I shouldn't have done that. I didn't think about pissing him off and him taking it out on you. But you said Professor Weiss had your back, right?"

"I hope so. So where else did you put the petitions?"

"I put the first one on the front doors of Old Main."

"Symbolic. It's where all this started."

"You read my mind. That's exactly why I did it. The second one went on the front door of the administrative building."

"Are you supposed to do that? I bet they took it down too."

"They did. It was just another symbolic act."

"I hope they don't symbolically expel you for that."

"It's free speech. The most they would do is warn me. Besides, I never put my name on it."

"Smart. So where else?"

"One on the bulletin board at the library and another at the bulletin board here at the student center."

"Let's check on it after lunch. You might need to add more paper to it."

After they had eaten, they went over to the bulletin board at the student center. Sure enough, the page was filled with signatures, every line. She pulled the push-pin and flipped it around. Several signatures were on the back. Below the signatures was a hand-written note. Someone from the Campus Crusade for Christ was offering the ministry's services if she needed help getting the word out.

"This is perfect," she said. "Look, even the Campus Crusade for Christ wants to help. I'll call them later today."

"How come you didn't tell me you were doing this?"

"Because I wanted you to be able to look Rahal in the face and tell him you knew nothing about it—without lying. This is all on me. I don't want you getting in trouble."

"Yeah, that might be a good idea. I don't mind helping, but we better keep it on the down low, if you know what I mean."

"That's right. You stay out of it. As far as they're concerned, this is my fight."

And Amari was far from surrender. She never told him about going to the dean's office either. And he certainly didn't know what she was about to do if Rahal didn't cave because of the petitions. But he would soon find out. Everyone on campus would soon find out.

Chapter 21

Ms. Embry set down her novel and lowered the reading glasses to her nose. "It's you again."

"Hey, Ms. Embry," Amari said. "I'm back."

"If you're here for Dr. Rahal, he's in a meeting. At any rate, he doesn't want to see you. And I think your boyfriend is talking with a client, but you can wait if you like," she said and pointed to a chair.

"Boyfriend? You mean Dr. Brenner?"

"He's a cutie. And so sweet. You're lucky to have him."

"He's not my boyfriend. We're just . . . regular friends."

Ms. Embry pulled her glasses off her nose and let them hang by the beaded cord around her neck. "Honey, I'm seventy-two years old. I wasn't born yesterday. I've seen you two together. I've seen how you look at him and how he looks at you. He's your boyfriend."

"No, seriously, we're just friends."

"That's what I said about my husband—at first. We've been married for fifty-two years."

"I'm pretty sure Kevin doesn't see me that way."

Ms. Embry held up her romance novel and fanned the pages. "I've read hundreds of these trashy things. You're talking to an expert, honey."

She hoped Ms. Embry was right, but she hadn't come there to discuss her love life. "Okay, whatever you say. So you have no idea when Dr. Rahal will be back?"

"It's hard to say. He's been gone for a while already. What's in that envelope you're holding? Another Applebee's gift certificate?"

"It's a petition, signed by a hundred and twenty-eight people who think Dr. Rahal should let me see his sample of the Shroud."

"So this is round two?"

"It's actually round three. Four if you include the dean. Round five is tomorrow if he doesn't give in."

"Well, put up your dukes. Here he comes now," she said and pointed to the front door.

Dr. Rahal stepped into the foyer and stood unmoving for a moment as he watched Amari. Maybe he was trying to decide what to do, whether he wanted another round with her, or maybe he would just escape while he could and go in the back door. Finally, he threw up his hands in exasperation and stalked toward her. "Have I not made myself clear? You are not welcome here. Now leave before I call security again."

Amari squinted her eyes defiantly. "I am not in your lab, Dr. Rahal. This is not a restricted area."

"Miss Embry, call security."

Amari handed him an envelope. "There are two petitions in that envelope. A hundred and twenty-eight other people demand you let me inspect your sample of the Shroud. A copy of those two petitions was delivered to the Dean of Science, and copies were also sent to the president of the university. If you don't want any trouble, you better stop hiding the truth and let me see your sample."

Dr. Rahal tore the envelope in two and tossed it into Miss Embry's garbage. "You have wasted the time of one hundred and twenty-eight people. Miss Embry, security."

"She's right, you know," Ms. Embry said. "This is not a secure area. She has a right to be here."

His misaligned eyes bulged. "She is causing a disturbance!"

"You're the one yelling," Ms. Embry replied. "Not her."

Dr. Rahal huffed and spun around toward his office. "I will have you expelled," he spat back at her.

"For what?" she yelled after him. "The first amendment says I can do this! You try to expel me and I'll slap a lawsuit on you so fast—" The door slammed shut and stopped her sentence short. Dr. Rahal had retreated back into the safety of his secured laboratory.

"Bite me," she said under her breath as she headed for the door.

****

Dan Rather wore an amused expression as a still shot of a campus protest was superimposed over his left shoulder, a blue-gray map of the world as the backdrop. "Apparently not everyone is taking the news about the Shroud of Turin's carbon date lying down," Dan said. "A student at the University of Arizona has organized a protest against the way the carbon date was handled. She insists that the results are invalid. We go now to our Tucson affiliate."

****

Sandra Davis stood on the court between the University of Arizona library and the long grass lawn that led up to Old Main. Crowds of students encircled the protest with curious grins on their faces. A young woman with sweat beaded on her face, her hair long and braided in a ponytail, shouted defiantly into a megaphone as several other students in red T-shirts held signs and chanted around her. Sandra's crew pointed the camera at her, taking in the protest behind her as well. The ornate, arched red brick front of the Bear Down Gym was in the background.

"The world deserves to know *all* of the truth!" the young woman shouted into a megaphone in one hand, while shaking a poster-board sign with a wooden post in the other. The sign read *The Shroud of Turin belongs to the world. The World Deserves the Truth.* "The WMS lab is holding a piece of the Shroud captive! There is evidence on that piece of Shroud that could prove the carbon date is wrong! Tell them to let me see the sample! The world deserves the truth!"

Ten other students wearing red Campus Crusade for Christ T-shirts hoisted similar signs and shouted, "If you have nothing to hide, then let us see the sample!" Others shouted, "Jesus did not die for a lie!"

Sandra got the cue from the cameraman. She raised the microphone to her mouth and began. "I'm here in front of the library at the University of Arizona where one of the students seems to be less than satisfied with the results of the carbon date performed on the Shroud of Turin, which some believe bears the image of the crucified Jesus Christ. You can see the zeal in this young lady's eye. She's not playing around. She claims to have evidence that there was a mistake made during the sampling of the Shroud, a mistake that makes the Shroud appear much younger than it really is."

The crew stopped filming for a moment. Sandra stepped over to the young lady as the camera crew followed. The girl noticed Sandra and silenced her megaphone. The camera rolled again and Sandra continued as she stood next to the girl. "So tell me, why are you making such a fuss over a medieval forgery?"

The young protester wiped sweat from her brow with the back of her hand. "I think they made a mistake when they took the sample for the carbon date," she said, catching her breath. "Dr. Rahal at the WMS laboratory has a piece of the Shroud used for the carbon date. All I want to do is look at it under a microscope. It's no big deal," she said and caught her breath again. "They can have it right back. But he absolutely refuses to let me see it. Why? I think it's because they're hiding something."

"That's a serious claim," Sandra said. "Do you have any proof?"

"I have evidence, but I need more to prove my case. I've tried reason, I've tried a petition, and now I'm trying this."

"And if this doesn't work? What will you do then?"

"I won't give up, I can tell you that. I'll keep raising public awareness until he caves. I may even have to file a lawsuit. If I have to, I will."

Sandra turned back to the Camera. "Well, there you have it. I'm Sandra Davis, WKLD News."

****

Ernesto Galliano sat behind his antique mahogany pedestal desk. A TV played from the bookcase on the opposite wall. He stroked his beard as he sat engrossed with the CBS Evening News. When the Tucson news reporter finished and Dan Rather came back to the screen, he slid open his desk drawer, removed the remote control, and clicked the TV off. The pendulum of an antique grandfather clock sounded a steady tick, tock as he deliberated his next move. *Tick Tock Tick Tock Tick Tock.* He sat unmoving until the clock chimed seven times. He reached for the phone and punched in the numbers. He pressed the receiver to his ear and waited.

"Hello," a voice sounded from the earpiece.

"Bonelli, I have a job for you and Parker. I saw something very interesting on the news. There's a student in Tucson, Arizona who claims she has evidence that discredits the carbon date on the Shroud."

"A college student in Arizona? How could a college student know so much about the Shroud?"

"That's what I'd like you and Parker to find out. Head down there and find out who she is and what she knows. Find out everything you can, but don't approach her. Just sniff around and get back to me."

Chapter 22

"I can't believe it, Kevin, I was on the news!" Amari said into the phone. "The lady from WKLD was there. You should have seen it! I think I did pretty good."

"I just saw it. Dan Rather had it on the national news too."

"Dan Rather! The CBS News? Are you serious? The whole world's going to know now!"

"Looks that way. Hey, I wanted to come watch you, but Rahal might have found out I was there. I was on the clock."

"So does he know? What did he say?"

"He hit the roof."

"Good, maybe now he'll listen. Hey, it's still early. Have you eaten?"

"I was just looking in my fridge when you called."

"Then take me to dinner. I want to celebrate."

"See you in thirty?"

"I'll be ready."

Steam puffed from the iron and Jenny rotated a skirt around the ironing board. "Are you and Kevin going on a date?"

"It's just dinner. It's not a *date*, date. We eat together all the time."

"Mind if I come along then?"

"Oh . . . I guess that would be okay. I mean, he's your cousin. I don't think he would mind."

"But you would."

"No, why would you say that?"

"I think you have feelings for Kevin."

Amari felt her cheeks flush. "What? *No*. Kevin? Be serious."

"He's cute. He's a sweet guy."

"Yeah, but he doesn't . . . I mean . . . has he ever even had a girlfriend?"

"Not that I know of." She sat the iron on its end and pulled the skirt free from the ironing board and clipped it to a hanger. "Don't take this the wrong way. I could be wrong. But I don't want you to get hurt."

"Why would I get hurt? We're just friends. It's no big deal."

Jenny held the palms of her hands together and rested her lips on her fingertips as she thought. Finally, she lowered her hands and spoke. "Some guys just aren't the relationship type. They have trouble connecting with the opposite sex. It's not that Kevin is gay, he really isn't. It's just that he's already married."

"What?"

"No, not like that. To his work. He's married to his work. He has a compulsive personality. His compulsion is physics. Guys like that are very single-minded and they just can't devote enough neurons to a relationship. I'm not sure you can compete. His brain just isn't wired like other guys."

"So? I like the way his brain is wired. Besides, it doesn't matter, because we're just friends."

"If you say so," Jenny said and pulled another skirt onto the ironing board. "I just don't want you to get hurt, that's all."

****

Amari rode the elevator to the seventh floor of the administrative tower, toward the office of the president. She had gotten a call to be there at noon. The elevator's door opened and she went down the hall and met the secretary. When she noticed Amari, she stopped typing. "Hello, Miss Johnston. I recognize you from the news. I hope you're ready for this. Everybody's in there waiting for you. Say a quick prayer and go on in."

Amari closed her eyes and prayed silently. *Father, if it is your will.* She opened her eyes and pushed through the door.

President Boling sat behind his desk. Plaques and awards decorated the wall behind him. The top of his head was completely bare, with two tufts of gray-white hair over his ears. He had kind looking, half-moon eyes that seemed to say she wasn't going to be expelled on his watch.

Dr. Schmidt, the Dean of Science who'd booted Amari from her office the other day, sat scowling next to a tense-faced Dr. Rahal.

Dr. Eastman from the microbiology department sat next to the window, eased back in his seat rubbing his hands slowly together as if he were rubbing lotion into them. His fifty-something face had wide cheek bones and his skin was leathery and sun-beaten. Amari met Dr. Eastman's eyes. He widened his tight smile and gave a slow, easy nod of approval.

Professor Wiess sat next to Dr. Eastman. He sat with an amused look on his face, one leg crossed over the other the way a woman does, rather than the usual wide leg position most men took, his laced fingers resting on his knee.

"Good afternoon, Miss Johnston," the president said. "I believe you know Dr. Rahal, Professor Weiss, and Dr. Schmitt. And I believe you've also met Dr. Eastman, professor of microbiology. I'm Henry Boling, the residing president of this university. Have a seat," he said and motioned to a chair.

Amari sat and smiled at Professor Weiss. He winked back at her. She didn't look at Drs. Rahal or Schmitt, but her sensitive cheeks could almost feel their anger radiating out to her.

"Miss Johnston, you've caused quite a stir over the past few days," Dr. Boling said. "My phone has been ringing off the hook. If this doesn't stop, we may have to change the number."

"Woops," Amari said, her eyes flashing around the room. "Sorry about that. I had no idea the news would show up."

"Yes, well, they did show up, and I've been taking a lot of heat. There are some that want you expelled. I believe Drs. Schmitt and Rahal might agree."

Amari glanced over at their glare. Yes, they agreed.

"Fortunately for you, not all the calls have been complaints. One of our wealthy alumni supports your cause and was very insistent that we let you see the sample."

"Is that what this has come down to?" Dr. Schmitt asked. "Money? Let me guess. He threatened to stop his donations. Is that why we're here today?"

"He's a very generous donor," Dr. Boling said. "Donors like him help pay your salary."

"I suppose money talks then, doesn't it," Dr. Schmidt bit back.

"He wasn't the only donor who called, I assure you. Besides, Drs. Weiss and Eastman have a right to be heard too. They don't share your opinion."

"He's right, Judy," Dr. Eastman said and scooted forward in his seat. "I have my own theory as to why the carbon date is wrong." He spoke slow and easy with a confident swagger, reminding Amari of an old John Wayne movie. "If Dr. Rahal and the College of Science would be so obliged, I'd like to get a gander of that Shroud myself. Why not make this easy and let us both see it at the same time?"

"And neither of you will find a shred of evidence that disproves the carbon date," Professor Weiss said. "All of this is silliness in my opinion and I can't understand Dr. Rahal's objection to a little further scrutiny. In the name of science, Dr. Rahal, just let these two have their look. They will find nothing and we can all move on."

"Every eye turned to Dr. Rahal."

"Very well. Take it. I'm sick and tired of arguing. If Miss Johnston had taken a more official, civil approach, I might have agreed sooner. However, if Dr. Eastman, a real scientist, rather than a disrespectful, Christian fanatic, had asked to examine the Shroud, I would have responded differently. But this young woman barged into my lab and used her looks to seduce one of my scientists into cooperating with her."

Amari sat up in her chair. "Seduced?"

Professor Weiss chuckled and clapped his hands in glee. "That is priceless. Is she a Christian or a succubus? I can't see how she could be both."

"Dr. Brenner is my roommate's cousin," Amari responded. "He did me a favor by answering a few questions—because his cousin asked him to, not because I *seduced* him."

"Knowing Dr. Brenner, I doubt he even noticed she was female," Professor Weiss said. "He is one of the most brilliant minds I've ever encountered. He is single-mindedly focused on science, not upon frolics with the opposite sex. You don't give him enough credit, Dr. Rahal."

"Okay, okay, fellas," Dr. Boling said. "Let's keep this civil. Now here's what I want to see happen. Dr. Rahal, take the piece of the Shroud you have locked in your office and deliver it to the biology lab so that Dr. Eastman and Miss Johnston can do their examinations. If it makes you feel better, you may take campus security with you."

"That scope in Dr. Kelley's lab won't cut it for me," Dr. Eastman said. "I need something more powerful. I might even have to cut off a sample for more tests."

"Testing of what kind?" Dr. Rahal asked.

"Staining. Biochemical testing," Dr. Eastman said.

"That is out of the question," Dr. Rahal said. "We may need that sample for further testing."

"Dr. Rahal, do you personally own that sample?" Dr. Boling asked. "Was it deeded to you by the Vatican?"

"Of course not," Dr. Rahal said.

"Then you have no cause to claim it for physics alone. We will discuss what Dr. Eastman has in mind later. But for now, let's satisfy Miss Johnston's curiosity before she goes on *60 Minutes*. The three of you agree on a time and get this done. Am I clear?"

Dr. Eastman locked his eyes with one of Dr. Rahal's misaligned eyes. "I'll look at the lab schedule and let you know a good time," he said and stretched his lips into a tight smile again.

Dr. Rahal stood and snapped his navy blazer taut. "If we're finished here, I have legitimate scientific business to attend to."

Chapter 23

Dr. Kelley fiddled with the scope as he worked to hook up the Polaroid camera. It attached to a tube that descended into the body of the gray colored microscope. Amari brought her own film so nobody could say the pictures did not belong to her.

Dr. Eastman opened the door and held it as Dr. Rahal entered the biology lab, followed by two campus security officers in their khaki brown uniforms.

"Did you really think we were going to steal this?" Dr. Kelley asked. "I think the campus police have better things to do, don't you Dr. Rahal?"

"I wouldn't put anything past her," Dr. Rahal said as he jabbed a finger toward Amari. "Now let's get this over with. My time is valuable."

Dr. Kelley held out his hand. "The sample?"

Dr. Rahal pulled a small, transparent plastic case from his pocket. Inside was a square piece of tan fabric, about a half inch in width. Amari eyed the fabric with awe. To think, she was in the same room with part of the cloth that covered the historical Jesus. And she was about to examine it under a microscope. She felt unworthy of the task, but somebody had to do this.

The two campus police stood off to the side, watching with their thumbs hanging on their belts. Dr. Eastman stood patiently with his hands in his back pockets. Dr. Kelley took the sample and set it by the scope. He turned his attention to Amari and said, "Now, from what I understand, you would like to inspect the fibers to see if there are cotton fibers mixed in with the linen."

"That's right," she said. "The cotton will probably look darker. They used dyes and a gummy mordant to fix the dyes onto the fibers. The mordant also helps the strands stick together."

"Then the first thing we need to do is free up some of the fibers," Dr. Kelley said. "If I put this under the scope the way it is, light won't pass through it, and it will be so thick you won't be able to tell anything. Dr. Rahal, do you have an objection if I scraped the sample to release some fibers?"

"Do what you must," Dr. Rahal said. "Just get on with it."

"Why don't you mosey on out of here if you've got things to do," Dr. Eastman said. "I promise we won't lose it."

Dr. Rahal pulled up a chair and sat. "I think I'll stay. I will enjoy seeing the look on Miss Johnston's face when she finds nothing."

"Suit yourself," Dr. Kelley said. He pulled the Shroud sample out of the plastic case with a pair of tweezers. Then he took a scalpel and scraped the sample with the sharp edge of the scalpel, causing the fibers to fall onto a glass microscope slide. When enough fibers were visible to the naked eye, Dr. Kelley transferred the glass slide to the microscope stage. He reached into the drawer and pulled out a small white box of thin glass coverslips. When he had the fibers secured under the coverslip, he flipped on the stage light. The glass slide glowed as light passed from the stage and up into the microscope's oculars. He pressed his eyes to the binocular scope and adjusted the focus. "Hmm. Interesting."

"What do you see?" Amari asked with excitement.

"Have a look." Dr. Kelley stood up and let her have the scope.

She pressed her eyes against the two oculars. Tiny transparent threads were randomly scattered about with brown colored fabric mixed in. She knew it! There is was, in plain sight. Dyed cotton fibers were mixed in with clear linen. She adjusted the stage to see more fibers. She gasped at the next thing she saw.

"What do you see?" Dr. Kelley asked.

Dr. Eastman moved in closer.

"Look," she said and moved her head out of the way. "You see those fibers?"

Dr. Kelley put his face to the eyepieces. "Well, I'll be darned. They're twisted together. One fiber is dark brown and another is clear and transparent."

"Yes!" she said. "Dark fibers are twisted onto colorless fibers. The dark fibers are dyed cotton. They did it that way because linen turns yellow with age. So they dyed the cotton to match the linen and then wove them together."

"Nonsense," Dr. Rahal said.

"See for yourself," Dr. Kelley said. "It's as plain as day."

"Can I see?" Dr. Eastman asked.

Dr. Kelley moved aside and gave Dr. Eastman the scope. "I'll be a monkey's uncle. Look at that. Seems to me there may be two reasons the carbon date is wrong. My theory is that bacteria formed biofilms over the years," he said and kept adjusting the stage, looking at other sections of the slide. "These biofilms contain younger carbon. We know this because mummies can date much younger than they really are. Biofilms are invisible. It's hard to prove my case, but your case is right there in plain view."

"Is the camera ready?" she asked.

"The film you brought is loaded up and ready to go," Dr. Kelley said.

"This proves nothing," Dr. Rahal scoffed.

Dr. Eastman offered to show him the image under the scope, but Rahal only sat in his chair with his arms folded across his chest. "My specialty is particle physics. I wouldn't know what I was looking at."

Amari slid back under the scope and started maneuvering the stage. When viewed from a distance with thousands of linen fibers bound together, it looked yellow or tan. But under the microscope, they looked relatively colorless. She snapped her first photo of a darkly stained cotton fiber lying next to a colorless linen fiber. The camera perched on top of the microscope whined as it ejected the photo. She took the photo and set it down on the counter and waited for it to develop. An image gradually emerged from a wall of gray, framed with a white border, thicker white at the bottom for gripping the photo without damaging the image. She maneuvered the stage and snapped another shot, then another, until the 10 pack of film had been exhausted.

By the time she had finished, the first pictures had fully developed. She held one up and showed it to Dr. Rahal. "You see, there's two different types of fibers. And this one," she said and pulled up another photo, "clearly shows two of those fibers wound together. Congratulations, Dr. Rahal, you just carbon dated a sixteenth-century patch."

"That proves nothing. Who's to say they didn't mix cotton and linen throughout the entire Shroud? We have cotton and polyester blends. Perhaps it was no different then."

Amari was amazed at his ignorance of ancient textiles. But why should he know? "That's not the way they did things back then."

"Then perhaps the forger wove dyed cotton into the Shroud intentionally so it would look older when it was brand new," Dr. Rahal said. "If linen yellows in time, they must have tried to match the color so it would appear old. Otherwise, the forgery would be obvious."

"Or," Dr. Eastman said, "they could have used an old piece of linen to make the forgery."

"You see, Miss Johnston, you have proven nothing." Dr. Rahal said. "You would need to get a sample from the middle of the Shroud for comparison. And I would like to know how you intend to do that. If you think you had trouble convincing me to hand this over, try asking the Vatican to let you cut a hole in their precious relic. Now you are wasting our time. Enough of this."

Rahal thought he had her, but he didn't. "You've heard of STURP, haven't you? The Shroud of Turin Research Project? They took tape samples from the middle of the Shroud in 1978. I know from a very good source that Los Alamos has some of those tape samples. I can look at those and compare them." She was careful not to mention that Kevin was that good source.

"Hah!" Dr. Rahal arrogantly laughed. "Los Alamos is one of the most secure government facilities in the country. You will never set foot in that building, I assure you."

"Oh yeah?" Amari said and scooped up her ten photos. "Well, I never give up," she said and made her way for the exit. The campus police held the door open for her as she left.

****

It was almost midnight. Amari sat next to the third-floor window of the university's main library. The window reflected her image like a mirror, illuminated by fluorescent lights.

Since the Shroud of Turin was obviously not a work of art, she'd decided to do her art history report on gothic sculpture instead. She'd come to the library several hours earlier to finish that report. Once she'd finished, shifted her focus back to the Shroud.

She flipped through the pages of an obscure book on textiles she had found after searching the card index for over an hour. Then the book wasn't where it was supposed to be. She finally found it but now it was getting late and they were about to close.

Before she got too excited about her find in the biology lab, she had to make sure she had all her evidence substantiated. She had to find pictures of cotton fibers, preferably dyed cotton fibers, so she could prove the images on her Polaroids were indeed cotton and not some other contaminating artifact. She only assumed they were cotton, after all. If she didn't make certain and have pictures to back up her claim, she would be discredited.

Frustrated, she flipped through the pages. She still could not find any microscopic images, only the fabric form. Keys jangled and she looked up to see Hokee approaching. Hokee, a library security guard, was a full-blooded Navajo Indian. He was also Amari's second cousin. When she was a kid, he used to come over to the house with his mother.

"I know, you're closing," she said. "I'll be out by midnight, I promise."

"You got five minutes," Hokee said and continued his rounds.

"Okie, dokie, Hokee," Amari said and giggled. Just like when they were kids.

"That never gets old, does it?" he called back to her as he moved down the hall.

"Nope."

"Seriously, Amari, hurry it up."

"Okie, dokie, Hokee, I won't be poky," she said and snorted a laugh.

"Very funny," Hokee called back. "*Four* minutes."

Amari flipped through some more pages. A sound from behind her startled her. She turned to see. Nobody was there. Must be another student packing up.

Grid by grid, fluorescent lights went dark, leaving only the occasional emergency light.

"Fine, Hokee, I'm going," she uttered and scooped up the book. She grabbed her backpack and went to the isle between bookshelves, carefully navigating in low light, heading for the shelf the book was supposed to be on. Another light grid went dark and she knew Hokee was messing with her. She strained to see, waiting as her eyes adjusted. She would have to drop the book in the return bin and the librarian could return the book to its proper place. She found the return bin sitting on a table next to a Xerox machine, directly across from the elevator. She set the book in the box. A door slammed shut, startling her.

"Hokee? Is that you?"

No answer.

"Okay, you got me."

No answer.

"You jerk, I'm telling your mother!"

No answer.

She stepped to the elevator. A crude handwritten sign made of copy paper hung on the sliding doors. *Out of Order.* She had just taken that elevator up a few hours before. Now it was broken? Or was it Hokee playing a prank on her, just like when they were kids? It didn't look like Hokee's writing. It was way too messy. Maybe they closed it for maintenance at night since nobody needed to use it. "Oh, well," she said to herself and headed down the darkened hall for the stairs. She was only three floors up, no big deal.

She swung open the stairway door and light flooded out, making her squint against her dark-adjusted pupils. "See you later, Hokee!" she called out and entered the stairwell. The door slammed closed, the clap echoing down the stairwell.

A large shadow fell over her. A crushing grip took her from behind.

Chapter 24

She opened her mouth to scream, adrenaline surging. A massive hand clamped over her lips, muffling her cries. Training kicked in. She dropped her backpack, gripped the hand over her mouth, and forced his middle finger between her teeth. She bit hard as she could.

"Ahhh," the man howled and let go.

She spun around, balled her fist, and punched at his throat. He deflected her blow and caught her by the wrists. She fought to free herself, yanking, pulling against massive hands. An angry giant's teeth gnashed through the mouth opening of a black ski cap.

"Let me go!" she cried and kicked his knee, square in the kneecap.

"Oouuww," he shrieked and released her. He grabbed her shoulder, spun her around, and shoved her into the stair rail. He pushed down on her head. Her neck strained against him. Her eyes widened to a three-story drop, the gap between stairs. One hand gripped her neck and the other grabbed her ankle and started to lift.

She reached over her head and clawed at the man's eyes. He howled and let go, falling back against the cinder blocks, his ski mask caught on her fingers. She pelted him in the head with the mask. His eyes were clenched tight, his hands rubbing them furiously.

She broke for the door and flung it open. "Hokee!" she screamed and stumbled out of the stairwell.

He grabbed her arm and worked to pull her back in. She came around with her knee and caught him in the groin. He hunched over from the pain and fell back. The fire extinguisher hung on the wall. She snatched it from its cradle, yanked the pin loose, and shot white powder in his face. He jerked his head away, flung the door open, and escaped into the stair landing.

Amari pursued him. She gripped the extinguisher like a bat and swung hard, connecting to his head with a loud *CLONG*. He stumbled backward and tumbled with thuds and clumps down a flight of stairs. The fire extinguisher clanged when she dropped it, echoing in the concrete stairwell. She broke through the door and sprinted down the hall. She plowed right into Hokee and knocked him to the ground.

"Sorry!" She grabbed his hand and helped him back up. "There's a guy in the stairway," she said frantically, catching her breath. "He attacked me. I got him, though. Hit him in the head with the fire extinguisher. He fell down the stairs. He's got to be hurt."

Hokee drew his revolver and crept for the stairwell. "Amari, stay back here."

She ignored him and followed close behind. Hokee flung the door open and lunged forward with his gun drawn. She stepped in with him. They both stared down at the foot of the stairs. He was gone. They heard another door slam, then silence.

****

The doorbell rang. Amari startled awake and came up from the bed so fast she felt dizzy. The doorbell rang again, then rapping on the door. It rang again, *rap-rap-rap-rap!* She snapped open the nightstand drawer and grabbed her gun, a compact 9mm Beretta registered to her dad. Who could it be? Her attacker from the library?

A muffled voice came from the door. "Amari, it's me. Kevin."

She sighed in relief and put the gun back where she found it. She hated guns, but her dad had insisted she keep it.

Rap-rap-rap-rap!

"Hold on, Kevin, I'm coming," she yelled.

She slid her feet into her slippers, then went to the bathroom and splashed water on her face. She was still stunned about what had happened, not even sure what had happened. It was like a dream—or nightmare. She hadn't had time to sort her emotions. She just talked to the police for a while, came home with her dad, and finally fell asleep with him still there. She vaguely remembered him kissing her on the forehead and leaving just before dawn.

And then Kevin woke her. She splashed more water on her face. She dried it with a towel and noticed her reflection in the mirror. She looked like crap, no makeup, her hair was a mess— and fear showed in her eyes. She wet a wash cloth and held the cool wetness against her eyes, hoping it would somehow ease the tension in her facial muscles. She couldn't let him see her fear. She had to put on a brave face.

The doorbell rang, *rap, rap, rap!*

"Hold on, I said I'm coming!" she yelled and put on her robe. She tied the belt around her waist as she made her way into the den. "Here goes," she muttered to herself. "I hope he buys it."

She looked through the peephole. She had visual confirmation. It was Kevin. She slid the dead bolt open, unhooked the chain, and opened the door.

"Kevin?" she said, squinting from the sunlight flooding in. "What time is it?"

"It's 10 o'clock."

"Oh," she said and stepped aside. She closed the door behind him.

"I heard what happened," he said breathlessly. "It's all over campus. That Shroud protest girl was attacked at the library. Are you okay?"

"Yeah, Kevin, I'm fine. This wasn't my first go around," she assured him—and herself. "I can take care of myself. You want coffee?"

"You almost got killed and you ask if I want coffee?"

"Uh, excuse me, but I beat the crap out of that guy. I'm surprised he's still alive. They found a blood trail so I know he's hurt. I need to ask my dad if they checked all the hospitals."

She rubbed at her eyes and yawned for effect, to show how relaxed she was. "I can't believe you saw me like this. Why didn't you call?"

"I did, all I got was a busy signal."

"Phone must be off the hook. Sorry."

"You've got a bruise on your chin. And look at your wrists!"

She held up her wrists and noticed it for the first time. Dark ringed bruises encircled both of them. It must have happened during the struggle. They didn't hurt but sure looked bad. "It's a little bruising, Kevin. Calm down."

He sat on the couch and rubbed his temples. "They have got to get a handle on crime at this university. The other day someone busted out Rahal's windshield."

"The university is perfectly safe. He probably just pissed somebody else off too."

"I wonder if you touched a nerve over the Shroud. You made quite a scene at the library the other day. Maybe someone's trying to send you a message. You better lay low for a while until this blows over. If you gotta be at the university at night, I'm coming with you. Understand?"

"Kevin, relax. I've never seen you this way before. You're always so laid back."

"There's a lot of sides to me you've never seen. Now, I'm serious. You call me if you're going over there at night."

That was so sweet. He really cared about her. She sat next to him and put her hand on his shoulder. "Fine, Kevin, I promise, I'll call you first. At least until this all blows over. But we don't know if this had anything to do with the Shroud. It could have just been a pervert."

"Did he say anything? What did he look like?"

"He was big. At least six foot, maybe more. He was Middle Eastern looking. Black hair, dark eyes. Bulky. Not muscular, but stout. He could stand to lose a few pounds. Maybe thirty years old."

"So what did the police say?"

"They don't know. I gave them the description."

"And your dad?"

"My dad's having a cow. He was here until daylight. Then he left to try to find this guy. I was up until five. I was going to call you as soon as I woke up. I promise."

"As long as you're okay."

"I'm fine. I don't think that guy was trying to kill me. Although there for a minute I thought he was going to throw me down the stair shaft. I honestly don't know what he was trying to do. But he hesitated, and that's all I needed to get the upper hand."

"What did you do then?"

"I clawed his eyes, kicked him in the groin, sprayed him in the face with a fire extinguisher, then used it like a bat to knock him down the stairs. I swear, I thought I'd find him dead, but he was gone. He must be pretty hard headed."

"*He's* hard headed."

"What can I say, I have a stubborn streak."

She got up and went to the coffee maker. "Jenny didn't get much sleep either, poor girl. She's got a test today. Hope she doesn't flunk it. Hey, I've got decaf if you want it."

He came to her in the kitchen. "Amari, I'm nervous enough as it is. I don't need coffee."

"You don't think Rahal is behind this, do you? He's the only one with a motive. This guy was Middle Eastern and so is Rahal."

"I can't imagine he'd go that far."

"Jeremy says he's dangerous—because he's a Muslim."

"If he is a Muslim, he doesn't seem very devout."

"Still, my dad thinks it's the only lead we have. He's the only one with a motive."

"That we know of," he reminded her.

"Yes, that we know of. Then again, it could just be a perv wanting to rape me. He got what was coming to him. Either way, my dad wants to talk to you."

"To me?"

"Well, yeah, because you work with Rahal. And he's with me about the Shroud. He thinks there may be something bigger behind this than Rahal's hurt feelings. I told him about the pictures I took. He smells a cover-up, just like I do."

"What pictures? What are you talking about?"

"I didn't tell you because I don't want you involved. I was afraid you would say something and then Rahal would know we're still talking. But the president forced Rahal to show me the Shroud sample. And guess what?"

"You found something?"

Amari went to her bedroom and came back with the Polaroids. "Right there, two kinds of fibers, just like we thought. I was at the library looking for some pictures to confirm that those were cotton fibers. I was going to tell you once I had all the evidence. Until then, it was just conjecture."

"Did you find any?"

"No, but my dad said I didn't need to. His crime lab has pictures for reference. They work with fibers all the time. I felt like an idiot. I should have thought of that."

"You're not supposed know everything. You haven't even graduated."

"Well, I know now. So can you come over?"

"Tonight?"

"No, tomorrow night. My dad took some of my photos to the crime lab. When he gets their opinion, he wants to meet with you. He's interested in what you know about the Shroud."

"I can tell him the science behind it, but I'm not sure how that's going to help."

"You said you knew how the sampling process went. You said they handled it like idiots."

"They did."

"Maybe they only want us to *think* they're idiots. Maybe this is a cover-up. Anyway, don't be surprised if he goes that route with you. So around seven?"

"Your dad's a cop. Do I have a choice?"

"Not really." She shot him a playful look. "We can do this the easy way, or the hard way."

"I'm all for the easy way. Hey, I better get back to work. Rahal doesn't know I left. I just wanted to make sure you were safe. I couldn't concentrate on work anyway." He hesitated, like he was thinking of something else to say. "Well, I'll see you tonight."

"No, it's tomorrow night," she reminded him.

"Let's do dinner tonight then."

"Sure."

"Well, better go," he said, standing there awkwardly like he'd forgotten something, like there was a natural inclination he didn't know how to handle.

Kevin might be oblivious, but Amari knew what he needed—and what she needed too. She stepped over and wrapped her arms around him and gave him a firm hug. He was rigid at first, then sort of melted into it and held her back. She pulled back and looked at his face. "Feel better now?"

The tension in his face eased up. "I do feel better."

Jenny was right. Kevin was a genius in a physics lab, but he was oblivious to the simplest of human needs. Amari would just have to teach him. "You know, Kevin, I worry a lot too. I may be hard headed, but I'm not made of stone. I'm just a girl. Or had you not noticed that?"

"Of course, I noticed."

"Well, girls like to be hugged from time to time."

"Even if we're just friends?"

"It's perfectly acceptable in our culture."

"Okay, I'll remember that. Hey, I better go before Rahal finds out I'm gone."

He was out the door before she could say another word.

Chapter 25

Pete gave the Phillips-head screwdriver a final twist and inspected his work. He slid the half inch, galvanized steel dead bolt back and forth to make sure it tracked smoothly. He'd meant to install extra protection on Amari's front door sooner, but the attack on his girl at the library sent it to the top of his to-do list.

"Dad, that guy doesn't know where I live," Amari said, her hands defiantly on her hips. "Assuming he hasn't learned his lesson. It was random. College campuses are a magnet for perverts. It was just a coincidence this happened now."

"Maybe it was, maybe not. Either way, I've been meaning to install this thing on your door. And I cut a broomstick to brace the sliding door in your bedroom. I'm going to put some security film over the glass so it'll be hard to break."

"It's not necessary, Dad. You're wasting your time."

At times, Amari seemed wise beyond her years, but other times she showed her age. Kids always thought they were invincible. It was a father's job to show them otherwise until they got enough scrapes to figure it out themselves. "Wait till you have your own daughter," Pete said, "then you'll understand. So what time is this guy supposed to show?"

The doorbell rang. "That's him," she said and slid open the newly installed dead bolt.

"Hold on, Amari. You see that peephole? Use it first. And if you don't see someone you recognize, don't open the door. They're either trying to sell you something or they're up to no good. Get your gun by your side and pretend you're not home."

The doorbell rang again.

Amari pouted for a second, then checked the peephole. "It's Kevin. Satisfied?"

"Not till you promise to do that every time."

"I promise. Can I open the door now?"

"Let him in. I'm eager to hear what he's got to say."

Amari snapped open the other dead bolt, removed the chain, and opened the door to let Dr. Brenner inside.

So this was the amazing Dr. Brenner, 1988's answer to Albert Einstein. To hear Amari talk, Carl Sagan came to this guy for advice. But he was just a long-haired dork with a silly smirk on his face. He didn't look like he'd be much help.

Amari went to the kitchen and came back with a can of Mountain Dew with a straw stuck inside. "Here you go, Kevin. Dad's got some heavy questions for you. I think you're going to need this."

"Well, hey, stranger," Jenny said as she walked into the room.

"Hey, Jenny," Dr. Brenner said. "How's school?"

"Pharmacology is a killer, but other than that, great."

Pete knew where this was going. They'd be yammering all night if he didn't butt in. "Hey, guys, I'll let you two catch up later. I've just got a few questions for Dr. Brenner and then I'll be out of your hair."

They all went to the kitchen and sat around the table. Pete wasted no time with pleasantries because there was nothing pleasant about someone trying to harm his daughter. "Now, Dr. Brenner, Amari tells me you know a lot of background information that could help shed some light on this case."

"I know some things," Dr. Brenner said.

"Good. Now, I'm not interested in having a religious debate. I respect the opinion of scientists like yourself, but I'm going to be up front and tell you that I'm a Christian. I believe the Shroud of Turin is the authentic burial shroud mentioned in the New Testament. I know this because of the evidence. There's no plausible way to make this forgery now, let alone with the technology they had six hundred years ago. So once you eliminate the impossible, whatever remains, no matter how improbable, must be the truth."

"Sherlock Holmes," Dr. Brenner said.

Amari pointed at him. "Elementary, my dear Watson."

Pete forced a wry smile and kept talking. "Like I said, we've established beyond any reasonable doubt that this was the burial shroud of Jesus Christ. That radiation that formed the image must have been from the energy shot out during the resurrection. It's the only plausible answer. Now, what concerns me is why they got the carbon date wrong. Dr. Brenner, Amari tells me you're familiar with the carbon dating process. Hey, Amari, run get me that poster with the pictures of the Shroud on it."

Amari went to her bedroom and came back with the poster with the negative image of the Shroud on one side and the positive image on the other.

"Thank you," Pete said and took the poster from her. "I was hoping you could shed some light on why they chose this corner of all places to take the carbon date sample." He pointed to the lower left corner of the tan, positive image of the Shroud. "This is the same corner that Amari found the dyed cotton. I had my CSI guys check out the pictures she took. They agree. There's two kinds of fibers in that corner. Linen and cotton. Now, as careful as these scientific types are, I can't believe the notion of a repair hadn't occurred to them. Amari knows her weaving, but she's not the expert she thinks she is. These guys should have known better."

"Hey," she objected.

"It's the truth, Amari, you've read a couple of books and your mother taught you some things, but that's the end of it. You're not paid to know everything, but these guys are. So either they're real idiots, or they did this on purpose. And if Amari has caught them red-handed, then they've got motive to keep her quiet. Maybe that's what the guy in the library was trying to do. That attack happened the day after she made her discovery in front of Dr. Rahal. That's too much to be coincidence. Maybe Rahal paid someone to rough her up as a warning. Maybe he was trying to kill her to shut her up. But she shut *him* up before he could say anything."

"Or maybe that guy was just a pervert and he has nothing to do with the Shroud," Amari said.

Pete knew she didn't want to believe the attack could be connected. It might make her think twice about going forward. And she had made it very clear—she was taking this to the Vatican.

Jenny broke into the conversation. "Can I say something? It might help explain why Dr. Rahal is being such a jerk."

"Then I'd like to hear it," Pete said.

"You have to understand that where Dr. Rahal comes from, the culture is entirely different. Women have fewer rights and they don't dare speak to men the way Amari challenged him. Honor is very important in his culture, and Amari insulted his honor by defying him."

"You think he would kill to protect his honor?" Pete asked.

"It happens all the time over there."

"This isn't over there. Surely a man in Dr. Rahal's position would never try such a thing."

"No, but he might hire someone to send her a message. It would be hard for him to just let her behavior go unpunished."

"Because she insulted his honor?"

"Because she is a *woman* who insulted his honor. That makes all the difference."

"That's certainly something to consider. Thank you, Jenny."

"Just doing my job," she said and walked back down the hall.

"Or it was probably just a random pervert," Amari said emphatically.

"I'm with Amari on this," Dr. Brenner said. "Dr. Rahal's a jerk, but he's not stupid. He could go to jail over that."

"I don't know what to think, Dr. Brenner. I'm just getting the facts. Jenny gave me some and now it's your turn."

"My brain is yours to pick. Have at it."

"Okay, forget the honor killing angle for now. Let's say that Rahal, or maybe even someone else for all we know, wants to keep Amari quiet about her theory. So we need to go back to the beginning and work our way forward. Now, Dr. Brenner, Amari tells me you're familiar with the process of collecting these samples. She says you implied there's some duplicity."

"You can call me Kevin."

"And you can call me Pete. So tell me, Kevin, give me a little history about all this."

Kevin sipped on his Mountain Dew and thought for a moment. "First off," he finally said, "only three labs ended up dating the Shroud instead of the seven that were originally agreed on. My lab was one of those three."

"How convenient," Pete said. "A cover-up would be easier with only three labs."

"The really strange part is how they pushed STURP out of the picture. That's The Shroud of Turin Research Project."

"I know who they are," Pete said.

"Okay, so you know that nobody knew more about the Shroud than STURP. These guys were the ones that suggested the carbon date in the first place. And these were the only guys who had the expertise to sample the right spot. Yet somewhere along the line, STURP gets completely pushed out. And the ones who finally got the samples ended up breaking nearly every protocol the world's greatest scientists had agreed on. In the end, they cut out a piece from the worst possible location."

"And you're implying that wasn't an accident?"

"All they had to do was look at some of the ultraviolet photos taken by STURP and they could see that. That corner was an anomalous area. It fluoresced dark green while the other parts were yellow, orange, and pink. The STURP guys knew that and the STURP guys would have said to cut somewhere else."

"So either they're idiots, or they did this on purpose."

"They're not idiots," Amari said. "These guys are Ph.Ds."

"Then I say they saw those ultraviolet pictures and cut there intentionally."

"Could be," Kevin said.

"So, Kevin, you know Dr. Rahal better than any of us. Do you think he was in cahoots with these guys who sampled the Shroud?"

"He's not supposed to be," Kevin said, "but he sure is defensive about it."

"Then I say he has motive," Pete said. "A Muslim wouldn't want proof of Christ's divinity known to the world. That's why he's so defensive."

"He doesn't seem the religious type to me," Kevin said. "I mean, I think he is a Muslim, but not very devout. Not enough to commit murder."

"You know him that well?" Pete asked.

"No, he hates me. He only talks business—or fusses at me."

"So is that all you've got? He's a jerk?"

"No, there's a little something else."

"Then let's hear it."

"All right, it's like this. When all the numbers from the three carbon date labs came in, it showed that the farther away from the body the sample was taken, the older the sample dated. And the closer the samples were to the body, the younger they dated. Amari thinks that's because of the uneven way they did the patch. The higher up part had more cotton. But whatever the cause, this sent up red flags because the dates should have been random."

"So you're telling me that the date they got depended on how far away the cloth was from the body," Pete said, just to clarify.

"Exactly," Kevin said. "They fixed this by reporting the averages for my lab's results and not the actual numbers."

"Explain that," Pete said.

"You see, they divided the original sample into four different pieces. Oxford got the left middle piece, Zurich got the right middle, and we got the two outer edges. When we tested our two pieces, one end was way different from the other end and that's how we saw the trend. So we only reported the average of the two numbers so nobody would notice."

"That sounds like intentional deception," Pete said. "Were you involved in that?"

Kevin held up his hands defensively. "No, sir. I only ran the test. I had no control over what was reported. I just knew what they did when I saw the published results."

"So if they went that far to cover up the truth, then maybe they would go even further. Like put a hit on Amari to shut her up."

"Dad, I really don't think . . . I don't know. I don't want to think about it."

"You have to think about it," Pete said.

"Trust me. I haven't stopped thinking about it."

"All right, guys, I think I've heard enough. Amari, remember what I told you. No dark alleys. I'll get your license to carry by the end of the week."

"Carry a gun? Do I have to?"

"If you're going to be a cop, you need to get used to it."

She gave a hard sigh. "I guess you're right. If it makes you feel any better, it's in my nightstand."

"Good. Now I want you to come with me to the firing range and practice. You'll need to do that before we get a license to carry. You'll have to be signed off."

"Fine, Dad. If it'll make you feel better."

"It would. And a patrol car should be outside most of the time at night. Starting tonight. At least until we get to the bottom of this. Meeting adjourned. I'll get back with you when I find out more."

"Hey, Dad. I promised Kevin all this would stay between us. He could get fired if they know he told us any of this. Don't mention Kevin or anything only he would know."

Pete looked over at Kevin. "Don't worry about a thing. Your secret's safe with me. All I needed to know was whether or not I should consider Dr. Rahal a suspect. I'll talk to him next, and I promise, I won't mention anything you just told me."

"Thank you," Kevin said. "I appreciate that."

Kevin went back to catch up with Jenny and Amari walked Pete to his car.

"You like this Kevin guy, don't you?" Pete asked.

"Sure, he's very nice."

"You're different around him, you know. You may not notice, but I do. And I haven't seen you wear that much makeup since the divorce. Honestly, you look better without it. That gunk just covers your pretty skin."

"It's Jenny's fault. She's trying to make me more fashion conscious."

"She needs the makeup. You don't."

"How am I different around him?"

"I don't know. You seem, softer. More feminine. Not so bossy. You actually let him finish a sentence without butting in. You have feelings for him, don't you?"

She started to deny it, but it would be a lie. And she hated lies. "Maybe a little. I'm trying not to, but I just like being around him. He makes me laugh. And he is kind of cute."

"Amari, I'm not trying to intrude in your personal life, but something about that guy bothers me. Call it a hunch, but he's hiding something. I don't think he's been completely honest with you."

"You don't think he has something to do with the guy in the library do you?"

"No, nothing like that. Like you said, he seems harmless enough, but there's something hidden behind his expression. I can't put my finger on it. He just seems to be too eager to throw his colleagues under the bus. Most people would be reluctant to answer my questions. But he just threw it all out there. Why would someone in Kevin's position bite the hand that feeds him?"

"You think he's trying to throw you off the scent?"

"I wouldn't say that, it's . . . I don't know. It seems strange to me, that's all. Just proceed cautiously, that's all I'm saying."

"Dad, I promise, he's harmless. He wouldn't hurt a fly."

"You're a smart girl. I trust you. Just something to consider." He leaned in to give her a hug. "Love you, baby."

"Love you too, Dad."

"And don't walk alone at night."

"Okay, Dad. I'll be fine, don't worry. Whoever that guy was won't feel like taking me on anytime soon. Did you check all the hospitals?"

"We did. There were no concussions from a guy matching your description. But the local ERs are going to keep an eye out. And you tell me if you see anything suspicious."

"I will. Don't worry about me. I'll be fine."

Chapter 26

Ernesto stood under the shade of his estate's veranda, watching the children play kickball on the lawn. The bouncy red ball ricocheted off the marble support pillar and hit a chair next to him.

"Foul ball," Ernesto shouted and kicked the ball back onto the playing field.

One of the servants hurried onto the veranda holding a cordless phone. She extended the silver antenna and handed it to him. "It's Bonelli," she said. "He says it's urgent."

Ernesto took the phone and paced down the veranda, farther away from the laughing children so he could hear better. "Bonelli, what's going on? Miranda said it's urgent."

"It's about the student in Tucson," Bonelli said.

"I'm listening."

"Her name is Amari Johnston. She claims she has evidence to prove the carbon date on the Shroud was done on a patch."

"A patch?"

"She thinks the section they used for the carbon date was repaired. Newer cloth was woven into older cloth and that's why the Shroud appears much younger than it truly is."

"Fascinating. I wonder if she's right."

"I think somebody's afraid she is."

"What do you mean?"

"She was attacked. She's okay, but somebody attacked her in the stairwell of the university library. I have a feeling somebody was trying to shut her up."

"That's not good. What do the police say?"

"They haven't made any announcements. But I did find this out. She's the daughter of a high-ranking detective for the Tucson Police department."

"Good, then she will have better protection."

"I'd say you're right. There's a police cruiser in front of her house at night."

"That's a relief."

"So what should we do? Are you ready for us to come back to Fresno?"

Ernesto pondered his decision as he walked back into the parlor of his estate. What if she was right about the patch? That would change everything. Perhaps he could use his influence with the Vatican. Maybe they would hear her out and agree to a retest on a different portion of the Shroud. He would make some calls and pull some strings, but navigating the complex Vatican bureaucracy was difficult and time-consuming. In the meantime, he had to keep that girl safe. "I tell you what, why don't you and Parker hang around for a few days. Don't get involved. I just want you to watch her back from a distance. Besides, if there is somebody trying to kill her and they know you're protecting her, they could try to remove you first. It's better to stay in the shadows."

"And keep the element of surprise."

"Exactly. By all means, intervene if she's in danger, but stay in the shadows until she does need you. Between you and the police, she should be in good hands until her attacker is caught."

"We'll do what we can."

"And keep me posted."

****

The sweet smell of fresh donuts filled Pete's nostrils as he sorted the pages. If he was going to interrogate Dr. Rahal, he had to have some evidence to go on. So he had Judge Hader issue a warrant requiring the bank to release statements for one Musa Rahal. Pete sat on a stool at the counter of Don's Donuts reading these statements as George dipped his donut into coffee.

Amari's attacker in the library seemed like an amateur, and the way he went about his attack made little sense. If he wanted her dead, why not shoot her in the back on the way out of the library? Why not follow her to her car? There were security guards on staff at that library. It was a reckless act and it was a stroke of sheer luck he didn't get caught. No, this guy was no pro, but he could have been desperate for cash. And the only person angry enough to put him on their payroll was Dr. Rahal.

"Find anything good?" George asked and brought the coffee cup to his lips.

"I Gotcha!" Pete blurted.

George flinched and spilled coffee onto his shirt and tie. "Dang, Pete, you want to warn me when you do that? Got coffee all over my clothes. I just bought this tie."

Pete handed him a napkin but never pulled his eyes from the bank statement. "Gotcha again, you miserable scumbag."

George dabbed coffee from his tie, careful not to rub it in. "What'd you find?"

"Big cash withdrawals. Two of them. Twenty-five hundred each time. And some other good sized checks."

"So let's go get him. Have someone pick him up and take him to the station. We'll sweat it out of him."

"I got a better idea. Let's go visit him at work. Maybe we'll spot something fishy while we're there."

George took his coffee and donut to go and they headed to the WMS laboratory.

When Pete stopped for a red light at East 6th Street and North Park, George wadded his donut bag and tossed it over his head into the back seat. "What did Interpol say?"

"That I was wasting their time," Pete said. He watched for the light to change through dark green, tinted aviator sunglasses. "Nine in the morning in Italy is one in the morning here. I spent most of the night trying to get someone to understand me. Mostly I sat on hold. I talked to the Director General of Public Security. He's sort of their Chief of Police. I talked to the ministry of interior himself. The guy spoke pretty good English, but he told me the same thing everyone else did. He's got a back log of cases that involved real crimes." The light turned green and Pete followed a line of cars left onto North Park. "He said if I wanted to chase after conspiracy theories, I needed to hire a private investigator or come over there and do it myself."

"He's got a point, Pete. We got nothing but the word of that geek your daughter's friends with. It's not real evidence. You need something concrete before they'll listen."

"You're right. I'm just grasping at straws. And speaking of that geek, I'm not so sure about Dr. Brenner either. You know he's got a record?"

"You're kidding? Hey, turn right on 4th Street."

Pete turned onto 4th and kept talking. "It's juvenile, so I can't touch it. Out in Knoxville, Tennessee, back in '79. He was sixteen at the time. I tried to get details, but they wouldn't budge."

"He probably egged somebody's house for all you know."

"Maybe, but still I'd like to know. I tell you, he's hiding something."

"Maybe something Rahal says will give you some clues. It's right here," George said as he pointed to the long, red brick building. "Take that spot."

Pete pulled into a parking meter slot next to the lab. "Hey, remember what I told you. You do the introductions. Don't tell him my last name. I don't want him making any connections that I might be Amari's father."

"Got it. I'll do all the talking."

"Not all the talking, just the intro. I'll do the rest."

"Right, you're the boss. Like usual, only I get to say a few words this time."

They dropped a quarter in the meter and went through the front door. An elderly lady with horn-tipped reading glasses sat at a reception desk with her nose in a book. Pete coughed for her attention.

"May I help you gentlemen?" she asked.

George pulled his sport coat back and flashed the gold badge clipped to his belt. "I'm detective George Sanchez. This here's my partner. We need to speak to a Dr. Musa Rahal."

"Is this about Amari Johnston?"

"Maybe," George said. "You heard of her?"

"Heard of her? Who hasn't? That's a feisty young broad if ever I've seen one."

Pete fought to suppress the smile tugging at his lips.

The receptionist picked up the phone. "Dr. Rahal, you have a visitor. No, it's not that girl again. It's the police." There was a long pause and then barely audible words. "Yes, I'll tell them."

"He said he would be right out. I think he's been expecting you. You know, I warned him about smoking all that hashish in his office. That's middle eastern marijuana in case you don't know."

Pete and George shot each other an incredulous glance.

"Yes, I'm just kidding," she said and pointed down the hall. "There he comes now."

Dr. Rahal strode toward them. He was a short, Arab-looking man with gray streaked, televangelist shaped black hair. His eyes pointed in different directions so Pete couldn't tell who he was looking at.

"May I help you, gentlemen?" Dr. Rahal asked.

"I was hoping so," George said. "I'm detective George Sanchez from the Tucson Police Department." He showed his badge and Pete did the same. "This is my partner, Pete. We'd like to ask you a few questions if you don't mind."

"Of course," Dr. Rahal said cordially. "Would you like to speak in my office?"

"That would be great," Pete said. They followed him down the hall, cut right, and stopped at the first door on the left.

"Come in, have a seat," Dr. Rahal said and pulled a second chair from the corner to join the one already in front of his desk.

Pete and George sat, and Dr. Rahal went behind his desk. Pete looked around his office. There were pictures of family, trinkets, lots of books and manuals, but nothing unusual.

"Do you know why we're here?" Pete asked.

"I suspect you're here about the attack on Amari Johnston. Our disagreement is well known. However," he quickly added and held up his index finger, "I assure you, I had nothing to do with that. In fact, I was concerned. I'm glad she was not harmed."

"So why were you so against her looking at the Shroud sample then?" Pete asked. "If you didn't have anything to hide, that is?"

"I had nothing to hide. I was simply following security protocols. That section of the Shroud comes from a priceless relic.

We can't have people come in off the street and demand to see it, can we?"

"I see your point," Pete said. The question he was about to ask may seem out of line, but he never beat around the bush. Sometimes the reaction to an inappropriate question said volumes about what's on a man's mind, no matter what came from his lips. "And I also see you're not from around here. I understand you're a Muslim. Your reluctance isn't because of your beliefs, is it? After all, if the Shroud of Turin is for real, then that sort of discredits your own religion, don't it?"

Dr. Rahal seemed a little offended, but not like Pete had hoped. He just leaned back in his chair with the slightest of a smirk on his face.

"First of all, detective, I am from here," Dr. Rahal said. "My parents immigrated to this country before I was born. I'm from Phoenix. Second of all, I am not a practicing Muslim. I'm an atheist. Any religious tradition in my family will have to be passed on by my son," he said and pointed at a picture frame on his desk. His son wore a white tunic and smiled for the camera behind a thick, neatly groomed black beard. "He is a devout Muslim. It's not the way I raised him, but unfortunately, he fell into the wrong crowd in college. I do not share his faith, so certainly that is not the reason for my opposition."

Pete absorbed his statement, wondering if he should believe him. Dr. Rahal was dressed like anybody else and his office was completely secular, not one religious trinket to suggest he was a man of faith.

"Listen," Dr. Rahal said. "I know I was a bit hostile toward that girl, but you must understand that I've been going through a very nasty divorce. I've been in a foul mood lately. Ask anyone who works for me."

"I can understand that," Pete said. "Been there, done that."

"Then you can understand my irritation when a young lady—who bears a remarkable resemblance to a young version of my own wife—comes in here and starts issuing commands like my wife did in divorce court."

"Okay, so you've been irritable lately," Pete said. "But your spending habits say you've been having a good time. We checked your bank accounts and saw some pretty steep withdrawals. Now, we have a hunch this guy in the library was a paid hit man—and not a very good one. Maybe you paid him to rough her up so she'd know her place."

Astonishment flashed on Dr. Rahal's face. "Gentlemen, I assure you, I did no such thing."

"So explain the large checks?"

"Attorney fees."

"All right, I'll buy that. But most attorneys I know don't get paid in cash. Care to explain the two $2500 cash withdrawals?"

"My wife got the house. I was forced to buy a fixer-upper. The contractor preferred cash. I can give you his number. He can verify this if you like." Rahal opened his desk drawer and pulled out a business card and handed it to Pete. "This is his number. Call him. He will verify what I'm saying."

Pete took the card. "I'll do that." Then he looked at George and George returned the knowing look. Dr. Rahal's story seemed solid. No holes whatsoever.

A thought occurred to him. It was a long shot, but it was worth seeing Dr. Rahal's reaction. "You're kind of a short fella. How tall are you?"

"I am five foot five. What does my stature have to do with this young lady?"

"It's another case. You don't happen to ride a motorcycle, do you?"

Rahal pointed his index and middle fingers at his own face. "With these eyes? Would you risk your life on a motorcycle if you had my vision? No, like the religion, I leave the motorcycle riding to my son."

"Your son rides?"

"He does. He's a student here at the university. He has no need for a car. He can borrow mine if he needs one."

"Interesting. You say he's a pretty devout Muslim?"

"Unfortunately. I try not to interfere. He gets extremely defensive."

"He does, does he?"

"What does my son have to do with any of this? You're investigating the attack of that young lady at the library. According to what I hear, he was a large man. My son is my size."

"Your son may have a buddy. Someone that shares his convictions."

"I assure you, gentlemen, my son was not involved in this."

"You're probably right, but I'd still like to question him. Maybe he knows somebody who was involved."

"Gentlemen, this girl was on the national news. Did you know that?"

"I heard."

"The entire country knows what she's up to. Everybody knows what she looks like and everybody knows she goes to college here. She brought this on herself. It could be anybody. But I promise you, it was not my son. Please, leave him out of this."

"If he's got nothing to hide, then he's got nothing to worry about. Now what's his name and where can I find him?"

Chapter 27

Amari walked out of Pizza Hut at a quarter past ten. She stopped and scanned the dark parking lot for anything suspicious. Satisfied, she headed for her car. Her dad had told her not to stay out late, but she had to work if she wanted to eat. Besides, whoever it was that had attacked her at the library had surely learned his lesson—or else he was lying in a coma. If he really wanted her dead, he would have used a gun or at least a knife. And then again, he could have just been a rapist looking for opportunity, having nothing whatsoever to do with her butting heads with Rahal. She was tired of worrying about this guy, tired of losing sleep. She'd relived those moments on the stairway enough. She'd prayed for protection. Now she tried to put her faith in God and just move on, but it wasn't easy.

She reached her car and put the key in the door when something caught her eye. A black car sat all by itself in the middle of the strip mall next door. The car was facing her. Two figures sat in the front seat, watching her.

"That's my dad," she said to herself. He'd promised he would have a patrol car around her house at night. He must have a couple of plain clothes officers watching her too.

She got in and flipped on the lights, casting her high beam into the direction of the unmarked police car. A Mercedes symbol jutted from the hood. That was no police car. Cops don't drive foreign luxury cars. And she had a feeling those guys weren't local. Maybe she was paranoid, but she'd take the back way home tonight. She cranked the car, backed quickly out of her spot, and drove toward the strip mall, taking the side exit out and into the adjacent neighborhood. She slowed to see if they followed. They didn't. They were probably lost, looking at a street map or something.

****

Amari pulled her car into Kevin's apartment complex and parked next to his car. It was nine o'clock in the morning and they had a long drive ahead of them.

She got out of her car and met him on the sidewalk. "Ready for this?" she asked and hugged herself over her down coat to stay warm. Fog blew like smoke from her mouth when she breathed.

"Is that a herringbone braid in your hair? Like the Shroud?"

"You're very observant. I told you, I can't get that thing out of my head."

"Or your hair."

"It's for good luck. So are you ready?"

"All set. Got my suitcase packed and confirmed the appointment time with Jeffery up in Los Alamos."

"These are the actual tape samples STURP took in 1978?"

"Not all of the tapes, but enough for us to see if there was cotton toward the center of the Shroud. If there isn't, then we know the samples they took for the carbon date are anomalous. You know, some of these tape samples have actual blood on them."

Amari felt a sense of awe. To think she was about to be in the same room with the blood of Christ himself—and look at it under the microscope. How many people could claim such an honor? "That's amazing, Kevin. I can't believe we're actually doing this."

"It's all in who you know. Like I said, Jeffery's coworker was on STURP. Maybe we can meet him too."

"That would be awesome. Whose car are we taking?"

"Let's see, mine's an '86 Honda Accord and yours is a 78 Camaro that keeps going into the shop. Mine's still under warranty."

"Mine will get us there faster."

"Mine will get us there," he replied matter-of-factly.

"Good point. I'll get my overnight bag." She retrieved her bag, tossed it onto his back seat, and met him at the front of the car.

He spread a road map out onto the hood. "You want to go the shorter way or the scenic route?"

"How long is the scenic route?"

"If my math's right, if we take highway 60 through the mountains, it will take about nine hours. If we take Interstate 10 and cut up to Albuquerque on I-25, we'll save about an hour."

"The meeting's not until tomorrow. An hour's nothing. Let's take the scenic route. I've never been up that way."

"Me neither. I was hoping you'd say that."

He moved to his car door, but stopped and started to pat down his pockets first. "Crap, forgot my ChapStick. It's so dry out here I spend a fortune on lotion and lip balm."

"You can have some of mine," she said and puckered her lips playfully. She didn't think he'd fall for it, but it was worth it to see his reaction, just to see if the thought even remotely crossed his mind.

He was oblivious to the hint. "No, I'll get mine," he said instead of kissing her. He started for his apartment, then stopped. "You know what? I just remembered I lost mine to the dryer. If you see wet looking smudges all over my shirt, you know why. Is the offer still good?" he asked and held out his hand.

"Sure," she said and handed him the ChapStick.

He applied it to his lips and handed it back. At least he wasn't afraid of her girl germs. She was making progress, but logic still told her to put it out of her head. If he wasn't a Christian, there would only be trouble in the future. Still, she felt what she felt and she couldn't shake the feeling that God wanted them together. She just needed to give him more time, that's all.

They got into the car and he reached behind his seat. He pulled out his maroon, vinyl cassette case and cracked it open. "I've got tunes for the road. Radio reception's going to be spotty. Why don't we have us a U2-athon on the way? We can start on *Boy* and work our way up. I'll plug in the Sony Discman and we can listen to *Joshua Tree* on CD—if the road's not too bumpy and it doesn't skip. We can do R.E.M and the Alarm on the way back."

"Sounds good to me," she said, scanning the titles in his case. "Is that Debbie Gibson?"

"I'm a complicated person. You know she wrote, recorded, and produced that album when she was seventeen?"

"*Tiffany*? She didn't write her own songs."

"Well, yeah, but—"

"Just drive, Kevin. You don't have to explain."

He cranked the ignition and backed out of the spot. "Like I said, I'm complicated. There's other sides of me you don't know about."

"I can see that. So did you have any trouble getting off?"

"Put on your seatbelt. Better safe than sorry."

"That's true," she said and buckled herself in. "So did you?"

"Nah, I think Rahal was glad to be rid of me for a couple of days. Jerry said he'd keep me posted on anything I missed."

They made their way through the Oro Valley and around the northern side of Santa Catalina Mountain. They chatted as U2 played quietly in the background. Kevin seemed more interested in her voice than Bono's, but it still seemed purely platonic. She'd asked him if they were getting separate rooms in Los Alamos and the "of course" look dented his face.

So if he had no romantic interest in her, then what was his secret agenda her dad had hinted about? She wished her dad hadn't mentioned that. Kevin was the only good thing in her life right now and her dad had to point out the obvious. He was being terribly accommodating. He was even paying for both rooms. It's bad enough she kept seeing that man from the library around every corner. She saw him every time she closed her eyes—those angry teeth snarling through the mouth hole of the ski mask. She hardly slept as it was, and now her dad questioned Kevin's motives too. And then to tell her that Kevin had a criminal record of all things. It was juvenile court, so the records were sealed. Why couldn't her dad keep his own mouth sealed?

They kept driving, chatting, listening to U2, absorbing the scenery of Tonto National Forest. She managed to stay awake until the Fort Apache Indian reservation, but her eyes got too heavy. Sleep deprivation, the drone of the car, and the sameness of the scenery eventually lulled her into sleep, her head propped up against her down coat as a pillow.

****

Something startled her awake. "I fell asleep."

"You totally missed *The Joshua Tree*."

"I heard it in my dreams."

"I bet you haven't been sleeping good, have you? That guy from the library still bothering you?"

"Jenny noticed it too. She says I was traumatized by what happened. That I'm only playing tough. She says repressing all my emotion keeps me awake at night."

"You were sleeping just then."

He was right, despite her dad's warning, she still felt safe around him. That was the best sleep she'd had in a while. A smile worked its way into her face when she thought about his juvenile record. He must have gotten caught rolling someone's house with toilet paper or something. Kevin, a criminal? That was hysterical.

He glanced over at her. "What are you smiling about?"

"You tell me."

"What? What are you talking about?"

"Nothing, Kevin. Are we there yet?" she said, changing the subject. When he wanted to talk about it, he would. Until then, she wasn't going to pry. "How much longer do we have?"

"We should be half way there. We're ten miles from Quemado. Once we get there, we turn north onto 36 and go about another 250 miles."

"We should have taken Interstate 10. We are literally in the middle of nowhere."

"It's scenic nowhere, ain't it?"

"The mountains were pretty, but past Show Low there's nothing. All I see is brown grass and scrubby little trees."

"Live and learn. We'll take Interstate 10 on the way back to tomorrow."

"That's a good idea. I don't like this. We're like the only car on the road."

"Not the only one. There's an 18-wheeler coming toward us. And then there's that idiot on my tail. He's been on my bumper for the last five miles. I'm going sixty-five now. That's ten miles over the limit," he said, his eyes narrowed in anger at the rearview mirror. "As soon as that truck goes by, I'll slow down so he can pass."

She turned her head to look. It was an older model, navy-blue, Lincoln Town car. And it was right on their bumper. "That's an old man's car. They don't usually speed," she said and turned back to face the road.

"Maybe they're trying to get to the hospital. I'll slow down so he can pass right after this truck goes by."

A blue object caught her eye. She snapped her head around. "That guy's in the emergency lane. He's right next to us!"

"It that guy crazy?" he said and slowed down so he could pass.

The Lincoln Town car slowed down too and stayed next to them. Her pulse hammered hard and she recalled the guy from the library. Could that be him? She strained to see the driver. The window was tinted. All she saw was black glass.

The car suddenly lunged left. It crashed into Kevin's car, knocking it into the path of the fast approaching truck.

"Kevin!" she screamed.

White smoke billowed from the truck's tires.

He jerked the wheel left. The car swerved into the emergency lane and just missed the truck. He lost control. The car fishtailed in the dirt and came to a rest, a cloud of dust blocking their view.

"You okay?" he asked in a panic. "That guy was trying to kill us!"

"I think he was!" she cried back at him.

The dust settled. They found themselves catty-corner to the road, the front of the car facing the highway. A dark car sat in the emergency lane. The 18-wheeler pulled over down the road.

"Get behind the car!" Kevin demanded. He pulled a black revolver from under his seat.

"You've got a gun!"

"Don't argue, just get behind the car!"

She yanked open the door and clambered out. Kevin got out and ran around to meet her.

"Get down!" he yelled. Using the car for cover, he crouched and cocked the revolver, aiming for the dark car.

She stooped down behind the car. "I can't believe you brought a gun!"

"I'm from Tennessee!"

"So?"

"And I'm a Republican!"

She peered over the edge of the car to get a view. "Kevin, that's not the car."

"What do you mean, it's not the car?"

"The car that hit us was a Lincoln Town car. I know my cars, and that's not it." She cautiously stood and inspected the car more closely. Recognition dawned. It was the black Mercedes. Two men sat unmoving inside.

"Then why are they just sitting there." He tensed his grip on the gun. "Why don't they come see if we need help?"

"Maybe it's because you have a *gun* pointed at them!"

"I'm sorry, but when someone tries to turn us into road pizza, I get a little tense."

She noticed the truck driver walking toward them. Suddenly, the Mercedes spat dirt from its tires and sped away.

He finally lowered his gun. "What was that about?"

"I've seen that car before. I think they've been tailing us."

"That can't be good."

"They're not the ones that ran us off the road," she reminded him.

"No, but maybe they were about to finish the job."

"You guys all right?" the truck driver in jean overalls asked as he approached. "I called to police on my CB. You guys need an ambulance too?"

"No," she said. "Thank you. Thank you for stopping."

"And for calling the cops," Kevin said.

"Well, of course, I did," the truck driver said. "If I didn't know better, I'd think that guy was trying to kill you."

Kevin locked eyes with Amari. "I think he might be right."

Chapter 28

Amari and Kevin gave their statements to the sheriff in Show Low. The truck driver gave a corroborating statement. Because Kevin's car was drivable and met safety standards, the sheriff let them go on to Los Alamos with the assurance that the state police would follow up on the issue.

They both sat in stunned silence a good portion of the way to Los Alamos. Was he thinking the same thing she was? Was somebody really trying to kill them over the Shroud? Was the man in the Town Car the same man as in the library? What about the Mercedes? Why were they following them? Amari had suggested they cut their losses and run back to the safety of Tucson, but Kevin wouldn't hear it. He'd said they were on a mission and no fender-bender was going to change that.

She cupped her face into her hands, forcing back the emotion. She couldn't show weakness in front of Kevin—not while he appeared so strong. Didn't it bother him that they both almost died? She wasn't ready to die. She was just twenty-two. Her whole life was ahead of her. And so was his, but you'd never know he was worried by the way he acted, now that the adrenaline of almost getting killed had worn off.

She glanced over at him. He sat there, face tensed with resolve. He seemed transformed, his goofy expression replaced with a courageous stare, his eyes squinting like Clint Eastwood. Maybe she wasn't attracted so much to his corny jokes that made her laugh as much as she was drawn to his inner strength, his absolute confidence that made him seem so laid-back.

How well did she really know him? Was there another side to him she'd yet to discover? He'd suggested there was. Still, she'd never expected he would carry a gun—but she was now glad he did. He didn't seem the type to confront danger head on, but he certainly proved himself on the side of that road. He would have used that gun if he needed to. He would have given his life to save hers. And she was supposed to be the strong one. She was the cop's daughter, she'd taken all the self-defense classes, yet he was the one telling her to get behind the car as he confronted the danger.

"You know that guy was probably drunk," he finally said. "Probably had nothing to do with that guy in the library."

"Do you really believe that?"

"I just believe, that's all," he said, eyes firmly fixed to the road ahead. "We'll be all right, Amari, I promise."

****

They had stopped for dinner in Albuquerque and it was already night when they reached the Holiday Inn nearest to the Los Alamos lab. Kevin pulled his car under the awning by the front desk of the hotel. He got out and opened Amari's door to let her out. The door stuck because of the damage, so he had to give it an extra hard yank.

She got out and inspected the car with him. "It's not that bad. I know a guy who can fix this pretty cheap."

"I got coverage. I'm not worried about the car. We better go check in," he said and moved toward the entrance.

She grabbed his hand.

He stopped and studied her face. "You okay?"

"You said you had reservations for two rooms?"

"Of course."

She squeezed his hand tighter. "Kevin, please don't get the wrong idea, but I don't want to be alone tonight. Would you please stay with me? We can get separate beds." She didn't want him to think the wrong thing, but she told the truth. She didn't want to be alone. Not after she nearly lost her life—again.

He hesitated. "If it'll make you feel better. It would save money."

"That's right. We can put that money towards your insurance deductible."

"It's kind of weird. I've never slept with a girl."

"I'm not going to sleep *with* you, Kevin, just next to you. On the *other* bed."

He stammered for words. "Oh, I didn't mean—"

"I know what you meant. It's okay. I just don't want to be alone tonight. I think we'll both sleep better after what happened today, don't you think? There's safety in numbers."

"When you put it that way, it makes a lot of sense. Jenny says I snore. Can you handle that?"

"She says I snore too. Yes, I can handle that."

"Then it's settled, I guess."

"And bring your gun inside too. Just in case."

****

After Amari showered, she put on her pajamas and robe, then sat on the edge of her bed and looked at Kevin. He was propped up with pillows against his headboard. "I'm so exhausted. I haven't been able to sleep lately."

"Well, lie here and watch TV with me," he said, pointing to her bed. "*Cheers* is about to come on. That'll *cheer* you up."

She just stared at him.

"Boy, you must be tired. Normally you pretend to like my jokes."

She laughed that time. He always found a way to make her laugh.

"Here, lay down next to me then. I promise, I won't try anything. I know we're just friends."

Well, there he said it again. They were just friends. She pondered her next move for a moment, wondering if it was appropriate to share his bed, even if it was just for TV. But he did offer, so it would be rude to refuse. She tightened the sash around her waist and climbed onto bed next to him.

"There you go," he said and flipped the TV back on.

A noisy commercial blared. She reached for the remote and pushed the mute button. "Kevin, I know we're just friends . . . but . . . could you just hold me? Just for a minute? I'm so scared," she said, water burning at her eyes. "We almost died today. Doesn't that bother you?"

He awkwardly put his arm around her. She moved into the cradle of his arm and chest. He took the remote and clicked the TV off. "But, Amari, you're so tough."

"People aren't always what they seem. That's just what I want people to think. It's just the way I act. I lose my temper sometimes and people *think* I'm tough. But it's not who I am, not really." Her defenses seemed to crumble in his arms. "It's not the way I feel right now."

"That's not true. You're tough as nails. The way you went against Rahal, wow, I could never do that."

"Rahal wasn't trying to *kill* me, he was just being a jerk. This is different. When you nearly die, everything changes. I thought God had my back, Kevin. I was sure he wanted me to do this. I was sure he would protect me, but I'm not so sure anymore." An aching sadness built within her. It burned in her eyes and spilled onto her cheeks. "I'm not sure what to think anymore," she said and sniffed. "I thought I had a purpose. I thought he needed me but now look. People are trying to kill me. *Both* of us." She couldn't control it anymore. She broke into bitter sobs, pushing her face deeper into his chest.

She felt his gentle, comforting stroke on her hair. "Shh, it's going to be okay. 'Be strong and of good courage, do not fear nor be afraid of them; for the Lord your God, he is the one who goes with you. He will not leave you nor forsake you.'"

She caught her breath between sobs. "What did you say?"

"'For I am the Lord, your God, who takes hold of your right hand and says to you, do not fear; I will help you.'"

She sat up straight. She pulled a tissue from the night stand and dabbed her eyes. "How do you know those verses?"

"'There is no fear in love,'" he said, calmly looking into her eyes. He took her hand and said, "'But perfect love drives out fear.'"

"You're not a Christian. How do you know all that?"

"In John 17:16, Jesus says 'they are not of the world, even as I am not of the world.' And if you're not of this world, then you're alien to this world. What I said to you was true. The Shroud of Turin was formed by an alien, alien to this world and our imperfections. But he loved this world and spent thirty-three years in this world to teach us, and then to die for us, so that we may have everlasting life."

"I don't believe what I'm hearing," she said, nodding her head in disbelief. "All this time, you were a Christian and you didn't tell me?"

"I was going to tell you today in the car. Got a little distracted."

"But why would you wait so long?"

"I had to be sure I could trust you with my secret. I was waiting for the right time, and God handed it to me just now. It's time you knew the whole truth about me. I know I can trust you now."

She moved over to her bed and rubbed her eyes with tissue. "Wow, this has been a long day. First I almost get killed—again. And now this?"

He swung his feet over and sat on the edge of his bed, elbows resting on his knees, looking intently into her eyes. "You have to understand, Amari, that in my profession, religious faith is career suicide. Science is God to these people. It's all they care about. Any hint of faith in something that can't be proven experimentally is scoffed at. It implies bias. Bias toward things that don't agree with the culture of science. If I revealed my faith, I would get blackballed. People talk, word spreads. If they had any idea about my true feelings, I would have never been hired to carbon date the Shroud. And then I would have never met you. There's a purpose in all of this, Amari. You have to believe that."

"But Jesus said you have to let your light shine. Put it on a lamp stand. Don't cover it up and leave the world in darkness."

"And I will. When the time is right. Someday, when I'm well established, when I've gained respect from my colleagues, when I have more evidence to back my claims, I will let my light shine. But not until it shines bright. When they respect me, they might believe my words. But for now, I'll only find myself without a career. Please, Amari, you can't tell anyone, okay? I told you because I trust you. Promise me."

She sniffed and stared at his pleading face. So this was his secret. If only her dad could see this. "I knew you were hiding something. My dad did too," she said and laughed to herself. "I'm just glad you're not in the mob or something. But it's not your only secret, is it?"

"What do you mean?"

"My dad says you have a juvenile record."

"Oh, that."

"What did you do?"

He swung his legs back onto the bed and lay back against the pillows.

"Kevin, tell me."

"When I was a teenager I started reading books like C.S. Lewis' *Mere Christianity* and Josh McDowell's *Evidence that Demands a Verdict.* I couldn't deny that Jesus was real. About the same time, I had a crush on this girl named Lisa. She invited me to her church and I was really getting into it until. . .well, you could say things turned a little sour."

"Did you love this girl?"

"Thought I did. Probably more like an infatuation. But I learned my lesson. You're the first girl I've trusted since then."

"Since what? Tell me, Kevin, why did you get arrested?"

He laughed and rubbed at his forehead. "Oh, gosh, it seems kind of funny now that I look back at it."

"What, Kevin? Tell me why you got arrested."

"Some people at this girl's church invited me to protest with them at the abortion clinic out in Knoxville. One of them had this crazy idea to cuff me to a light pole just to show how serious we were. When the police came, they scattered and left me there. Lisa just abandoned me. She laughed about it later. So I got arrested for refusing to disband. I told them I didn't have the key, but they took me in anyway."

"How could they do that to you? That's not the way Christians are supposed to act."

"You know, Mahatma Gandhi loved Jesus. It was Christians he had a problem with. At least some of them. Not everybody plays by the rules. Now you can see one of the reasons I haven't been back to church. I don't know who I can trust anymore. Until I met you."

"They're not all like that. I can't believe they did that to you."

"I don't think the older ones realized I didn't have the key. The younger ones, like Lisa, were just scared of getting arrested."

"Don't make excuses for them. What they did to you was wrong."

"It was. And ever since then I've been a loner. Just me and God. I realized then that I didn't need to go to church to believe."

"Of course not, but it certainly helps. Look, I understand, it's hard just walking into a church full of strangers. Especially for someone like you. You had a bad experience and nobody's invited you to have a better one. You can come to church with me. You'll see, church is great. It's not what you think."

"You might need that, but I don't. Besides, like I told you, it would be career suicide."

She could see he was traumatized over this, so she decided to drop it. They'd had enough trauma for one day. "I get it, Kevin. You're not ready. I'm cool with that."

"Thank you for understanding."

"Thank you for being here for me. You have no idea what you mean to me . . . I mean, how much help you've been with the Shroud."

"So now you know why I'm helping you. We have the same goal in common. We both want the world to know the truth about the Shroud."

"Yeah," she agreed as the sad realization sank. She'd had a flicker of hope he was helping her because he cared about her, not her mission. She'd hoped his feelings for her was the real reason he'd thrown his profession under the bus during her dad's interrogation, the reason he bit the hand that fed him. But now she knew the real reason he did it. It was his love for God, not for her.

"Hey, what's wrong, Amari? I thought you'd be happy."

"I am, Kevin. I am. I'm just really tired, that's all."

"You don't look so happy."

"Haven't you ever been so happy you want to cry?" she said, the tears welling in her eyes again.

He went over to her bed and wrapped his arms around her. "It's going to be okay, Amari. I promise, everything's going to be okay."

****

The gated entrance to Los Alamos National Laboratory was way out in the woods, not anywhere close to the laboratory itself. They patiently waited their turn as the cars ahead worked through security. Amari had slept a full eight hours last night, no nightmares about the man in the library, no flashbacks of a Lincoln Town Car running them off the road. She felt refreshed and energized. Of course, Kevin had been a perfect gentleman. Like Jenny said, he wasn't wired like other guys.

She was half-ashamed, half-glad she'd lost control in front of him last night. She was ashamed because he saw the true Amari—just a young girl with anxieties and fears like anybody else, a young girl who tried to act tough and live up to her dad's reputation and the reputation of a warrior chief whose blood flowed in her veins. But she was glad she could let go in front of him. It made them closer. It gave them a bond. And now she knew

Kevin was a Christian. She had no moral qualms about taking the relationship to the next level—if only he shared her feelings.

He pulled the car forward and stopped in front of the gate. "Hey there," he said. "Name's Kevin Brenner. I have an appointment with Jeffery Jenkins."

The stone-faced security guard ran his finger down a page stuck on a clipboard. "Here you are, Dr. Kevin Brenner. Says your permission to enter was revoked."

"Revoked?" Kevin said. "What do you mean, revoked?"

"Somebody pulled your clearance."

"Look, call Jeffery, he'll tell you I'm good."

"Pull your car over to the side," the guard said. "You're blocking traffic. I'll call and see what I can do."

"Thank you, officer," Kevin said.

"I'll let the gate up so you can turn around," he said. "Park over by the curb and I'll send someone to talk to you."

The gate rail went up and Kevin moved his car forward. "Maybe I ought to make a run for it."

"Don't you dare. We can't do anything inside federal prison."

"Fine," he said and pulled his car back around and out the exit gate. He moved his car over to a parking space by the curb.

After a few minutes, a security car pulled up. Two men got out and walked up to the car. One was wearing jeans, but the other was armed security. Kevin noticed them and stepped out of the car to meet them. She stayed put, but she could still hear them through the open window. "Hey, Jeffery, good to see you again," Kevin said and shook hands. "I thought you said we were good to go." Jeffery wasn't much older than Kevin. A mess of brown curly hair fell back past his shirt collar.

"You were, Kevin, I promise. But someone from upstairs got wind of this and pulled the plug."

"But why?" Kevin asked. "We weren't going to take the tapes. We just wanted to look at them."

"I don't know what to tell you. They were fine with it one minute, then at the last minute, they pulled the clearance. I wonder if someone called or something. Maybe someone thought you were a security risk."

"So there's no way you can get us in?"

"Sorry, buddy. Sorry you had to drive all the way out here, but I tried. They wouldn't budge."

"I understand. Thanks anyway, Jeffery," Kevin said and got back into the car. Jeffery and the guard went back to their car.

"I can't believe this. All this way, for nothing," Amari said. "We almost got killed for nothing."

"I wonder if someone called them and told them why we wanted to see those tapes."

She narrowed her eyes in anger. "Rahal."

"He didn't know we were coming up here. It couldn't have been him."

She winced. "Actually, I might have let it slip back at the biology lab. He told me I'd never get into this place. I bet he called them to make sure I didn't."

Kevin hammered the steering wheel with his fist. "That jerk! That's got to be it then."

"I'm sorry, Kevin, I shouldn't have told him. It just slipped."

"That's all right. We'll find another way."

"Oh, no," she said and buried her face in her hands.

"You're thinking Rahal knows I'm the one who took you up here. Otherwise, why would they block my clearance?"

She pulled her hands away and looked at him apologetically. "They never even asked my name. It's the only thing that makes sense. Kevin, I'm so sorry. Rahal's going to fire you over this."

"So what if he does? I ain't worried about it."

"How can you be so relaxed about this? Your whole career could go down the drain? Because you helped me."

"Maybe, but not till after we carbon date the Dead Sea Scrolls. He'd be screwed if he fired me now."

"And what about after that?"

"He'd still have to get Dr. Weiss's approval to fire me."

"You think Dr. Weiss still has your back?"

"Maybe."

"And what if he doesn't?"

"One day at a time, Amari. Sometimes you just gotta live by faith."

****

Kevin pulled his car into his apartment complex and took the spot next to Amari's Camaro.

"Interstate 10 was definitely better," she said.

"And nobody tried to kill us," he said. "That's refreshing."

"Well, Kevin, thank you for taking me up there. I'm sorry it didn't end the way we wanted."

"Something will work out. I'll call Jeffery and see if there's another way."

"And thank you for being honest with me, you know, about your faith."

"I should have told you sooner. I just didn't know how to bring it up."

"Is there anything else you want to tell me? This would be a good time."

"Now that you mention it, there is a little something. I haven't been *totally* honest with you."

"Well, spit it out. Nothing surprises me about you anymore."

"I'm not really a Republican. I mean, I voted for Bush this time, but I voted for Mondale in '84. I go either way, really."

"I'm serious, Kevin. No jokes. Is that it?"

"Fine, I'll ante up. But I'm afraid you're not going to like it."

"Try me. Your last secret was a pleasant surprise."

"Okay, but remember, friends stick together through thick and thin. Promise you won't get mad. I've seen you get mad before, and it ain't pretty."

"I promise, I won't get mad."

He held out his right pinky. "Pinky promise?"

"You really think I'll be mad?"

"Not furious mad, but maybe a little disappointed I didn't show you this earlier."

"If it's anything like your last secret, I promise, I won't get mad." She linked her pinky into his. "Pinky promise."

They held their pinkies together for several seconds and his eyes drifted to her lips. This was it. He wanted to kiss. All the emotion from the trip finally brought his feelings to the surface. Now or never, Amari told herself and leaned forward.

"You got something on your lip," he said. "It's been driving me nuts. I think it's a cracker crumb."

She let go of his pinky and swiped at her lips. She pulled away the crumb he had used this very intimate moment to bring up. He was right. It was a crumb from the cheese cracker she'd eaten a few minutes before.

"Hey," he said. "If you're still hungry, let's go grab a bite to eat.".

"Oh, no you don't. You told me you had another secret. Show me now. We eat later."

"Okay, but you promised. You won't get mad."

Chapter 29

Kevin's apartment was a mess. The floor needed to be vacuumed and books and magazines littered the couch and coffee table. It reminded Amari of her own place before Jenny moved in.

"No wonder Jenny wanted out," she said.

"Organization is not my forte," he said.

"Mine neither. So what's the big secret?"

"It's in my bedroom. I kept it hidden in there so Jenny wouldn't see. Uh, hold on a second before you come in."

He slipped into his bedroom and shut the door. She heard thumps and rustling and then he reemerged.

"It's good now. Come on in."

A pile of clothes was on the bathroom floor and the comforter was wrinkled and hastily thrown over the pillows. He pointed to his book shelf. On the top shelf was every book she had read about the Shroud along with several more. The second shelf had history books about the Roman Empire, Medieval Europe, a thick one called *Life and Times of Jesus the Messiah*, and other books by the historian Josephus. There were also three different translations of the Bible. The King James version looked a hundred years old. The next two shelves were lined with science books—physics, chemistry, anatomy and physiology, astronomy, and math.

"I kept the religious books in my closet so Jenny wouldn't see them. I put them back on the shelf when she moved out."

"She's a Christian. Why go to all the trouble of hiding this from her?"

"Because I don't trust her. She'd go blabbing it to everybody back home."

"I promise, I won't tell."

"I know you won't. That's why I told you and not her."

Her eyes went back to the top shelf. "Well, I see why you think I should be mad. All this time you were just humoring me. You know more about the Shroud than I do. You just let me go on like I was discovering America when you'd been living there the whole time." She should have been furious, but when someone tries to kill you twice, it's hard to get excited about something like that.

"I never said I *didn't* know what you were talking about either."

"I noticed you didn't seem all that surprised."

"Now you see why I got this job. I knew over a year ago the Shroud sample was coming to Arizona. I worked hard to get my position. I pulled strings, made phone calls, and called in favors. It's no coincidence I'm here. The thought of being in the same room with a piece of the Shroud thrilled me, especially the thought of experimenting with it."

"Okay, Kevin. I forgive you. I'm not mad. But I am hungry. Buy me dinner and all's forgiven."

"Actually, I'm not done."

"Somehow, I didn't think you were."

He pulled a box from under his bed. "I keep all this in a fire safe. Just in case." He took his keys from his pocket and opened the thick, insulated door. Stacks of journals filled the inside. He pulled the top one out and handed it to her. "That's what you're going to be mad about."

She flipped through it. Math calculations, statements, and diagrams painted the pages. In between the pages were various photos of the Shroud, shot from different angles and even different wavelengths. Still more calculations and atomic symbols covered the last few pages.

"That's my latest volume. Earlier drafts and theories are in those other journals. I've got a ton of other stuff on my Mac."

She fanned the pages. "So what exactly is this?"

"I've been working on this since last June, day and night, ever since we did the carbon date."

"I still don't get it. Why is this stuff supposed to make me mad?"

"Because this is *my* theory as to why the carbon date is wrong. You're going to be mad because it doesn't agree with yours."

There it was, the anger he had feared. She felt it in her cheeks first, then her jaws tensed. "Kevin, you saw the fluorescent photos," she said sternly. "You saw the cotton. You agreed with me. The carbon date was done on a patch."

"Maybe."

"Maybe! What do you mean, maybe?"

"Hold on now, Amari. Hear me out."

"You were just toying with me?"

"No, that's not it at all. I do think that section was fixed. The evidence clearly shows that. What I can't believe is that those few contaminating fibers could throw the date off as much as it did."

She couldn't believe what she was hearing, but she did pinky promise him. She wouldn't get mad. "Okay, fine. You half believe me then. So what's your theory?"

"Okay, now we've settled the fact that radiation of some kind caused that image. It's the only way it could have been formed. Now, there's different kinds of radiation. One kind is proton radiation. It's non-penetrating radiation. I think that's what caused the cellulose in that linen to denature. But another kind of radiation is neutron radiation. Neutron radiation is much more penetrating. It passes right through things. In the process, it messes with the atomic structure."

"This isn't helping much. Keep it simple."

"You took chemistry, right?"

"General Chemistry."

"Okay, you remember how nitrogen has seven neutrons and seven protons. It's called nitrogen-14. When nitrogen-14 gets hit by neutron radiation, sometimes a neutron is added to the nucleus so now it has eight neutrons. This causes instability in the atom, so it ejects one of its protons. The result is carbon-14, with six protons and eight neutrons. And the closer to the source of neutron radiation, in this case, the body of Jesus, the more carbon-14 you'll find. Don't you get it?"

"Still don't get it, Kevin."

"Neutron radiation is what caused the wrong carbon date. Human blood has much more nitrogen than cellulose. If you sampled a portion of the blood, so much carbon-14 would be created, it would date into the *future*."

She felt her heart sink as he kept yammering. She moved to his bed, sat down, and cupped her hand over her forehead.

"You are mad, aren't you?"

She pulled her hand away and looked at him. "No, Kevin, I'm not mad. I just realized that I *do* get it. I see what you're saying. I had no business taking this so far," she said and looked out the window. "I'm just an amateur. Some kid whose mother taught her about weaving, some criminal justice major who thought she had a hot lead that would change the world. But look at you. You've spent your life preparing for this. God hasn't called *me* for this, he called *you*."

He sat next to her and gripped her knee. "No, Amari, not just me. Us. He pulled us together for a reason."

She knocked his hand off her knee. "Don't touch me. I'm mad at you."

"Listen to me, Amari. Finish hearing what I have to say and maybe you won't be so mad."

"Fine, Kevin, I'm listening."

"Okay, all you have to do is look at the condition of the Shroud and you know it was hit by neutron radiation. Haven't you ever been curious why the Shroud is in such good shape after two thousand years?"

"I just figured God preserved it."

"Yes, he did—with neutron radiation. Neutron radiation would cause molecular bonds in the linen to break and reform in the non-crystalline parts of the linen's cellulose. That makes the molecules cross-link, which makes the Shroud more durable. It's less soluble and more resistant to oxygenation."

Amari gave him a blank stare. "Now you're just showing off."

"I know this may be over your head but hear me out. I can prove carbon-14 cannot be used to date the Shroud. Not only that, but I can prove the image was made with proton radiation, and that is *not* natural. It's *super*natural. All I need to do is figure out how to measure the ratio of chlorine-36 to chlorine-35, and maybe even calcium-41 to calcium-40—if I can get enough sample. And I can do all that from the burned pieces of Shroud. That way I don't have to damage it anymore. But perfecting my tests is going to take time and money. A lot of money. I can't do that on my own."

"So get an investor. I can't help you with that. I can't even pay my own tuition."

"Nobody's going to throw that kind of money at me when they're convinced the carbon date is right. That's where you come in. Your theory is so simple and easy to prove. All we need to do is get our hands on those tape samples at Los Alamos and we'll prove it. If we publish those findings, the Vatican may authorize another sampling of the Shroud. Then maybe somebody will fund my experiments. But none of that is going to happen unless we can prove the carbon date is wrong."

Time seemed to stop as realization dawned. Kevin didn't really care for her. She was just a means to his goal. She stepped away and gave a slow, disbelieving shake of her head.

"Amari, what's wrong?"

"You're using me. All this time, I thought you cared about me. But you were just *using* me." Hurt swelled from her core and pressure built in her eyes.

"No, I do care for you, I really do."

"No you don't, you said it yourself. You were just using me!" she said and headed for the front door.

"But what about dinner?" he called after her.

"I'll go to a drive-thru," she yelled back and slammed the door behind her.

Chapter 30

Amari cranked her ignition and revved her Camaro's engine. The passenger door came open and Kevin plopped into the seat next to her.

"Kevin, get out of my car. I'm serious."

"Then you need to learn to lock your doors. What if I was that lunatic who tried to run us off the road?"

She pointed at the door. "Out."

"You promised me you wouldn't get mad. I trusted you."

She turned off the ignition and stared out the driver window. "Just give me some time."

"Look, maybe I was utilizing you to get what I wanted."

"You mean *using* me."

"All right, but no more than you've been using me. Why did you come into my lab that day? Because you thought I'd be fun to hang out with? No, you needed something from me. You still do. And you offer something I need. That's not using each other, that's called teamwork. We help each other. That's what teams do. They count on each other. I need you, and you need me. Together we can go to the Vatican. Together, we can prove this is the authentic burial Shroud of Jesus Christ."

"Okay, Kevin, I get it. I know we need each other for that. But I thought I was more than just your business partner. I thought you cared about me. About me, not what I could do for you."

"Rahal is my business partner. You see me going to movies with him? You see me eating lunch with him every day? You see me sleeping in the same *room* with him? Give me a break. If all I wanted was a business relationship with you, I would have said so."

Amari turned to face him. "You mean that?"

Kevin put his hand on her shoulder. "Heck, yeah, I do. You're like my best friend."

"So you keep reminding me. I'm your best bud."

"I told you I was afraid you'd be mad."

She looked into his oblivious eyes. "Anger isn't the emotion I'm feeling right now."

"Then what is it?"

"I don't think you would understand. You know, you're great at physics and everything, but I wonder if Jenny was right about you."

"What did she say?"

"That you're not wired like other guys. And I think she's right. If you were, then you would know why I'm upset. But you really don't have a clue."

He just sat there watching her in silence, the gears in his head turning.

"I really need to check in with my dad."

"But what about dinner?"

"Fine, Kevin, you can take me to dinner. Maybe I'll feel better once I eat."

"Where do you want to go?"

"Are you buying?"

"Of course."

"Then somewhere expensive."

"Fine, it's the least I can do."

"You got that right."

****

The gun sounded, then again. *Pop, pop, pop, pop.* Amari unloaded the rest of her bullets at the target. She holstered her weapon, removed her earplugs, and waited for her dad's reaction.

"Not bad," Dad said, eyeing the holes in the concentric circle on the paper target at the end of the range. "Not as good as Kevin here, but not bad at all. Reload and try again. But this time I want you to try it with the gun in your purse with the safety on. When I say go, pull it out and unload another magazine. When you're done with that, I want you to try it again with your purse on the ground, like it's been knocked out of your hand. When you're done with that, we can call it a day. Then I want you back out here again next week, then again, a week later. Practice makes perfect."

Amari drove Kevin home from the firing range in her Camaro. His car was in the repair shop, but it didn't go until after the police worked to lift forensic evidence from it. Even a flake of paint from the navy-blue Town Car would be helpful. The truck driver involved was also interviewed. Unfortunately, there was a glare on the Town Car's windshield so the driver couldn't help with a description.

Kevin inspected her license to carry paperwork. "Pretty much the same as in Tennessee. You know, I was afraid your dad would be upset with me for taking you up to Los Alamos and almost getting you killed."

"Actually, he thinks you're a hero. Since you told him why you acted suspicious during his interrogation, he's completely changed his tune about you. He thinks risking your career for your faith was brave. And he said your fast thinking with the car saved my life."

"That's good. I wouldn't want to be in his crosshairs. That's why I fessed up to him about being a Christian. Did you tell him about the Mercedes?"

"I did. He doesn't know what to think. It could be a coincidence. A lot of people drive those."

They pulled into his apartment complex and headed toward his unit. "Hey, stop here and let me check my mail," he said. He got the mail, hopped back in, and sorted the envelopes. "Yes!"

"What is it?" she asked as she parked in front of his unit.

"This envelope is from Jeffery in Los Alamos. If it's what I think it is . . ." he said and tore it open. "It is!" He pulled out several Polaroid pictures and a typed letter.

She gasped. "Oh, my gosh, those are pictures of the tape samples!"

She leaned over and they inspected them together. He held the first one. Just linen, no cotton. He flipped to the next one. Same thing. Then the next one, nothing but linen. The next one, only linen. "That looks nothing like the photos I took," she said.

He held out the letter and read, mumbling the words to himself until he started reading out loud. "After careful examination of every tape sample, although pollen and other artifacts were noted, I could find absolutely no evidence of cotton fibers, nor any other textile fiber, other than linen."

She clenched her fists in victory. "Thank you, Jeffery."

"Well, there you have it. I think we have all we need. It's time to talk to the bishop."

Chapter 31

Friday, December 23, 1988

Pete and George had checked with Dr. Rahal and the student dormitory on three different occasions over the past week. Unfortunately, Anwar Rahal was nowhere to be found. The fourth attempt was on the Friday before Christmas. George had taken off to be with his family, so Pete made the call by himself.

Pete stood at the front desk of the Coronado Residence hall, over in the Park District. He waited for his turn at the house phone so he could call Anwar's room. The hall was mostly deserted for Christmas. A few students remained, two sitting on a couch watching the communal projection TV in the lobby. Most of them looked foreign. They either didn't celebrate Christmas or couldn't afford to fly home.

But he didn't kid himself. The only connection Anwar had to the arsons and murder of the priest was his religion and the fact that he rode a motorcycle. The only reason Anwar's religion was a factor was because of the word *jihad* painted on the sidewalk. And the only reason Anwar might be after Amari was because of the way she had disrespected his father. He was a long shot, but it was all he had.

Unfortunately, anyone could be behind it because the crime against the priest and Amari had a common thread. The priest had written an article in support of the Shroud of Turin's authenticity. Amari had declared her belief in the Shroud on national television. They were both public statements made in support of the Shroud's authenticity. The coincidence was impossible to ignore. That meant that anyone with a newspaper or a television was a potential suspect.

Still, Anwar had to be eliminated as a suspect first. And if Anwar wasn't guilty, maybe he could suggest other suspects. The Muslim community in Tucson was relatively small compared to big cities. And in small communities, people talk. If Anwar wasn't there this time, he'd ask some of these students if they knew his whereabouts. But for all he knew, Anwar had gone to Mexico for vacation. Classes were out, so why not?

The girl on the phone hung up and he reached for it but hesitated. If Anwar was guilty, what were the odds he would stick around knowing a cop was in the lobby? He could flee down the stairs and Pete would never catch him with his bad hip. He scanned the directory, and instead of looking for his phone extension, he looked for his room number.

Pete went up to Room 428 and put his ear to the door. He heard a television, then a toilet flush. He reached inside his sport coat and pulled back the Velcro strap that held the gun secure in his holster.

He knocked twice. "Anwar Rahal?"

Light showed through the peephole, then was blocked by a shadow. Pete stepped to the side, away from the door, just in case a high caliber bullet decided to come through. "May I help you?" a voice came from within.

"Anwar Rahal?"

"Yes."

"My name is Detective Pete Johnston, from the Tucson Police department. Mind if I ask you a few questions?"

"I can't see you through the peephole. How do I know you're really from the police?"

Pete pulled out his ID and held it to the peephole. A moment later, the lock snapped open, and the door swung inward. Anwar stepped out into the hall. He was unarmed.

Pete let go of his revolver. "Anwar Rahal?"

"Yes, I spoke to my father. He told me you might want to speak with me." Anwar was early twenties with dark Middle Eastern features. He had heavy black eyebrows and a long face that was made to look even longer with the three-inch beard that spread from his ears down. The mustache part of his beard was little more than an afternoon shadow. He wore a white tunic that cut off just below his pant pockets and a white cap on his head that clearly had religious significance.

"Do you mind if I come in?" Pete asked.

"Do you have a warrant?"

"No, I just have a few questions."

"We can speak in the hall. I have nothing to hide."

Pete glanced around Anwar and into the room, but the kid closed the door before he could lock eyes on anything.

"You act like you have something to hide."

"My room is a mess. I'm embarrassed. You said you had questions."

"You're a short fella, just like your father. How tall are you?"

"I'm five foot six. Why do you ask?"

"More like five-five if you ask me. I always exaggerate my height too."

"Is there something I can help you with?"

"You can start by telling me where you were this last week. Neither me nor your father could find you."

"After I took my last final, I joined my brothers in a retreat."

"Like a religious retreat?"

"Yes, in Tempe."

"Can you provide witnesses to verify this?"

"You can call the imam. He will confirm it."

"You didn't happen to drive a navy-blue Lincoln Town car up that way, did you?"

"I rode with a friend, in a Pontiac Fiero. Why do you ask?"

"Are you familiar with a student named Amari Johnston?"

"Everyone on campus is. What does she have to do with me? My father is the one who has a problem with her."

"Maybe so, but since you're apparently a devout Muslim, I was hoping you had some insight as to who attacked her in the library."

"I wish I could help you. But I don't know anything."

"What comes to mind when I mention The Shroud of Turin?"

"It's a fake."

"It wouldn't upset you if someone tried to prove it wasn't a fake?"

"No, I couldn't care less," he said flatly.

There wasn't the slightest hint of emotion from this guy, not like you would expect if you thought the police were about to expose your crimes. He showed no anxiety, no remorse. But, then again, psychopaths are skilled at hiding their feelings. "So is that your motorcycle out front?"

"The BMW?"

"Yeah, the red one with the two luggage boxes." George didn't get a good look at the bike at the synagogue, but he did notice the luggage boxes. The light was too dim to differentiate color.

"Yes, that one is mine."

Bingo, Pete said to himself. Now he was getting somewhere. "You mind coming down with me to have a look at it?"

Anwar glanced at the door to his room.

"Tell your girlfriend we'll be right back. This won't take long."

"One moment," he said and went back into the room. Seconds later he came out with a young lady. She had a scarf over her dark hair. "She needs to go. She's not allowed in the halls without a male escort."

"Bring her, then. We'll escort her out."

When they got downstairs, Anwar said goodbye to his friend and joined Pete at the motorcycle. The bike was parked next to the tall, red brick dorm tower, in a motorcycle only section, next to a cluster of bicycles that were chained to racks beneath tall, spindly palm trees.

"I've got bad timing," Pete said, referring to Anwar's girlfriend. "Sorry about that."

Anwar said nothing.

"So how long have you had this bike?"

"About four years."

"BMW, huh? Sounds expensive."

"I bought it used."

Pete frowned down at the front wheel. "Did you know one of your spokes is broken?" They weren't like regular motorcycle tire spokes, but made of formed metal that created a series of X's around the rim. One X had a leg broken to make it look like a lowercase y.

Anwar bent over to look at it. He passed his hand into the space where the spoke should have been and then stood, rubbing his beard. "I hadn't noticed."

Pete stooped down and fingered the broken metal. "It's like something hit this and snapped it off. Something coming at it with a lot of velocity. Something lead. Like a bullet."

Anwar scratched at his beard again. "Why do you think it was a bullet?"

"I'm just speculating." He walked around to the rear of the bike. "Somebody knocked me over with a door a few weeks back. You might still see the lump on my head. He took off on a motorcycle. My partner took a couple of shots at him. Sound familiar? This person didn't like Jews. Some Muslims don't care much for Jews. What about you?"

"We both share Abraham as our father."

"We're all sons of Adam too. One of Adam's sons killed the other. You would never think of killing another person over religion, would you?"

"Murder is a sin. Allah does not condone murder."

"Unless, of course, it's in war. Like a jihad. Then it would be okay, right?"

"Why are you asking me these questions?"

"Why not? Am I making you uncomfortable?"

"Yes, you are."

"You said you had nothing to hide, so relax. You carry your books around in these luggage boxes?"

"Sometimes."

Something caught Pete's eye. On the maroon-red gas tank, just to the right of the BMW symbol, was a black smudge. He rubbed the smudge with his finger. If it was oil, it would smear. It didn't budge. It was clearly dry black paint. He felt his blood pressure going up again. "You know, Anwar, when you use a can of spray paint, sometimes you get a little on your index finger. Or the glove of that finger. Anything you touch, like this gas tank, would get paint on it. You been doing some painting lately?"

"No, when would I have time? I was carrying a twenty-hour course load this fall."

Anwar moved in next to him and inspected the tank. "That wasn't there before."

"When's the last time you rode this bike?"

"It's been several weeks. I walk to class and my girlfriend drives me if I need to go somewhere."

"I see. You mind opening this box up for me?"

"I don't keep it locked."

"So you don't mind if I take a look inside?"

"It's empty."

Pete flipped the luggage compartment lid open. He reached in and pulled out a can of black spray paint. He quickly dropped the can back into the box and gripped his revolver with his right hand, but fell short of pulling it out. "I think you need to put your hands behind your back."

Chapter 32

Tuesday, December 27, 1988

St. Augustine Cathedral had stood in downtown Tucson for over a hundred years. It was sandstone in color and had an elaborate frontal façade that rose over the arched, wooden doorway, sandwiched between two Spanish colonial towers with domed roofs. Kevin had never been to the cathedral before, but Amari had gone there to get books and papers about the Shroud from the bishop's library.

The bishop was eager to see her findings, so he agreed to meet with them the Tuesday after Christmas. She and Kevin parked in the lot behind the cathedral and made their way to the bishop's office. They stepped through the door and went to the secretary's desk. "We have an appointment to meet with the bishop," she said.

The secretary stood and opened his door. "He's waiting for you. Go right in."

Bishop Patrick McClure sat at his desk, jotting down something on church stationery. He was in his late fifties, thinning gray hair parted on the side. He wore the standard priest's black uniform, except he had a silver chain around his neck and a jeweled ring was on his right ring finger, signifying his marriage to the church. Behind him, two bookends parted a sea of books to make room for a crucifix perched on a stand.

He came around to greet his guests. "Amari, come, come, have a seat," he said and motioned to the chairs in front of his desk. "And this must be Dr. Brenner." He shook hands with Kevin while simultaneously patting him on the forearm. "Sit, please."

"I brought back the books you loaned me." Amari set the books on the desk and took a seat next to Kevin. "They were very helpful. Thank you so much."

"You're very welcome. I should be thanking you. You're the talk of the diocese. Your brother, Jason, told me you were a pistol. I see he wasn't exaggerating."

"Thank you, but I've had a lot of help," she said and tilted her head toward Kevin.

"Yes, Dr. Brenner, Amari told me all about you over the phone. I have to say, I was concerned the cardinal in Turin would never lend his ear to a college student with no science background, but when she told me about you, I realized we had a leg to stand on. No offense, Amari."

"None taken," she said. "I agree one hundred percent. Kevin has the clout to make a difference."

"Her theory's every bit as good as mine," Kevin said.

"Great," the bishop said. "So let's hear it."

Amari presented her case, recounting her knowledge of ancient weaving techniques and why she thought the Shroud was patched. She then showed her photos she'd taken at the biology lab and compared them with the ones from Los Alamos to back up her story. Then Kevin started rattling off scientific jargon and formulas as he turned pages and pointed to hand drawn illustrations. When they both had finished, the bishop sat in stunned silence as he soaked it all in.

"So when can we see the Pope?" Kevin asked. "Once he sees what we've got, I'm sure he'll agree to more tests. He speaks English, don't he? I heard him once on TV."

Amari elbowed him and gave him a stern look.

The bishop grinned. "Dr. Brenner, I'm afraid it's not that simple. The protocol involved for getting permission to study the

Shroud is very long. They may be unwilling to remove the Shroud from its casket for another round of tests that may prove just as disappointing to the church. The other evidence speaks for itself. They may decide to leave well enough alone."

"The other evidence will talk louder if we can prove the carbon date is wrong," Kevin said. "I think I can prove my theory if I just had a little more money to develop some tests. We've all heard about the Vatican's deep pockets. Let me show them what I've got and maybe they'll ante up."

She elbowed him harder.

"Ouch," Kevin said and rubbed his forearm. "See, your most reverend? She is a pistol."

She whispered angrily in his ear. "I thought I was doing the talking. You're not helping." She turned back to the bishop. "I'm sorry, Kevin's a genius when it comes to physics, but only at the expense of his social skills."

Kevin nodded in agreement. "Can't have it all."

Bishop McClure chuckled. "I think he just likes to make people laugh. The world could use more humor."

"Sometimes he only thinks he's funny."

"Hit and miss, I guess," Kevin said. "But seriously, what are the odds of us talking to someone from Rome?"

"Dr. Brenner, the wheels of Vatican bureaucracy grind slowly. Fortunately, you've both made a very compelling argument. But I'm not sure how the Vatican will react right now. The result of the carbon date was a hurtful wound, so this could go either way. On the one hand, they may be delighted to have the results refuted so soon. On the other hand, they may be more skeptical of scientists than ever. They may simply decide to leave it as a matter of faith and refuse all future scientific intrusions."

"But if the carbon date is wrong, the truth needs to come out," she said.

"And they may well agree with you. Give me a few days and I'll make some calls. If all goes well, you may indeed have your audience with the Pope, Dr. Brenner."

"That would be awesome," Kevin said. "He seems like a great guy."

"We like to think so. But I suspect your first meeting, if there is one, will be with Cardinal Ragazzi of Turin. You may even have to go through his scientific advisor to the Shroud of Turin Research Project first. I believe his name is Professor Messina, and he won't be easily persuaded."

"I would like to try," she said.

"I will do everything in my power to ensure that you do," Bishop McClure said. "Give me a few days and I'll get back to you."

They left the bishop's office and strolled back to the car. "I didn't mean to elbow you that hard, Kevin, I was just trying to get your attention."

"I'm sorry, Amari, I didn't keep my side of the deal. I should have let you do all the talking. You're the one that knows the guy. I just want to do this thing so bad I can't stand it."

"Me too, Kevin. Me—hey!" She pointed to a parking spot. "There's the car!"

"What car?"

"The black Mercedes that's been following me."

She pulled Kevin to the cover of a nearby van. She flipped up the flap of her purse and pulled out her gun. "Stay out of sight," she said and peered around the corner of the van. She locked eyes on the passenger, searing his face into memory. He had kinky brown hair and one of those short, stubby beards like Sonny

Crockett wore on *Miami Vice.* He was talking on one of those new mobile phones. The sun visor blocked the driver's face. The passenger had words with the driver and the car quickly pulled out of the spot and sped toward the exit to the parking lot.

Amari slid the safety back on and set the gun back in her purse. "I got a look at one of them that time. I couldn't see the driver, but I saw the passenger. He was talking on one of those new mobile phones. You know, the real thick ones?"

"Those things cost nearly four thousand bucks. They must have some deep pockets."

"They're driving a Mercedes. I think they can afford it."

"I guess so. What do you think they want?"

"I don't know."

"You think they're the ones trying to kill you?"

"You mean *us?*" she pointed out.

"You said they weren't the ones who tried to run us into that truck."

"No, they weren't. If they wanted us dead, they could have shot us both just now."

"So what do they want?"

"I don't know, Kevin. I seriously have no idea. But if they're on our side, they should introduce themselves instead of spying on us. I say they're up to no good."

Chapter 33

The German Shepherd named Foster sat at attention with drool dripping from his black lips as he panted. His long, pink tongue hung out from under his nose and his ears stood on end, pivoting toward the source of sound. He was a retired police dog. Amari's dad had brought him home for extra security.

"Hey, there, Foster," Jenny said in her squeaky voice. "You like your new home? You're such a good boy."

Amari huffed in frustration. "Dad, that's a very sweet dog. I'm glad you brought him. But I can't believe you let Rahal's son go."

"You think he's sweet now, but just see what he does if he hears someone at the door. Only an idiot would try to come in here. He's a trained attack dog. And he's only seven years old. That's *my* age in dog years. He's got several good years left in him. I don't care what the policy says."

"I'm sure he is, Dad. He reminds me so much of Max. Thank you. But you still didn't tell me why you let Rahal's son go."

"It wasn't my call," Dad said. "He's got a good lawyer."

"But the evidence!"

"All we got is a broken spoke and a paint can. Anybody could have put the paint smudge on his gas tank and planted the can in his luggage box. He didn't even have it locked."

"Oh, come on, who would do that?"

"He passed a polygraph and he's got an alibi. The night the priest was shot he was at the movies with his girlfriend. He has a ticket stub to prove it. *A Nightmare on Elm Street*. Number four."

"And the fire at the synagogue?"

"He was in the library with a study group, cramming for an exam the next day. Three of them confirmed he was there until the library closed."

Amari digested the evidence for a moment and came to the only logical conclusion. "Then someone really is setting him up."

"Looks that way. When the forensic guys went over his motorcycle, they found clear evidence the ignition system was tampered with, and more than once."

"So it was hotwired."

"It appears so. Somebody was watching him. They knew he didn't ride his bike much and wouldn't notice it missing for a couple of hours."

"It must be his father then."

"Why would you say that?"

"Because you said they had differences of opinion. And he's a psychopath. That's why."

"Baby, I know you want this to be over. But we have to look somewhere else."

She closed her eyes and shook her head. "And his alibi checked out when the Town Car ran us off the road?"

"It did, Amari, I'm sorry. But we'll get this guy, I promise."

"So did you find out anything about the Mercedes?"

"It would have helped if you got the license tag."

"They were too far away."

"I told my guys to be on the lookout for a black Mercedes with two men, but so far we've got nothing. We can't pull over every Mercedes we see. Besides, they haven't committed a crime. Are you sure this whole thing hasn't made you paranoid? Maybe you're making connections that aren't there."

"I know what I saw."

"Could be private investigators for all we know. That stunt you pulled on campus has gone all over the country, maybe even the world. A lot of people have a stake in the Shroud of Turin. Maybe you've attracted more attention than you think."

"Then why don't they just talk to me?"

"That's the part that smells rotten to me too. You had your gun with you?"

"I had it in my hand. And I would have used it."

"Now don't be too trigger happy with that thing. Nobody's likely to hurt you in the light of day. I've got a police car on your street twenty-four-seven now. And from now on, you may notice them following you. Everything's going to be all right, I promise."

Foster let out a loud woof.

"You see there. Foster agrees with me."

"I think he just wants his treat."

Foster woofed again and scarfed the treat out of Jenny's hand. He crunched it loudly with content.

"There you go, Foster," Jenny said. "Such a good boy. I just met you, and I'm already going to miss you."

Amari looked Jenny's way. "I hope you're not mad. It's too dangerous for you to stay here."

"That's right," Dad said. "It's better that you stay clear of here for now. When this is all over, you can come back if you want."

"I'd love that," Jenny said. She came over and hugged Amari. She pulled away but still held hands. "I think you should get out too, I really do. Leave town, at least until this guy is caught."

"But I have Foster now. And my dad and the entire Tucson police force. I'll be fine."

Jenny let go of Amari's hands and went back to petting Foster. Then she looked up and said, "I'll be praying for you."

"Thank you for your prayers, Jenny. It means a lot to me. So where are you going?"

"Graduate student housing. It's more expensive, but you're right. It beats living in a war zone. It's really hard to study here."

Chapter 34

Christ Chapel was a white, wood-frame church no bigger than a house. It was off I-10 in northwest Tucson, right next to a neighborhood of mobiles homes. Flames devoured the church as two fire trucks nearly as big at the church itself churned out a forceful, white stream of water through a hole in the roof that billowed smoke. On the sidewalk in front of the church, black spray paint scrawled out what they now knew was Arabic for jihad. In front of the word were the numbers 1253.

Pete and George stood next to Sandra Davis and her WKLD camera crew. Sandra prepared to go on air.

"We shouldn't have let that guy go," George said. "Every one of his witnesses were Muslim. I bet they're covering for him."

"It wasn't my call. The guy had Joe Halsey for his lawyer. We couldn't get the charges to stick."

Sandra Davis started her broadcast. "I'm standing here in front of Christ Chapel where, as you can see, flames engulf the tiny church. Witnesses say the church's minister is missing and they fear his body may lie inside. This just four days after Anwar Rahal, a known radical Muslim, was arrested for suspicion of committing two counts of arson and the murder of a Catholic priest. Rahal was released from custody early yesterday morning without bail. Police haven't said if there is a connection with the other two fires. I'm Sandra Davis. Stay tuned to WKLD for details as they emerge. Back to you, Sam."

"Well, there goes the neighborhood," Pete said.

"That's not good," George said. "Every Bible thumper in Arizona's going to be breathing down our necks over this."

"Or worse, they may be burning down the mosques."

"Shouldn't have let him go."

"We'll pick him up again and question him. But I'm telling you, George, for once I'm with Halsey. I don't think the kid's lying. I can smell a lie and all I smelled on him was his girl's perfume. Somebody's setting him up, I can feel it. It's no coincidence the real killer waited until Anwar was released to commit this crime. Anwar seems like a smart kid. Even if he was guilty, he wouldn't be dumb enough to burn this church down right after he got out."

"And kill the minister."

"I hope you're wrong about that. We'll find out when the smoke clears."

****

Pete sat flustered, pondering three photographs aligned vertically on his desk. The top photo was of the black spray paint on the sidewalk in front of Holy Ghost Catholic Church—the numbers 1035 and the Arabic word for jihad. The second photo was the one taken of the sidewalk at the Jewish synagogue up in the Catalina Foothills. It read 76 and the Arabic word for jihad. The third photo was one taken three days ago, at the little Christ Chapel next to Gardner Estates. Black paint on the sidewalk said 1253 and the Arabic word for jihad.

"What's the connection?" Pete uttered to himself. What did those numbers mean? They were a clue the killer had intentionally left. He was sending a message. But what? What was this lunatic trying to say?

George stepped into Pete's office. "You figure it out yet?"

"Nobody has it figured out. Not even the FBI. This just blows my mind."

"Maybe it doesn't mean anything. He could be toying with us. Why give us a clue that helps him get caught?"

"I don't know. You might be right. Is that the ballistics report in your hand?"

"It is," George said and handed him the papers. "It was a .38, same gun used on the priest."

"That's no surprise."

"Only, the minister was shot in the chest. Twice."

"Any other evidence? Witnesses?"

"Nope."

"Anybody say they heard a motorcycle?"

"No, but get this. I showed a picture of a '78 Lincoln Town Car, like Amari said tried to run her off the road. One of the neighbors thinks he may have seen a car that looked like that on the next street over from the church, but he wasn't sure. It was dark."

Pete rubbed the back of his neck. A sense of dread overcame him.

"Don't worry, Pete. You got twenty-four-seven protection on Amari. The priest and the minister weren't armed. They never knew what hit them. At least Amari's on the lookout."

"That's true."

"You ever think about getting her out of town? Put her in hiding somewhere?"

"I mentioned it once to her, but she wouldn't go for it. Besides, if I did that, I couldn't have a patrol officer protecting her. What if this guy just followed her out of town and got her where she had no protection?"

"You could go with her."

"Then who's going to find this killer?"

"I don't know, Pete, I'm just thinking."

"I appreciate that. By the way, you hear anything about the whereabouts of Anwar Rahal?" Shouting from down the hall interrupted Pete. He went to his door and closed it. "Anyway, I talked to his father and he hasn't heard from him and neither has anyone at the dorm."

"I haven't heard anything. Maybe he pulled one last job and skipped town."

"I don't think so. My gut tells me no. And his mother is really worried. He was at her house the night before the church fire, but he never showed the night of the fire. She made his favorite dinner. He was supposed to be there but went missing."

"You got a BOLO out on him, don't you?"

"Of course, he's the prime suspect. But he's vanished."

"You mean escaped," George clarified.

"Wherever, he's gone, that's all I know. And what's all that racket going on down the hall? I can hardly hear myself think."

"You haven't heard?"

"Heard what? I've been busy trying to decipher this crazy code." More clamor came from down the hall, muffled by the closed door. "So what's going on down there?"

"They just brought in some nut-job from Avra Valley. He's got an arsenal in his house."

"One of those survivalist types?"

"Something like that, only this one apparently needed cash and was caught selling illegally. As you can hear, he's not happy about it. ATF is on the way. And get this, he had military stuff. Don't know how he got it. Machine guns, hand grenades, even some of those fire grenades."

"You mean incendiary grenades?"

"That's right. You ever use one of those? I know you were in the army."

"Once. In Korea. I threw one down the barrel of enemy artillery. Wanted to make sure they couldn't reuse it. They've got thermite in them. Melted the barrel right off."

"Wow, that's hot."

"This guy had some of those?"

"And regular grenades. He was selling them out of his trunk for a hundred bucks a piece."

"So where did he get them?"

"Stolen, I guess. That's for the ATF guys to figure out."

"You know what bothers me? It's who would have bought some of those? I'm afraid after the ATF guys are gone, we'll be dealing with this later."

George pointed to the pictures on Pete's desk. "You're right. This guy likes fire. I bet he'd be in the market."

Apprehension built within Pete and he knew it was time to up the ante. "All right, that clinches it. I've got a phone call to make."

"Who you calling?"

"A friend in Washington DC."

"Someone from the FBI?"

"No, someone from the police academy."

"Washington police academy? What's that got to do with this case?"

"I'll tell you later."

****

Amari and her dad sat on her couch watching the evening news. She glanced out the window and saw Kevin coming to the front door. She got up and let him in. "Hey, Kevin, my dad's here already. We're watching the news."

He came inside and tipped his orange baseball cap to her dad.

"Have a seat," Dad said. "I'll show you those pictures in just a minute. I want to see this next story first."

Kevin sat next to her and waited for the commercial to finish. Finally, Sam Brown of WKLD came on the screen, an image of an angry mob as his backdrop.

"Turmoil in Tucson erupted today as members from several area churches picketed outside of both area mosques. We have reports that the imam of the mosque on Speedway Boulevard was badly beaten by one of the protesters. Things don't look any better at the mosque downtown. Sandra Davis has the story."

The shot switched to Sandra. "I'm standing here at the Islamic Community center near campus, and let me tell you, things are getting ugly. As you can see, police have arrived to break up the protest and I even watched the police arrest a protester who waved a gas can over his head and threatened to burn the mosque to the ground. 'An eye for an eye' is what I heard him say."

The screen switched back to Sam. "In the aftermath of two clergy member murders and the burning of two Christian churches and a synagogue, this reaction comes as no surprise because the main suspect in this case is a Muslim named Anwar Rahal. The latest attack occurred just one day after he was released from jail for suspicion of committing the other three crimes. Coincidentally, after the murder of Christ Chapel's minister and the burning of his church, Anwar Rahal has gone missing. Clearly, many people are not happy about that. We here at WKLD pray that things will settle down soon before anybody else gets hurt." Sam turned his attention to the weather girl. "Betty, what's the weather looking like tomorrow?"

Dad grabbed the remote and flipped off the TV. "That's just perfect. I was afraid of this."

"So you really don't think Rahal's son was behind this?" she asked.

"No, Amari, I don't. I was there when they did the polygraph. He's not lying."

"Then why did he skip town?"

"I don't know. But I have a bad feeling about that."

"A house divided, will not stand," Kevin said.

"What's that?" Dad asked.

"The news. How the Christians and the Muslims are fighting each other. It just reminds me of Matthew 3:35. Jesus said, 'a house divided, cannot stand.'"

Dad furrowed his brows and pondered Kevin's words. "Hold that thought," he said and went into the kitchen. He came back carrying an envelope. "These are the pictures I wanted you to look at. Now I'm wondering if these numbers could be Bible verses."

"I'll give it a look," Kevin said. "But I'm not sure I can help."

"Don't sell yourself short. Amari tells me you got the social grace of an Amazon piranha in a swimming pool, but you got a brain like a computer. Put these numbers in your head and see what happens."

She rolled her eyes at her dad. "Kevin, I promise I didn't say that. I just told him you were . . . special, that's all. I told him you might be able to help us with this case."

A wide grimace spread on Kevin's face. "That's hysterical. Piranha in a swimming pool. Can I use that sometime?"

"Be my guest. I'll put it on a T-shirt for you if you can help solve this case."

"I'll help If I can. I brought my thinking cap," he said and pointed to his bold, orange cap with the capital white letter T. "I bought this the day Tennessee beat Bama in 82. Broke a twelve-year losing streak. I've worn it for every test I've taken since. Never fails me."

"Then let's see how it works," Dad said and handed him the three pictures. "Now, we know that is Arabic for jihad, but what we don't know is what those numbers mean. Do those numbers mean anything to you? Any Bible verses come to mind?"

"Hmmm," Kevin said and rubbed at his afternoon shadow. His eyes darted back and forth between numbers.

"Take your time," she said. "Just relax and see what comes to you."

"Hmmm," Kevin said again and tapped his finger against his lip. "Amari, hand me that Bible on your book shelf, will you?"

She handed him the Bible and he flipped to Matthew 10:35. "Yep, just what I thought. That number 1035 refers to another verse in Matthew. You see, it says, 'For I came to set a man against his father, and a daughter against her mother, and a daughter-in-law against her mother-in-law.' And you see right next to the verse it says to also see Micah 7:6. That other number is 76."

"That's the one for the Jewish synagogue," Dad said. "That must be why he refers to the Old Testament."

"Let's see," Kevin said and flipped the pages to Micah 7:6. "Right here, 'For son treats father contemptuously, Daughter rises up against her mother, Daughter-in-law against her mother-in law.' It says the same thing basically, only this was for the Jews. And I think that other number refers to Luke 12:53." Kevin flipped the pages to that verse. "Yep, says basically the same thing. So the two Christian churches get the New Testament verses and the synagogue gets the Old Testament one."

"That is amazing," Dad said. "All this time the FBI's been on this, and you figure it out in a few seconds."

"You have to know the Bible to know the verses," Kevin said. "They would have had better luck asking Billy Graham."

"So how does this help us find the killer?" Dad asked.

"I think we know his motive now," Kevin said. "That's something."

"I don't see motive from those verses," Dad said.

"I see it," Amari said. "It's what Kevin said earlier. 'A house divided will not stand.' He's trying to make the religions fight against each other. He burns the Christian and Jewish churches, then blames the Muslims."

"And the Christians and Jews play right into his hand and oppose the Muslims," Dad said. "He's trying to kill two birds with one stone. Maybe he thinks he's going to start some kind of holy war. Kevin, you're a genius."

"Must have been my lucky hat."

"Then can you use that hat to tell us who's behind all of this?"

"Not from what you gave me. What I did was the easy part. All I can tell you is this guy knows his Bible."

Dad took the photos and dropped them back into the envelope. "And he's got a serious beef with people who believe in that Bible."

"And the Quran," Kevin said. "He doesn't care for Muslims either."

Chapter 35

Amari pulled her Camaro onto campus and headed toward the student union parking garage. A Tucson Police Department cruiser followed close behind. They followed her everywhere, even to work at Pizza Hut, where the officer sat inside during her entire shift and followed her home afterward. She hated being followed. It was a creepy feeling. Still, she knew it was for her own good. Even though she missed her privacy, she was glad they had her back.

She pulled up to the Second Street parking garage and waited her turn to enter. She glanced into her rearview mirror. Where was the police cruiser? She must have lost him at the last red light. It was okay, she told herself. The university was crawling with campus police. Nobody would try anything in broad daylight.

She found a spot on the top level and parked. She retrieved the student parking hang tag from her glove compartment and hung it on the mirror post so she wouldn't get a ticket. She'd gotten the hang tag the day before when she paid her spring semester tuition—with the help of her dad—and prepared to start her last semester before graduating with a bachelor's in criminal justice. Classes started next week. Of course, she may need to skip class for a few days so she and Kevin could fly to Turin and speak to the cardinal, but she was more than willing for her grades to take the hit. So far, the bishop had not called, but she remained hopeful.

She exited the parking garage and walked to the student union. She was meeting Kevin for lunch. She had put any notion of a romance between her and Kevin out of her head. If he had any feelings other than friendship, he would let them show in his own time. Rushing him was counterproductive. Besides, she was happy being his friend. It was better than nothing.

She glanced around and did not see the patrol officer. She'd lost him, all right. That was okay, wasn't it? She was in public now, lots of people. What could happen?

She continued into the food court and met up with Kevin. They bought their food and went out to eat on the patio. It was a cool January day, but Kevin always needed some fresh air after being stuck inside all day.

She set her burrito down. "So any news about Rahal's son?"

"Not a word," Kevin said and dipped a chip into salsa. "Rahal seems pretty sensitive about it, so I dare not ask."

"You think something bad happened to him?"

"I don't know. I'd like to believe he really is the killer and he skipped town before he got caught. But apparently, your dad thinks he's being set up."

A fire truck screamed down the street. She craned her neck to see. She smelled a hint of smoke, from somewhere close to where she'd parked.

"It's always something," she said, tilting her head in the direction of the fire. "I'm still a little worried about you. Have you noticed anything, had any threats? Whoever ran us off the road ran us both off the road."

"I saw a black Mercedes at my apartment complex the other day."

"You serious? That means they're following you too."

"I think they must live there. I've seen it several times. It's a common car."

"If you could afford that car, would you be living where you are now?"

"Good point. Maybe it's a rich guy dating someone there. Who knows. It's a common car. Don't worry about me. I wasn't the one on the national news, remember?"

"That's true."

The smoke got heavier and she could see it now, billowing from the parking garage. A campus police officer cupped his hands around his mouth to amplify his voice. "Does anyone own a white Camaro? Correction, *did* anybody own a white Camaro?"

****

Dad, George, several fire fighters, and half the Tucson police department stood with Amari and Kevin as they watched the smoldering remains of Amari's 1978 white Camaro Z28. Used to be white. Everything but the front and rear bumpers was charred black.

Dad put his arm around her shoulder. "I'm sorry, baby. I know you loved that car. I'm just glad you weren't in it."

"You know I just paid $800 on the transmission," she said.

"At least you have insurance."

"It's just liability insurance. It only pays the other person if I hit them."

"I'll help you buy another car."

"And I'll drive you around until you get one," Kevin said.

"You see there," Dad said. "Kevin will help in the meantime. Come on, I don't like you out in the open. I'll drive you home. There's something we need to talk about."

Kevin went back to work and George stayed to finish the investigation as Dad drove her home. She sat with weary eyes watching the buildings go by. She was going to miss that car.

She'd had it since she learned to drive back in '81. But her dad was right about one thing—at least she wasn't in it.

"You think that was one of those fire grenades?" she asked. "You told me a guy was caught selling them."

"It's the only thing that could produce that much heat, that fast. Fire guys said whatever it was burned a hole in the bottom. Melted the metal clean through. Amari, it's not too late to get a refund on your tuition, is it?"

"I think I have a couple more weeks," she said with resignation. She knew what her dad was about to say. It was time to get out of Dodge.

"You know you have to go into the police academy before you can make detective, right? Just getting a degree won't cut it. You gotta pay your dues."

"I know the procedure," she said as they pulled into their neighborhood street.

Two squad cars were outside the house and an officer was checking the windows. Foster barked frantically from within.

"What are they doing to my house?" she asked.

"They're checking the perimeter. Looking for signs of forced entry. Just in case."

She cupped her face in her hands and fought to hold back the tears. She had to be strong. She couldn't show weakness, not in front of her dad. Courage, she told herself. Trust in God. He is your strength.

She felt her dad's hand caress her back. "It's okay, baby. Everybody has their breaking point. Even me." He pulled her head under his chin and held her close. "I'm going to get you out of here. I've got a plan."

She pulled her hands from her face and looked at him through tear-blurred eyes. "So what's your plan?"

"Washington DC. It's about as far away from Tucson you can get while still being in the States. I've got connections with the police academy there. The next class starts January 18. If you're not safe in a police academy, I don't know where you would be."

"But I can't leave," she said, stunned by the suggestion. "What about school?"

"Work as a beat cop during the day and take night classes at George Washington University. They've got a criminal justice program there. Or work at night and take day classes. You'll figure that out later. For right now, we need to keep you safe. Once this guy is caught, you can move back home if you don't like it out there."

"I don't know, Dad. That's a big move. What about Kevin?"

"What about him? You're just friends, right? Once you two make your case with the Vatican, you'll probably go your separate ways."

It tortured her to admit he was right, but she knew he probably was. "I guess you're right. But what about Foster?"

"I'll take him. I'll move back into the house. I can apply the rent I'm paying now toward your rent in Washington."

"I don't know. I'll have to think about it."

"All right, then why don't you go stay with your mother's parents on the reservation? Nobody will be able to find you there."

"At the reservation? I hardly know my grandparents. I've seen them maybe three times my whole life. They're strangers to me."

"And that's a shame. Maybe it's time you got to know them better."

"Okay," she said reluctantly.

"Okay what? You'll go to the reservation?"

"No, okay to Washington."

"All right, then. I'm going to double up on police at the house while you pack. We head out next week and find you an apartment. Police academy lasts about six months. They don't offer female housing, so you'll need a place to stay."

"It would be nice to see snow every once and a while," she said, trying to sound upbeat. "And trees, real trees that bloom in the spring, trees that change colors and lose their leaves in the fall. I've always wanted to see that. And it's right next to the FBI. Quantico is just a few miles away. Maybe I could join the FBI someday."

"There you go. You see? Everything works out in the end."

"But what about the Shroud? What if the bishop calls?"

"What if he doesn't? What if they don't agree to talk to you? You can't stay here."

"I guess I could fly out there over a weekend or something. If they ever call, that is."

"Or just mail them what you've got and talk to them over the phone. You'll figure something out. For now, keeping you safe is all that's important. You go start packing and I'll give my friend in Washington a call and tell him to expect you."

Chapter 36

Amari folded clothes in her bedroom and stacked them into a suitcase. She couldn't believe she was leaving. She was going to miss Kevin so much. Of course, she could always call him—every day if she wanted to. She could write and send pictures. Maybe she would fly back one weekend and surprise him. People do it all the time, she reminded herself. It didn't mean they couldn't still be friends.

She flinched at the sound of the doorbell. Foster sprang from the floor and dashed to the front of the house, barking. She went to the door and saw Kevin through the peephole. "It's okay," she soothed Foster. "He's my friend, remember? Sit." She pointed at the ground in front of the dog. He promptly complied, his pointy ears at attention.

She unbolted both bolts and chain, then opened the door.

A police officer stood next to him. "Do you know this guy?" the officer asked. "I patted him down. He's clean."

"Thank you, officer, but he's my friend."

The officer tipped his hat and walked back to the patrol car.

Kevin stepped inside and grinned. "That guy got a little too intimate."

"Sorry, Kevin. They're all terrified of my dad. He's probably making them do that."

"Hey, I'm glad they're so thorough," he said, one arm behind his back. He was hiding something. "Anyway, I thought I'd swing by here after work and check on you. Make sure you're okay."

"Like my dad said, I'm just glad I wasn't in the car. So what's behind your back?"

He pulled out a bouquet of flowers, red roses garnished with white baby's breath.

She caught her breath. "What's that for?"

"It's for your loss. I know how much you loved that car."

She took them and caressed them like a newborn. But red roses weren't for the grieving. Didn't he know that? Red roses were for love. "That's so nice. Nobody's ever brought me roses before. Let me go put them in water."

She filled a vase with water, dropped the flowers in, and set them on the coffee table. "They're beautiful. Thank you."

"They reminded me of you when I saw them. So what's with all the boxes? Are you going somewhere?"

There was no easy way to do this, so she sighed and let it out. "I've decided to drop out of college for now. I'm going to the police academy instead."

"Are you serious?" He let the words sink for a second. "I can see you doing that. Beats Pizza Hut, I guess. But you're not going to finish school? You had straight A's."

"Not in my art classes."

"Still, it's not like you to give up. Remember, your name says you can't give up."

"I'm going to finish, eventually. I'll go part time when I start working. I'll make more money then. Besides, I have to be a cop before I can be a detective."

"So is that nine to five? You still get weekends off, don't you?"

"I'm sorry, Kevin," she said, her voice cracking. She looked away from him and stared at the roses, hoping he wouldn't notice the moisture building in her eyes. "But I'm not staying in Tucson. I'm moving to Washington DC."

"Washington?" he blurted. "That's on the east coast!"

She turned back to face him. "Kevin, I have to get out of here before it's too late. It's too dangerous. My dad set this all up. He wants me out of Tucson, to somewhere safe."

He was silent as the thoughts churned in his head. "You know what, I agree one hundred percent. Let's get out of here. My lease is up. I'm paying month to month."

She was astonished. Did he think he could just tag along? "You can't just follow me to Washington. You have a job, responsibilities here."

"I'll get another job. I'll bus tables if I have to."

"Don't be silly. This is your post doc. You can't just quit."

"I can do whatever I want."

"Kevin, we're just friends."

"Stop calling me that!" he snapped, his fists clenched.

"Calling you what?"

"Your friend, stop calling me your friend."

"Then what am I supposed to call you?"

"Amari, I didn't buy those roses because of your car. I bought them because I'm trying to tell you something, only I don't know how."

A surge of joy gushed from within. She had prayed so hard for this moment. Could it be? "What? What are you trying to tell me? Just say it."

"Look, I don't know what love is, Amari. I've never been in love before. All I know is this. I think about you all the time. I can't stand the thought of being without you. And the other day when we came back from Los Alamos, you know, when you had that cracker on your lip?"

"Don't remind me."

"That day, I wanted to kiss you so bad, I couldn't stand it."

She threw her hands up in exasperation. "Then why didn't you?"

"Because you're so beautiful, Amari. It's a privilege to be in the same room with you."

"Kevin, that's so sweet."

"But look at me. I'm just some backward hick from Tennessee. And I don't even go to church. What would someone like you see in a guy like me? I was afraid you didn't share my feelings. What if I chased you off? Then we would never get to the Vatican. Our mission was too important for me to risk it."

"And I'm just some half-Navajo cop's kid from Tucson. What does that have to do with anything? Of course, I share your feelings. How many hints do I have to give you?"

"Well, I didn't know. Sometimes you acted a little flirty and then you'd turn around and call me your friend. Why do you girls have to be so complicated? I swear, quantum mechanics has nothing on you."

She shook her head and laughed. "We're not that complicated."

"Well, you are to me. So I went and asked Ms. Embry for some advice."

"Ms. Embry? The receptionist? What did she say?"

"She told me to get my head out of my behind and do something before I lost you. She's the one that told me to buy the roses."

Happy tears welled in her eyes. She plucked one of the roses from the vase and breathed in its aroma. "Because roses aren't for friends. Roses are for love."

Suddenly, Kevin pulled her in close by the small of her back. His spearmint breath was hot on her face and she dropped the rose onto the floor. "Kevin, this isn't like you."

His gaze fell to her lips. "I've been crunching the numbers."

"What numbers?"

"About how I was gonna kiss you for the first time. I've gone over and over it in my head, playing out every hypothetical scenario."

"And?"

"In real life, it's a whole lot simpler than I thought."

"An how's that?"

"In the real world . . . it all boils down to one thing."

"And what's that?" she said and gently pulled him closer.

"I just can't seem to help myself," he said and eagerly pressed his lips onto hers.

She kissed back, lost in his soft, warm embrace. And in that moment, she believed what he had been telling her all along—everything was going to be okay.

****

"You think these books will be too heavy?" Amari asked. She had brought a couple of boxes to the lab to help Kevin clean out his office. "Or should we put them in another box?"

"Actually, those stay here. Property of the university."

"What about the computer?"

"Theirs too. I'm taking the floppies though."

"Dr. Brenner, what is she doing here? Did I not warn you what I would do if I found her here again?" It was Rahal. The eye that focused on her was bloodshot. He sounded more weary than angry.

"You haven't been to your office yet?" Kevin asked. "Slid my resignation under your door. Saved you the trouble of firing me."

She thought he'd blow his stack when Kevin laid that on him. Instead, worried panic showed on his face. He moved over to Kevin's chair and sat. "Can we talk about this?" he asked. "If you are angry about the way I treated your girlfriend, I offer my apologies. But she put me in a difficult position," he said, glancing up at Amari. "I wish you would reconsider. We have to finish dating the Dead Sea scrolls. We have a deadline. I cannot meet that deadline without you."

She felt an unexpected wave of pity for Rahal. Clearly, the trouble with his now missing son had affected him, perhaps shown him what really matters in life.

Kevin walked over and looked down at the little man. "Before you say anything else, I want to ask you something."

"I'm listening."

"Was that you who got my clearance pulled at Los Alamos?"

"So you did go there. I thought you might. Dr. Brenner, I'm sorry, but Miss Johnston should have shown me more respect."

"So now you know I'm helping her. You still want me to stay?"

"My wants have nothing to do with this. We have contractual obligations."

"I need to let you in on another secret. Did you know that I'm a Christian?"

"As long as you give us accurate numbers from the Dead Sea scrolls, I don't care if you practice witchcraft on your own time. So will you stay a little longer? Just until we finish this project?"

"No-can-do," Kevin said. "I'm moving out of town. I'll give you the numbers of a couple guys who can help if you want."

Rahal stood and moved to the door. "If you will not reconsider, then, yes, I would appreciate those numbers," he said and walked slowly, quietly down the hall.

"Wow," she said. "I thought this would be a lot more fun."

"Yeah," he said, a perplexed, sad look on his face. "Now I feel like the bad guy. Did your dad ever find out what happened to his son?"

"Nothing yet. They still don't have a clue."

"Then I guess we should keep him in our prayers. Remind me next time we go to church."

She caught him by the wrist. "Kevin, are you serious?"

"Well, you heard me. My cover's blown now. What do I have to lose?"

She pulled him in for a hug. "Thank you, Kevin. You don't know how much that means to me." She let him go and reached for his hands. "The couple that prays together stays together."

"Just don't make me sit up front."

"I don't care where we sit, as long as you're sitting next to me."

"And don't make me sing either. Cause I can't sing."

Chapter 37

Dad stood in the doorway with drooping eyes and a red nose that looked worse against his pale face. He held an overnight bag in his left hand and a box of tissue in the other.

Amari bolted the door closed behind him and led him to the couch.

"Let me guess," she said. "You never got your flu shot."

"It's not just me," he said through stuffy nostrils. "Half the precinct has it. I'm sorry, but they don't have the extra manpower to leave a car outside. That's why I'm sleeping on your couch tonight."

"Lot of good you're going to do me like that."

"I can manage."

"How about you let me take care of you this time." She put her hand to his head. "You got a fever. I'll get you some medicine. I have a can of chicken soup in the cupboard."

Dad sat his gun holster at the base of the couch, slid off his shoes, and laid down. Amari went to her closet and came back with a pillow and a blanket.

"Thank you, baby. Don't you worry. Anyone comes through that door, I'll take him out," he said, an arm hanging off the couch, patting his gun.

"Just get some rest. Foster and I can handle this. Anyway, what are the odds of this guy hitting us tonight, of all nights? The patrol car has been out there for days. I think he gets the hint. He won't even think to come by here."

"You're probably right," Dad said. "I'm sure he got the message. But just in case, I'll feel better if I stay here."

She gave him some cold medicine with antihistamine to clear up the drainage and help him sleep. He took his medicine, ate the soup and crackers, and passed out on the couch.

"Come on, Foster. It's bedtime," she said. The loyal German Shepherd followed her to her bedroom. She closed the door to muffle her dad's snoring.

Later that night, she laid in bed reading the Bible. Foster made his bed on an old quilt comforter on the floor next to her. Lately, Scripture was the only comfort that helped eased her into sleep. She drifted in and out, on the edge of sleep, determined to finish Second Peter before she placed her bookmark.

Foster sprang off from the comforter and startled her. He went to the sliding glass door and whined to go out.

"Seriously, Foster? I thought I let you out already."

He scratched at the door and whined again.

"Hold on," she said and placed her Bible on the nightstand. She climbed out of bed and went to the door. She pulled back the drapes and surveyed the illuminated back yard. It was clear. She removed the broomstick that braced the door shut, clicked open the lock, and slid the door open. Foster bolted out and dashed to the corner of the fence, passionately sniffing at the ground. Could it be the neighbor's cat again? A horrible vision of her having to explain the dead cat to poor old lady Crawford flashed in her mind. She stepped out into the dark. "Foster!" she yelled. "Just do your business and get back in here. Leave that cat alone!"

A noise from behind startled her. She spun around.

A heavy shoulder shoved her through the open door. She lost her footing and fell to the floor. A hulking man in black slammed the door shut behind him.

Foster attacked the door, scratching, barking, and gnashing teeth.

He snatched a gun from his waistband and leveled at her head, hand clenched tight, quivering. "I warn you! You no listen!" the large, Middle Eastern man said. A deep, red scar crossed his forehead. The man from the library.

"Wait!" she said, slowly coming to her feet. "Please, don't do this!"

"Shut your eyes!"

"Please, you don't have to do this!"

Foster growled, barked, and clawed.

"Please, shut your eyes . . . *please!*"

She opened her eyes even wider, pleading for mercy.

Resolve fell away from the man's face. He relaxed the grip on his gun and moved the barrel to the temple of his own skull. "I am sorry for this." His eyes billowed with tears.

"What are you doing? Are you crazy? Just put the gun down!"

"I have no choice."

"Yes, you do have a choice."

Dad crashed through the door, gun drawn.

She dove at the man's arm and yanked it down. The gun toppled to the floor. She wrenched his hand to the small of his back, thrust upward, and shoved him against the wall.

"Ahhh!" the man cried.

Dad brought his gun steady against the man's head. "Get him to the ground," he said, then kicked the assailant behind his knee. He sank to the floor and she came down on top of him, still shoving his hand up to his shoulder blades.

"You hurt me!" the man cried.

"Hold him there while I get my cuffs." Dad went back to the couch and rushed back in with the handcuffs. He stooped down and wrenched the other wrist to the small of the back, cuffed him, and clamped them tight. Dad sank onto the bed while Amari kept her knee on his back. Foster still clawed at the door.

"We got him, baby," Dad said. "We got him."

****

Ambulance lights flashed out in front of the house. Dad laid on a gurney. He had passed out shortly after calling this in. Adrenaline and fever didn't go together well. They were taking him to the ER for IV fluids and observation. The Middle Eastern man sat in the back of a squad car, sad eyes fixed on Amari.

Kevin slammed the door of his Honda Accord and ran toward her, nearly knocking her over with his hug.

"It's okay," she said, hugging him back. "We got him. It's over now, thank God. It's finally over."

"I hope you're right," he said.

"Hope I'm right? Don't you see him? That's him in the police car."

"Well, yeah, but your dad thinks he was being paid. Sorry to burst your bubble, babe, but whoever was paying him is still out there."

Chapter 38

Pete stayed overnight at the hospital and was discharged around noon the next day. Amari and Kevin picked him up in his Regal he'd left at the house the night before and took him back to the house so he could continue his recovery. Pete knew he was fine. A little flu never killed anybody. He wanted to get back to work, only they wouldn't hear of it.

When they got to the house, Amari came around to Pete's door and tried to help him out.

"I'm not an invalid," he said and used the door frame to steady himself as he got out. They went inside to the couch and Amari stuck a thermometer under his tongue. She set an egg timer and when it went off, she pulled out the thermometer and announced the reading, "You're down to a hundred. How do you feel?"

"Still a little achy, but I'll manage."

"I'll get you some ibuprofen."

"Just ibuprofen. Nothing to make me drowsy. You should never have given me that cold medicine. If I'd known it would knock me out, I never would have taken it."

"He wasn't going to shoot me. He couldn't make himself do it."

"Still, it wasn't a good idea."

"Do they have him on suicide watch? If I hadn't knocked the gun away, I think he would have pulled the trigger. I could see it in his eyes."

"I don't know. I hope so. If someone paid him to do this, we need him alive. That's another reason I should be at work."

"Why do you think he was paid to do this?" she asked. "Why can't this just be over? We got the guy, didn't we?"

"He's too tall, Amari. The guy who shot the priest was shorter. The guy that started the synagogue fire was shorter, thinner, and faster."

"Then the two cases aren't related. Why do you think there's a link?"

"I hope you're right. Maybe Rahal is lying and he paid this guy. Maybe someone else put him up to it."

"Why do you insist that he was being paid?"

"He didn't have the heart to kill you. Otherwise, he would have done it. But he didn't want to do this. He was pressured. Maybe somebody is blackmailing him, who knows?"

Kevin brought some ibuprofen and a glass of water.

Pete took the tablets, downed them with the water, and snatched his keys off the coffee table.

"Where are you going?" she asked. "The nurse said you had to stay in bed for two more days."

Pete went to the hall closet, got his overcoat, and headed for the door.

"Dad, where do you think you're going? Get back on that couch. Doctor's orders."

"Where do you think I'm going?" he said and closed the door behind him.

****

Pete moved carefully down the hall toward the holding cell, steadying himself against the wall. George saw him coming and rushed to his side. "Pete, what are you doing here? You should be in bed, man. You got the flu."

"I'll sleep when I'm dead. Now out of my way. I need to talk to that guy."

"It's no use. He's not saying anything."

"Nothing?"

"Absolutely nothing. He had no ID. We don't know how he got to the house. We have no idea who he is. But what we do know is this. That gun he had pointed at Amari, it was registered to the minister at that little church."

"Then the preacher must have had a gun stashed in the church and our killer stole it."

"Seems that way," George said. "If that's true, then maybe this guy's our serial killer."

"Or it means our serial killer paid this guy and gave him the stolen gun to use. That way it couldn't be traced back to the killer."

"Or that."

"All right, get him to the interrogation room. I'll meet you in there."

"But, Pete . . . "

"Now!" he yelled, cringing at the pain in his head.

"I'll meet you in there."

Pete went to the interrogation room and waited with a wad of tissue in his hand. Finally, George brought the prisoner in, hands cuffed behind his back. Two other officers came in with George for extra muscle in case there was trouble. After they sat the prisoner down, the two officers stood sentry by the door. A surveillance camera pointed at the table from the top corner of the ceiling.

The beefy Arab sat with his shoulders hunched, dressed in orange, jail issued coveralls. His vacant eyes were red and swollen. A purple scar was on his head, a visible dent underneath. Amari's fire extinguisher.

Pete looked up to George. "I hope you have him on suicide watch."

"We do."

Pete studied the guy for a second. He could have been a NFL defensive tackle, but his eyes, bloodshot and sad, seemed to have no fight left in them. They held a distant stare at the table, refusing to make eye contact. His hulking body moved only slightly with the slow rise and fall of his breath.

"Listen, fella, I can see you're sorry for what you did," Pete finally said. "I know you didn't want to hurt my little girl. Somebody put you up to this. Somebody didn't give you a choice."

He just sat there, face of stone despair.

"Okay, listen, pal. It's not as bad as you're thinking. Here's all we got on you. Assault at the library and assault at the house. You didn't even break in, so there no charge there, right? You weren't trying to kill her because the last place you pointed the gun was to your own head. Judge might give you two years at the most, maybe three. Maybe they have you see a shrink while they're at it. Hey, look at me," Pete said and lowered his head to try to meet the man's gaze. "I bet we can work a deal. Maybe we can do six months if you tell me who put you up to this. Who knows? If the prosecutor feels like it, maybe we can even let you walk on probation. It's called working a deal. If we think we can land a bigger fish, we do it all the time."

But the man refused to look up.

Pete slammed his fist on the table. "Talk to me!" Pain pulsed in his head.

"Hey, Pete, before you go offering him a deal," George said, "I forgot to tell you something."

"I'm listening."

"That guy who was selling grenades from his trunk?"

"Yeah, I know who you're talking about."

"Well, that guy made a positive ID on our mute friend here. He says this guy bought three grenades. One regular, two of those fire grenades."

"Incendiary," Pete corrected.

"Yeah, that."

"So you're the guy . . . look at me when I'm talking to you!" Pete yelled, sending another pulse of pain to his head. He closed his eyes until it passed. Pete opened his eyes and saw the guy still staring at the table. "Are you the guy who firebombed my daughter's car?"

Finally, the beefy Arab raised his head and met Pete's stare. He finally spoke, but said only one word, his baritone voice tinged with sarcasm. "Jihad."

"Oh, yeah," George said. "He did say that. But that's all he would say."

Pete leaned back in his chair and stared back. "That confirms it then. Jihad was painted on the sidewalks. I doubt this guy is our killer, but he was definitely being paid by him."

"Makes sense," George said.

"Listen," Pete said. "Tell us who you are. We can work something out."

The man lowered his chin to his chest and let out a deep sigh.

Pete looked over to George. "Nothing on the prints, right?"

"Nothing local. Still checking. FBI's on it too."

"What about Interpol? Did you fax the prints to them?"

"FBI said they would."

Pete's chair barked when he scooted it backward. He stood and rotated his neck, trying to release some of the tension. Finally, he put his hands on the table and leaned in closer to the man. "Listen, I know you think this is hopeless. I know you think you have nothing to live for, but it's not true. We can work something out. Please, for the love of God, talk to me. We can get you some help. But you have to help yourself first."

The man met his gaze. "Jihad," he said with a weary tone of resignation.

Chapter 39

Friday, January 6, 1989

"Thank you for coming on such short notice," Bishop McClure said. "As I mentioned on the phone, in four days, Cardinal Ragazzi is leaving Italy for a conference in Buenos Aires. He's scheduled to visit several other South American cities after that. I could suggest you meet him in South America, but he needs input from his scientific adviser, Professor Messina. Unfortunately, Dr. Messina can't leave town because he's a professor at the University of Turin. He has classroom obligations. So unless we want to wait another month, I suggested we meet before the cardinal leaves. Also, there is the matter of . . . .well, you know."

"The guy who's trying to kill me," Amari said.

"To be blunt, yes. Apparently, your discovery has hit a nerve. I informed the cardinal about your situation. In light of this, he felt he should meet with you as soon as possible."

"Before it's too late," she said.

The bishop paused to consider his words. "Once you've revealed your findings to the church, the cat will be out of the bag. Hopefully, whoever is stalking you won't see the need to keep you quiet anymore."

"That's right," Kevin said. "Why risk getting caught after that?"

"Precisely," Bishop McClure said. "Now, of course, that was the logic I used with the cardinal. But now that you have this man in custody, this is a moot point."

"It ain't as moot as you think it is," Kevin said. "They think this guy was a hired hitman. The real culprit's still out there."

"Oh, my," Bishop McClure said. "Then you really do need to talk to the cardinal as soon as possible."

"When do we leave?" she asked. "Soon, I hope."

Bishop McClure removed two envelopes from his drawer and dropped them on the desk in front of her. "An anonymous donor has paid for everything, plane tickets and hotel. You said you had passports, right?"

"I got mine for a trip to Canada," Kevin said. "Amari's been to Mexico."

"That's good," the bishop said. "Because you leave in three days, this Monday. Better get packing."

"We've already started packing," Amari said, referring to their move to Washington.

"Good. Your plane tickets and instructions are in those envelopes. It's not the greatest flight times, but it's the best we could do on such short notice. It's mostly at night, so at least you can sleep on the plane. A driver will meet you at Milan. He'll be holding up a sign for you when you get there, so keep your eyes open. It's about a two-hour drive to Turin. There's a half million lire for spending money. It's about two hundred and fifty dollars in American cash. Complements of the Diocese. Buy some souvenirs and do some sight seeing while you're there. Now, most of the people in Italy speak at least some English, so language shouldn't be a problem."

"I bought me a book on Italian," Kevin said. "Just in case we got the call. Do vay el bag no?" he asked in an exaggerated Southern accent.

"I think you mean, Dov'è il bagno," the bishop said in an articulated, Italian accent as he pointed to his private restroom. "You can use mine if you like."

"Kevin, I'm begging you," Amari said. "Please don't embarrass me over there."

Bishop McClure chuckled.

"But you don't talk Italian like I do," Kevin said and flashed a big toothy grin.

"Then I'll find someone who speaks English." She stood and tugged on his shirt. "Come on. You're embarrassing me here too."

Before they left, she turned to the bishop. "I don't know how to thank you."

"If this goes as I hope it will, the Church won't know how to thank you. God be with you. Every Catholic church in Arizona will be praying for you. Some of the Protestant churches as well. They're all behind you. May God bless your journey."

With their fingers laced together, they strolled toward Kevin's car in the long parking lot behind the cathedral. "I'm so excited," she said. "I've never even been on a plane. In three days, I'll be flying to Italy!"

They stopped when they reached the car. Wheels barked from behind. She dropped his hand and spun around. Lincoln Town car, coming in fast.

Chapter 40

Kevin grabbed Amari's arm and yanked her out of the way.

The Town Car barreled past, just missing them.

Without thought, training kicked in. Amari snatched her gun from her purse. She took the Isosceles Stance, feet shoulder width, knees flexed, both hands on weapon, out in front. She followed the car through the gun sight. In front of the car, a white brick wall. The shot was safe. Car, front sight and rear sight aligned. *Pop! Pop!*

The Town car broke left, then right again into traffic, angry tires screaming.

Another car sped after the Town Car. A black Mercedes. Two men in the front.

She caught her breath. "I think I hit his car. Did you see the Mercedes?"

"I did. I saw it at my apartment again. Once at work. I think they're tailing me too. You think maybe they're on our side?"

She slid the gun back into her purse. "If they were on our side they would have stopped to see if we were okay. The reason they sped out of here is because they saw my gun—just like they did when you had your gun out on the way to Los Alamos. I say they're up to no good. Otherwise, they wouldn't be afraid of getting shot."

"I don't know what to think," he said. "But we better go back inside and use the phone. Call your dad and tell him what happened."

Amari's dad showed up a few minutes after her call and his men immediately started working the crime scene.

"Amari, why didn't you tell me you were coming down here?" Dad asked. "You're supposed to have a police escort. I know we're short because of the flu, but I could have gotten a car."

"Kevin's with me," she said. "We both have guns."

"The escort is a deterrent. He wouldn't have tried this if a squad car was here."

"I'm sorry, Dad. I was just so excited when the bishop called. I let my guard down."

"All right, that settles it. As soon as you two get back from Turin, I want you both out of here," Dad said emphatically. "You can let your guard down then. I'll go to the U-haul place and rent a truck. I'll drive the truck and fly back when you unpack. I'll put both your apartments in my name. That way they won't be able to track you. You keep your Arizona tags and stay away from the DMV. I don't want any public record that says you're in Washington. Until then, I want the two of you spending the night in a hotel, both rooms in my name. We'll get a downtown high rise with interior corridors. I'll try to get an officer to stand guard, but if I can't, I'll do it myself."

****

Monday, January 9, 1989

The airplane was big as a ship. Amari couldn't believe such a huge chunk of metal could make it off the ground. Yet the plane taxied down the runway nonetheless. It rounded a corner and paused momentarily. Suddenly, the engines screamed to life. An unseen forced pulled her back into her seat. Faster, faster, and she sank deeper, deeper into her seat. The faster the plane accelerated, the harder she squeezed Kevin's hand.

"That kind of hurts," Kevin said over the noise. "Relax."

"Sorry, I've never flown before," she said, cringing.

The plane drove faster still down the runway. Seat tops in front of her bumped and vibrated, the overhead carry-on bins rattling. Suddenly, the cabin hushed and she sensed the plane rising upward, feeling the lift in her stomach. She chanced a look out the window and watched Tucson drift away as the plane rose higher. A noisy rumble came from below her.

Kevin uttered something to her, but she couldn't hear over the muffled roar of the jet engines, the rush of wind over metal. She tapped at her earlobe so he'd know she couldn't hear him.

"That's just the landing gear going up," he reassured her in a louder voice.

Once the unnerving process of getting off the ground subsided, her heart rate slowed and she felt an odd peace overtake her, a slight easing of her anxiety. She was out of Tucson now. Nobody was trying to kill her at 30,000 feet. Feeling strangely reassured, she loosened her grip on his hand, but held it gently instead, comforted by its soft warmth. Before long, she would present her case to the Catholic Church. She was still nervous about that, but at least the church didn't want her dead.

Kevin had helped her type out a formal paper that explained how and why a repair might have been carried out, and why such a patch would seem invisible to the naked eye. She included photographic evidence to prove her point. Then he would offer his theory as well, show them all his postulations and calculations about how neutron radiation had formed the extra carbon-14 that made the results invalid. Then he would inappropriately ask for cash to fund his research on chloride isotopes, or whatever he was talking about. It was over her head. Maybe he would ask for breakfast with Pope John Paul the next day. She wouldn't put it past him. Hopefully, they would know he was kidding. But either way, whatever the church decided to do with the information, whether they agreed to further tests or simply chose to keep the Shroud locked away and leave well enough alone, she could rest, knowing that she had done everything in her power. The rest was up to the Vatican—and to God.

****

It was two in the morning, New York time, and for the third time in eight hours, Amari felt the pull in her stomach as the air lifted the plane skyward. First out of Tucson, connecting in Salt Lake City, and now out of JFK. In another eight hours, they should be in Milan, four in the afternoon Italy time. They would meet the limo driver and two hours later they would be in Turin.

Kevin sat next to her, reading *Popular Science* from the tiny spotlight that shown from the base of the carry-on storage. She had the window seat and watched a billion lights that made up New York City fade into the distance. There was no turning back now.

****

Pete stood next to George, looking down into the ravine. It was a few hundred yards past a hairpin hilltop curve on Gates Pass road, just west of Tucson. A squad car blocked the right lane, and officers waved motorists past as cars took turns using the lane next to the mountain bank. The sun beat down on Pete as he watched the rescue squad rappel over sand, rock, and flat-leafed, prickly pear cactus. Slender Saguaro cactus stretched for the sky and Creosote bushes sprouted like weeds.

A truck driver had spotted it yesterday morning and thought it was a white garbage bag reflecting in the sun. On the way home last evening, he noticed the vultures. Bobcats and coyotes don't wear white, so he called the police. When police arrived, binoculars confirmed the dead body. The crime scene guys had gone down with ropes earlier to collect evidence, and now the rescue squad was pulling the body up the hill in an orange emergency basket.

When the basket came to the top, Pete stared down at the blanket-covered body with dread. He had a bad feeling about who laid underneath. George pulled the blanket back and revealed the face. A wave of nausea hit Pete when he saw the swollen, decomposing, vulture-plucked face of Anwar Rahal. He wore the same white tunic he had on when Pete arrested him the other day. He couldn't help but wonder if this kid would be alive if he hadn't brought the media's attention to him. Guilt added fuel to his nausea.

"I've seen enough," Pete said to George. "I think you should drive this time."

Chapter 41

Pete sat at his desk and massaged his jaw muscles to release the tension. One of the hardest things about his job was notifying family about the murder of a loved one. He had just completed that grim task with Dr. Rahal. Even though Rahal was the jerk who had mistreated his daughter, it was still an emotional drain to tell him his son was dead.

From what they knew so far, Anwar Rahal was shot in the back. He probably never knew what hit him. The reason he was shot was hypothetical, but it may be so Anwar would disappear after the last church fire and murder. Then the public would pin the crime on him, and by association, on Islam itself. If they had brought Anwar back in for questioning and he came up with another alibi or passed another lie detector test, the public would know it was a setup and, if anything, find sympathy for the falsely accused Muslim community. As it turned out, Anwar did not have an alibi for the time of the Christ Chapel murder. He had gone missing several hours earlier.

Pete leaned back in his chair. He wondered about Amari and Kevin. She'd called from the Milan airport and left a message on his answering machine around nine, but he had been out at Anwar's crime scene and missed the call. Everything was fine, she had said. Don't worry, she'd told him. But he did worry. After the Town Car tried to run his daughter down three days ago, he knew for certain the real killer wasn't sitting in that cell refusing to talk. The real killer was still out there. Fortunately, the news never broke about her trip. As far as he knew, the public at large was unaware that they were in Turin. And if the public didn't know, chances are the killer didn't know either—not unless he had other sources of information.

George rattled a piece of paper, startling Pete from his thoughts. "We got him!" George said. "FBI matched his prints with a green card application. We got an ID."

Pete and George hurried to the interrogation room and waited. Finally, two officers brought the prisoner in. Pete's anger swelled at the sight of him. Now that he wasn't weak from the flu, he suppressed the deep desire to beat the truth out of him with a police baton. But that approach was frowned upon by the department. "Sit him down," Pete said, a fake pleasant smile on his face. "And take the cuffs off. We may be here a while and I want him to be comfortable."

"You sure about this, detective?" the officer said. "He could be dangerous."

"You two can stay in here unless you got other business. I think he'll behave, won't you, Hasan?"

The prisoner closed his eyes and he let out a deep breath. He'd been caught. Game over.

"Go on," Pete said to the officers.

An officer removed the cuffs and set the prisoner in a chair on the other side of a table. He went back around the table and joined two more officers standing sentry by the door.

"Want some coffee?" Pete asked Hasan.

The prisoner rubbed the red handcuff marks on his wrists. "I take water," he finally said.

"Good, you can speak English," Pete said. "More than just 'jihad.'" He motioned for one of the officers to get some water. He held up his report and read it as he spoke. "FBI says your name is Hasan Ghaffari. Says you emigrated from Iraq two years ago. You live in a trailer next to your brother and two cousins off West Curtis Road. You know, your brother turned in a missing person's report. You should have called him. I bet he was worried."

The officer set a Styrofoam cup of water in front of Hasan. "Thank you," he said and drank the entire contents.

"You want some more?" George asked.

"No," Hasan said.

"So you emigrated from Iraq in '86. You've been working odd jobs, mostly painting. A 1974 Dodge van is titled to you, which I presume you use for your painting jobs."

"Yes."

"So how did you get here? One day you're painting houses, the next day you're trying to kill my daughter. It doesn't make any sense. The FBI report says they interviewed your brother. He says you believe in God, but you're no radical. So if your motives aren't religious, then it must be money."

Hasan broke pieces off the top of the Styrofoam cup, rolled them in his fingers, then dropped them into the cup. He did this for several more seconds, saying nothing.

"You're going away for a long, long, time," George said. "If you talk to us we can work a deal. Come on, man, just give us something."

"He's right," Pete said. "We can talk to the prosecutor. If you give us who hired you, maybe you can be free in two years."

"Then I deport back to Iraq," Hasan said and kept working on the cup. "Saddam men, they torture and kill me if I return. I take prison."

"We can work on that too," Pete said. "Maybe you do three years and you can stay. Who knows? We'll never find out if you don't give us anything. You gotta give us something to work with here."

Hasan pushed the cup aside. His eyes grew tense and his nostrils flared. "Saddam Hussein. He torment my family. I had to get out, or I die. I come to United States. My brother, he help me.

My wife, she die after Saddam men rape and torture her. My daughter, she still in Iraq. She twelve when I leave. She stay with uncle. He tell me she sick, tumor in head. She die in year if no remove it. We are Shia Muslim. Doctor in Iraq no operate. Even if willing, he no have knowledge. He kill her if he try."

"I see," Pete said. "So you were trying to make money to bring her here?"

"Saddam men say they free her for government fee. In American money, it five thousand dollars. I save one thousand. It enough for plane ticket, no more."

"This is good," George said.

"What's good about his dying daughter?" Pete asked.

"No, the prosecutor's daughter had some kind of cancer," George said. "I think he'd feel sorry for Hasan."

"That's a good point, George. What do you say, Hasan? You tell us who hired you and we cut your sentence and maybe give you political asylum."

"He say, if I arrest, he give money for daughter anyway. I only need to say I am terrorist. Say I am on jihad. If he get arrest, then he no help me."

"And you believe him?"

"If he no pay, I help police. He know this. It was deal."

"This guy is a brutal murderer. You can't trust him," Pete said. "Can't you see that? He's playing you for a fool."

"He is only hope to save my daughter."

Pete slammed his fist against the table. "What about *my* daughter? Tell me who hired you!"

Hasan's eyes fell back to the table. "You give me money. I tell you."

"You got it," Pete said without a moment's thought. "You give me who hired you, and I'll give you *six* thousand. But you got to tell me today."

"Pete," George said. "Isn't that against the rules? Can you do that?"

"I don't give a crap about the rules. I want this guy off my daughter. I'll give both my kidneys and one of yours if I have to." He focused back on Hasan. "I'll have to borrow against my retirement. It may take a few days, but I promise, I will give you six thousand dollars if you give this guy up."

Hasan locked his eyes on Pete's intense stare. "Are you Christian?"

"Devout," Pete said.

"Swear to Jesus you pay me, and I help you."

"I swear to Jesus, God the Father, the Holy Spirit, and to your Allah. Tell me who hired you and your daughter will live."

Hasan held out his hand. "Shake first."

A grin spread on Pete's face and he shook Hasan's hand. "Deal."

George mashed Play on the tape recorder and nodded for Hasan to begin.

"I no want to kill your daughter."

"I know that," Pete said.

"When I see her in house, when I point gun to her, and I see fear in her eye, I see Sabeen. My own daughter. The fear I see in your daughter eye, it is same fear I see in my daughter eye when Saddam's men come to house. I could not kill her. My Sabeen would not want me to."

"Is that why you wanted her to close her eyes?"

"I see Sabeen in her eyes. I prefer to take my own life."

"I saw that. Let me help, Hasan."

"At first, he say, just scare her. Tell her be silent about Turin Shroud. Maybe slap her, give her warning."

"That was at the library. But she said you never said anything to her."

Hasan pointed at the dent in his head. "She no give me chance. Head still hurt."

"That's what you get when you mess with Amari," Pete said. "Now go on."

"Then he say, she no listen. Follow them to Los Alamos. Kill her there. Both if you can. But I refuse."

"Okay, hold on a second," Pete said. "How did he know they were going to Los Alamos?"

"I do not know. I will not do it, so he say, he do it."

"That doesn't make any sense. If he's not afraid to draw his own blood, why does he even need to hire you in the first place?"

"He is small man. He say she recognize him. If he fail, he go to jail."

"And since he only wanted her roughed up, he had to use a big guy like you."

"Your daughter kill him, with bare hands. She almost kill me."

Pete cracked a smile. "I spent a lot of money on self-defense classes. I see it paid off."

"It did."

"So from what you're saying, if Amari would recognize him, then she knows him. Was he an Arab looking guy? Did his eyes look funny, like they were looking in two different directions?"

"He have beard, black glasses. I no see his eyes."

"Then it could still be Rahal," George said.

"Could be," Pete said, "but let him talk before we jump to any conclusions. So what next, Hasan? If he gave up on you, then how did you get back into the picture?"

"He contact me again. Say he have another job. But I refuse. Then he say if I no do job, he tell police I attack your daughter in library. He say, your daughter recognize me and I go to jail, then I deport to Iraq. Then Saddam kill me. And my daughter die."

"All right, I understand," Pete said. "You did what you had to do. Just tell me about the job."

"He give me three hundred dollars. He say buy three grenade from man selling. Then he say take grenade that make fire and burn her car. I watch long time before chance in parking garage."

"She loved that car, you know that?" Pete said.

"He make me do it."

"We'll have time for that later. Just tell me the rest."

"Then he say, police gone from house. Go now, before it too late. Or you go to jail. He give me gun and I go."

"Okay, Hasan. I think from what you told me we can work a deal with the prosecutor. But you still haven't told me who he is."

"He drives big, blue car. He has long beard. I think it not real. And he wear black glasses."

"Is that it?"

"No, he is Catholic priest."

"A *priest?* Are you sure?"

"I do not think he really priest. His clothes . . . not fit good. He *pretend* to be priest."

"That's our guy!" George said. "From the fire at Holy Ghost. It's the same guy the imam saw outside his mosque. That's why he stole the uniform before he torched the body. He wanted it for a disguise."

"Okay, I get it, George. Is that all you can tell me? Where did you first meet this priest? And better yet, who knew you were desperate for money?"

"I tell people."

"Then who was the last person you told before you were hired?"

Hasan pondered the question for a moment before he spoke. "I work painting a house. I tell the owner. He say if I do good job, he give me extra two hundred. I tell him I can use money and tell him about daughter."

"So this guy knew you were desperate. When were you approached by the priest?"

"Next week, after I finish painting, I am on way home and stop for gas. The priest talk to me there."

"And that's all you know?"

"I no see his face. He have black glasses and beard. I recognize his voice if you find him."

"All right, so tell me about your last job then. The guy who knew you needed money."

"He live in house near Silver Bell Road. His name is . . . Weiss. He is old man. I think he teach at college. He tell me, call him Albert."

"Albert Weiss. Do you remember the address?"

"I have it in home."

"Never mind, we'll use the phone book," Pete said. "Officers, you can take him back now." Pete started to leave, but turned back and said, "Thanks, Hasan. You did the right thing. If this pans out, check's in the mail."

Chapter 42

Amari and Kevin stepped off the plane and stretched their limbs as they stood in the crowded concourse gate. The Italian language yammered all around them as they contemplated their next move. Adrenaline-fueled excitement masked the exhaustion she felt from the sixteen-hour flight. This was Italy—where the Roman Empire began. It was a big deal for a girl who'd never been farther than Disneyland in California.

"We're not in Kansas anymore," Kevin said. "Over here." He pointed at a green sign. "*Uscita*. It means exit."

She followed him down the hall, dodging hurried passengers as they worked toward the baggage claim. He was a seasoned traveler, so she followed him blindly. They showed their passports at the customs desk, then went through a long hall that terminated in a massive baggage claim area. Once they retrieved their bags, they followed the *uscita* signs to a large bay with TAXI signs on the front door. Several men stood facing the exiting crowd, holding up white signs.

"Look for a priest," she said.

"That's him over there," he said and pointed.

A priest, in traditional black wardrobe, stood with a white sheet of copy paper with the names Amari and Kevin written on it.

They walked over to the priest and introduced themselves. He wasn't your typical priest. This one had a thick jaw, dark, heavy brows, and an athletic build. Blue veins bulged in his hands. He looked like Clark Kent, only without the glasses.

"I hope you had a nice flight. I'm Jacob," he said.

Amari was surprised at his American accent. "You're American?"

"Is it so obvious?" he said with a friendly smile. "My assignment is in Turin. Since my English is so good, they asked me to come get you. My Italian isn't bad either. I'm going to be your guide while in Turin."

"And our translator?" she asked.

"E il traduttore," the priest said. "And your translator."

"That won't be necessary," Kevin said. "I memorized I-tal-yon on the plane."

Amari made a weary face. "They said it's two hours by car to Turin?"

"To your hotel? More or less, depending on traffic."

"Then you're in for a long two hours."

****

Once they got to Turin, Father Jacob drove them around town, showing them all the local landmarks. The sun had set by then, but the streets were well illuminated, and Amari got a good sense of the place. Turin was a mix of old world charm and modern annoyance. Motor scooters buzzed back and forth. Roman style buildings with ornate trim and balconies lined the streets. Overhead, a canopy of electric wire cluttered the skyline to provide power for street cars.

A gentle rain had started to fall when Father Jacob stopped briefly in front of St. John the Baptist Cathedral. Amari was in awe.

"Get a closer look. I'll stay with the car," Father Jacob said and handed Kevin an umbrella.

An open space of paver stone was in front of the church, and still more contact electric wires for the trolley stretched overhead. They got out and walked under the umbrella to the foot of some steps that led to the front doors. The massive façade glowed grayish white, bathed in floodlights. A large, carved wooden door was in the center. The Latin letters DO RVVERE CAR S CLE were engraved above the door, part of an elaborately carved marble door frame. Two smaller doors of similar design flanked the large center door. A gigantic bell tower stood off to the left.

To think, just inside, was the cloth that covered Jesus, God made flesh. God's very blood in its fibers, his image etched onto those fibers, the greatest testimony to the most important event in history. And it was right behind those walls.

Kevin reached for her hand. "That's pretty neat, ain't it?"

She squeezed his hand, but words escaped her.

Lightning streaked the night sky and thunder clapped, startling her from her trance. The rain intensified, angrily pelting the top of the umbrella.

"We better go," Kevin said.

They hurried back to the safety of the car and climbed inside.

"That's odd," Father Jacob said. "We don't usually have thunderstorms in January."

"I hope God's not trying to tell us something," Kevin said with a smirk.

"Don't even joke about that," Amari said. "I just hope it's not raining tomorrow."

"I know, I was hoping to do some sightseeing after talking to the cardinal."

"Me too," she said as she craned her neck, watching the church disappear behind other buildings. She made a note of the way back to the cathedral so they could go back to their room after the meeting, put on their street clothes and walking shoes, and do the tourist thing before leaving for Tucson the next day.

When they got to the hotel lobby, Amari felt like she was in a palace. Father Jacob spoke with the registration desk as she and Kevin gawked. An intricately molded ceiling soared overhead. The floor was complex, with colorful patterns of marble. Lavish red drapes hung over massive windows and elaborate flower bouquets sat atop carved, marble pedestals.

"Fancy," Kevin said. "Mmm, mmm, mmm. We have arrived."

"I wish my mother could see this," she said. "She dreamed of coming to Europe someday. She would be so happy for me. Someday in heaven, I'll tell her all about this."

A bellhop set their bags on a luggage cart and Amari, Kevin, and Father Jacob followed him to their room.

When the bellhop opened the door, they stepped inside.

"Holy, moly," Kevin said. "It's like we won the lottery."

White walls with detailed wooden molding contrasted a vibrant blue oriental rug. The yellow curtains were like fine tapestries. Red velvety couches and chairs were against the walls and a gold painted desk sat in front of the window.

"Now, since you aren't married," Father Jacob said, "this suite has separate bedrooms. Why don't you shower and change out of your travel clothes and meet me downstairs for dinner?"

"I don't think we got enough *lire* for the restaurant I saw downstairs," Kevin said.

"Complements of the church, Dr. Brenner. This is an all-expense paid trip. Even this room is under my name, paid for by the church."

"The bishop said this was paid for by an anonymous donor," Amari said.

"He made the donation to the church. Then the church signed the checks."

"So who is this donor?" Kevin asked.

"He said anonymous," Amari said. "That means he doesn't know."

Jacob gave a friendly smile. "I'll meet you downstairs in an hour."

After she and Kevin had cleaned up, they found themselves in one of those restaurants with several forks, sitting across from Father Jacob. She wore a simple cream-colored blouse with shoulder pads while Kevin wore khaki pants, dockside boat shoes, and a blue blazer with a maroon bow tie.

When the waiter offered water, he bowed slightly and spoke English. "With gas or without?" he asked.

"Sparkling water or plain," Father Jacob clarified.

"Well, I don't know about the gas," Kevin said with a satisfied grin. "I haven't eaten yet. Ask me in a few hours."

Amari crimped her lips to keep from laughing out loud. She considered kicking him with the sharp point of her shoe but figured she'd let him have his fun. It wasn't like anyone knew them there.

After dinner, Father Jacob escorted them back to their room.

"I know you've got to be exhausted," Father Jacob said. "Get a good night's sleep. I'll pick you up first thing in the morning. It will be a breakfast meeting, so there is no need to wake up early. Your meeting with the cardinal is at 8:00. What you are wearing now would be fine. I'll meet you out front with the car at 7:30."

"That sounds perfect," Amari said. "Thank you so much for everything. We'll see you at 7:30."

Father Jacob shut the door on his way out. She frowned at Kevin standing there in his blue blazer and silly bow tie. "Well, that was embarrassing. Food was good, though." She went over to him and straightened his tie. "Actually, I thought you were funny. Don't ever change." She pinched him on the cheek.

"What you see is what you get."

"We better get to bed. We've got a big day tomorrow." She put her arms around him and gazed into his eyes. "We're really here, Dr. Kevin Brenner. About to make history."

"Maybe so," he said and kissed her on the lips. He withdrew and hiked his brows playfully. "You think Father Jacob would come back up here and marry us real fast? I don't want to sin the night before we meet the cardinal."

She released her embrace. "You're terrible, Kevin." She turned and made a suggestive glide toward her room, exaggerating the sway of her hips, peering back, eyeing him playfully. "And I'm going to lock my door, just in case you get any ideas."

Chapter 43

Pete drove while George read directions from a road map. They took I-10 to West Grant, then took a right onto Silver Bell Rd. When they arrived at Neosha Street, which was barely more than a dirt road, the sun had just set over the mountain range west of Tucson. Blue light glowing from the mountain peak faded into the darkness to the east, where stars made their first appearance. They drove slowly until they found the right street number on the mail box, then turned right into a gravel road with a thicket of saguaro cactus in the center of a circular drive. The home was a flat roofed, tan brick rancher. Another section of driveway led around to the back of the house.

Pete had considered coming by in the morning, but Weiss would probably be at work. Besides, even though he'd asked the bishop to keep the news about Amari's trip to Turin a secret, just on the off chance the killer might have some insider information and follow her there, he wasn't wasting any time. He'd already looked up the Turin police department's number and he wouldn't hesitate to call if there was the slightest chance his daughter was still in danger.

Pete rang the doorbell and waited as George scanned the scene, looking for anything remotely incriminating. After a few moments, a lanky elderly man with bifocal glasses and combed over hair came to the door. "Are you Albert Weiss?" Pete asked.

"Yes, I'm Dr. Weiss. May I help you, gentlemen?"

Pete flashed his identification. "I'm detective Pete Johnston, and this is my partner, George Sanchez. Do you mind if we ask you some questions?"

"Certainly," Dr. Weiss said. "Please come in." He led them to a distressed-leather couch in the den. Book shelves lined the walls with hundreds of books, everything from heavy science books to Shakespeare.

"May I offer you gentlemen something to drink?"

"No, we won't be long," Pete said. "I know it's getting late already, so I don't want to keep you."

"It's no trouble at all. I want to keep the streets safe. Tell me, how can I be of service?"

"I understand you teach at the university."

"I used to. I currently serve as the professor emeritus. I'm retired from teaching, but still involved in the operations more or less."

"So what department do you work? From the looks of your books, I'd say something in science."

"The physics department."

"You don't say? You must know Dr. Brenner then? And Dr. Rahal?"

"Dr. Brenner, of course. I had a hand in hiring him. Brilliant young experimental physicist."

"I know the guy. He's sharp, all right."

"You know Dr. Brenner too?" Dr. Weiss said, his face registering surprise. "It's a small world."

"Boy, it is, isn't it?" Pete knew it wasn't that small. This was no coincidence. His gut told him he was about to crack this case wide open. It was time to push a little harder. "What do you think about Dr. Rahal?"

"Honestly, I try not to think of him."

"I've met the guy. I see what you mean."

"Hey this is a big coincidence," George spoke up. "You know, you being a professor at the physics lab."

Dr. Weiss gave George a curious stare. "Coincidence?"

"Sure," Pete said. "Dr. Rahal is a suspect for the attack of one Amari Johnston."

"You said your last name is Johnston," Dr. Weiss said. "Any relation?"

"She's my daughter."

"Then I see where she gets her spirit. I've met the young lady. In fact, I helped convince Dr. Rahal to let her see the Shroud samples. She is very persistent. Misguided persistence in this case, but still I admire her tenacity. Is that what you came to talk to me about? The attack on your daughter?"

"It is, actually. Now, don't get me wrong, I don't see you as a suspect. I'm more interested in the guy you hired to paint your house. He's the guy who led me to you."

"You must be referring to Hasan. Did he get into some kind of trouble?"

"You could say that."

"I'm afraid I don't know much about the man. I have his address on an invoice if that will help."

"We already know his address. We're more interested in something he told you. You know, he has a daughter in Iraq. She's dying and he wants to get her here for medical care. Only he can't because he doesn't have the money. You could say he's desperate for cash."

"Yes, he did tell me that."

"So the question is, did you tell anybody else this information?"

"Let's see," Dr. Weiss said and rubbed at the stubble on his chin. "My grandson was home at the time. He may have overheard us."

"That must be him," Pete said, pointing to the side table by Dr. Weiss's recliner.

Dr. Weiss glanced over at the photo. "Yes, that's Jeremy. He's my grandson."

"Mind if I see that picture?" Pete asked.

"Certainly," Dr. Weiss said and handed him the picture frame.

"He sure does have some blue eyes," Pete said.

George leaned over for a peek. "Looks like one of those Alaskan Husky's eyes, don't it?"

"He gets those from his mother," Dr. Weiss said. "Jeremy's father was my son. Unfortunately, my son died shortly after Jeremy was born. Jeremy's mother remarried a year later."

"I'm sorry to hear about your son," Pete said. "That must have been very difficult. So how did he die, if you don't mind my asking?"

"Suicide, I'm afraid. He was having some, well, problems."

"Then I'm real sorry to hear that," Pete said. "Was he depressed?"

"That among other issues. He had psychological problems. But I know you didn't come to discuss my son. He's been dead for twenty years."

"Sorry, I get a little off track sometimes," Pete said. "Then again, sometimes you have to go off the trail to find the right evidence."

"If you wish to pursue this evidence, then I would like to see a warrant. I don't want to discuss my son. The memories are too painful."

The air got tense, so Pete changed the subject. "I understand, Dr. Weiss. Again, I'm very sorry for your loss." Pete looked back at the grandson's picture. "I think I saw your grandson when I interviewed Dr. Rahal. He was wearing a lab coat. I assume he works there. Or maybe he's a student."

"He's a full-time student and works there part time," Dr. Weiss said. "He has an interest in physics, so I got him a job as a research technician. That way he could learn the ropes before he committed himself."

"That's a smart move," Pete said. "He do okay in school?"

"He passes his courses, I suppose."

"You must be pretty close to help him so much."

"I'd say I am. He lived under my roof for five years, until he went to college and got an apartment near campus."

"You help him with college? UA is pretty expensive. I ought to know."

"I give him money for tuition. He gets $10,000 a year, and he supplements his cost of living with his job at the lab."

"Ten grand a year, huh? That's generous."

"I don't want him to graduate and have student loans. Besides, I'm a widower, so he is the sole heir to my estate. The money will go to him sooner or later."

"That's good logic. I'd do the same thing if I were you and had the money. So what happened to his parents? I mean his mother and stepfather."

"It's another tragic story, I'm afraid. His stepfather died in a house fire. It destroyed Jeremy's home. He and his mother, Belinda, came to live with us after the fire." Deep sadness dented Dr. Weiss's face.

"That's rough," George said. "You've been through a lot."

"It wasn't all bad. The death of Belinda's husband was a blessing. The tragedy was Jeremy's mother. Shortly after she moved in with us, she contracted the flu."

George smacked Pete on the arm. "You know what that feels like, don't you, Pete?"

"You know I do," Pete said.

"I see you survived," Dr. Weiss said. "Belinda was not so fortunate. She went into the hospital and died a week later from pneumonia."

"I'm sorry to hear that," Pete said.

"Yeah, me too," George said.

"Jeremy never fully recovered, I'm afraid. To this day, he is afraid to shake hands, afraid of the germs."

"He's a germaphobe?" George asked.

"That is a crude term for his condition, but I suppose he is."

"We all got our thing, I guess," George said. "I hate spiders. You don't seem so sad about your son-in-law."

"That's because he was a tyrant. To be blunt, I'm glad he's dead. Belinda should never have married the man. If Jeremy's father hadn't died, she never would have. And Jeremy would not have been abused by that man's hand for eleven long years before he came to live with me."

"A tyrant, huh?" Pete said. "Abusive you say?"

"He was a religious fanatic. A zealot of the worst kind. He beat that child without mercy. He made Jeremy memorize entire sections of the Bible. He would beat him with a belt for the slightest infraction of Biblical law. Yet he, himself, was an abusive drunk. Not very Christian, if I understand the doctrine."

"Not all Christians are like that," Pete said. "Sounds like he only thought he was. Got what was coming to him. So what caused the fire, if you don't mind my asking?"

"They believe he fell asleep while smoking. Passed out drunk, I suspect."

"And they know this for sure?"

"It was from Jeremy's testimony."

"That's all they went by? Just Jeremy's testimony?"

"It was a small town, with scant investigative resources."

"That's interesting, don't you think, George?"

"It is," George said.

"Was Jeremy friends with Anwar Rahal?" Pete asked. "They're about the same age and both students at the university. Maybe Anwar came around the lab sometimes to talk with his father."

"I wouldn't use the word friends."

"I take it they didn't get along?"

"Apparently, Anwar Rahal is a religious terrorist. A pyromaniac, murdering extremist, if what I hear on the news is correct. Naturally, they didn't see eye to eye."

"Did you know Anwar was found dead this morning? It hasn't been made public yet. We found him not far from here. Just over that hill."

"Oh, my," Dr. Weiss said and sank back into his recliner as the news settled. "I didn't know about that. It must have been suicide then. Perhaps he couldn't live with his conscience."

"We have other theories," Pete said.

"At any rate, I must remember to offer Dr. Rahal my condolences."

"I take it you don't like the guy," George said. "So why be nice to him?"

"Social etiquette, of course."

"You know, my daughter says Jeremy doesn't like Dr. Rahal either," Pete said. "She says Jeremy warned her to stay away from Rahal because he was a religious fanatic, that he was dangerous."

"That sounds like Jeremy. I'm afraid the trauma with his stepfather has made him a tad paranoid when it comes to religious people."

"So religion didn't stick with Jeremy," Pete said. "Despite his stepfather's efforts."

"I made certain it didn't," Dr. Weiss said in a scolding tone.

"I take it you're not a religious man," Pete said.

"Of course not," Dr. Weiss said sharply, his face turned pink. "I am a man of science. Religion is folly. A weak-minded person's escape from reality. Fairy tales, as far as I'm concerned."

Pete glanced over in time to see George's eyes flash wide. Did this man just say that? Either he had no concern over who he offended or his feelings came from angry resentment and his response was a knee-jerk reaction. Pete had obviously hit a nerve. Maybe he'd irritate that nerve a little more and see where it led. "I call myself a Christian, Dr. Weiss. Are you calling me weak-minded?"

"Surely, detective, you can appreciate the harm religion causes. All the wars that have been fought over religion? Powerful men use it as a tool for persuasion, not for good."

"I see a lot of people getting fed because of it, getting a roof over their head. And a lot of people finding hope. Guess you got a different perspective. You teach your perspective to Jeremy?"

"I had to undo the damage done by his stepfather. Naturally, it wasn't easy. We even resorted to calling him by his middle name instead of his first. His first name is Robert. His stepfather called him Robby. Calling him Jeremy helped him put his dreadful past behind him. It helped teach him a new way of looking at things. A new reality, if you will."

"And that seemed to help?"

"I think so. It took years, but he seems to have come around."

"He sounds like a tormented soul."

"Sadly."

"You ever take Jeremy to a shrink?" George asked.

"I had considered that, but he seemed to be responding to my methods. As long as it worked, why change the formula? You saw what the psychiatrists did to my own son. I wasn't going to make the same mistake twice."

The more Pete heard, the louder the alarms rang. Most serial killers came from abusive homes. That Jeremy kid could well be the psychopath behind all this. "Are you sure Jeremy used that ten grand a year for tuition?" Pete asked. "Have you seen his grades? How do you know he really goes to class?"

"You're not suggesting he used that money for drugs, are you?"

"I wish that's all I'm suggesting," Pete said.

"Is Jeremy good on a motorcycle?" George asked.

"He uses one every day. Occasionally, he comes over to use my old car if he needs groceries, or perhaps if the weather is bad."

Pete scooted forward on the couch. "What kind of car would that be?"

"It's just an old Lincoln Town Car," Dr. Weiss said dismissively. "Rather than trade it in, I kept it for his use."

Pete and George came off the couch at the same time. This was the guy. It had to be. Dr. Weiss stood with them and met Pete's stare. "Is something wrong?"

"Does Jeremy have a passport?" Pete asked.

"We occasionally visit my family in Germany."

"Ever go down to Italy?"

"Occasionally."

"Where can we find Jeremy? I want to know where he is, *right now.*"

"I haven't heard from him. I just tried calling, but he didn't answer. Is he in some kind of trouble?"

"I need to see that Town Car. Can you tell me where it is?"

"It's just around back. Jeremy keeps a blue tarp over it. He wants to protect the finish from the sun."

Pete and George left Dr. Weiss without another word. They retrieved two flash lights from their car and hurried around the house. A blue tarp laid on top of a vehicle with rocks to hold it down against the wind. Pete went over and tossed the rocks into the yard. George ripped the tarp off, sending dust and dirt into a cloud. Pete waved away the dust and shined his flashlight on the car. The driver's side of the car had scratches and a long, shallow dent.

"He's been in an accident," Pete said.

"Like the kind you get when you run someone off the road," George said.

Pete went around to inspect the back, while George opened the driver door and pulled out a newspaper.

Pete moved his light side to side on the trunk. "George, we got bullet holes! Two of them!"

"Then you're not going to like this," George said as he read the newspaper by flashlight. "This is the Campus Newspaper. Says here the reporter talked to the secretary at St. Augustine Cathedral. Says Amari is going to speak with the cardinal in Turin. Oh, crap, Pete. Jeremy was reading this!"

Chapter 44

Amari stepped onto the sidewalk in front of the hotel lobby. Cars and trucks clogged the streets and motor scooters buzzed by, traveling within the narrow space between vehicles. A cold breeze bit her skin and she tied her overcoat's sash tightly around her sweater. She opted for casual flats instead of heels in case she had to do a lot of walking.

Sunlight broke through the clouds and warmed her cheeks. Instead of comfort, the sun made her feel uneasy, more exposed in the light, an easy target. She imagined every window was a sniper's nest. Even though she was thousands of miles removed from the killer in Tucson, she couldn't shake the anxiety that followed her to Italy. The only way she would let her guard down was if the killer were dead or in jail. Kevin didn't seem worried. He just stood there with his blue blazer and bow tie, totally aloof, clutching the black briefcase that held their research.

Almost there, she told herself. Once she made her pitch to the cardinal, the killer would back off. Maybe her dad would catch him. And surely, he had no idea she was in Turin.

Just then, Father Jacob pulled up to the curb in his black Alfa Romeo sedan.

"Here we go," Kevin said. He went to the curb and opened the back door for her.

"Such a gentleman," she said.

"Careful with the storm drain," he warned her. "You'll need to step over it to get in."

She made a long step from the curb and into the car. He closed the door, went around to the other side, and let himself in.

"Are you ready for this?" Father Jacob said from the front.

"Ready as we'll ever be," she said.

Glass shattered. Kevin's window exploded inward, tempered glass shards flying. Amari recoiled in defense. Something hard and heavy struck her thigh. An object the size and color of a bumpy avocado laid in the seat next to her. An avocado with a handle. A *grenade!*

"Kevin! Look out!" she screamed.

"Open your door!" he yelled back.

She pulled the lever and shoved the door open. She started to climb out, but he fell atop of her and lunged the grenade through the open door, into the storm drain. He slammed her door and grabbed her into his lap, covering her head with his arms.

A sound like thunder exploded from below. The car shuddered.

"What was that?" Father Jacob called from the front.

"He knows we're here!" she screamed. "Kevin, we have to get out of here!"

Father Jacob revved his engine. "Put on your seat belt!"

The car lurched into traffic. Tires screeched, followed by the sound of violently crushed metal and the bite of breaking glass. The car flew back against the curb. Father Jacob's head rested against the steering wheel, his hand holding the side of his face.

"We gotta go!" Kevin said and clutched her hand.

He pushed through his door and pulled her out with him. They stepped around the car that had collided with theirs and dodged traffic as they went to the opposite sidewalk. She glanced over to see Father Jacob with a bloody gash on his head. He thrust his finger in a panic, pointing to the narrow alley between buildings.

He was saying something. Her ears rang from the blast. What was he saying? Run, he was saying—*run!*

She tugged Kevin into the narrow, paver-stone ally—too narrow for traffic, away from the street. Balconies hung over graffiti-stained storefronts along the path.

"The cathedral is this way," she said.

A man dressed in black hurried toward them, locking alert eyes with Amari. He had kinky brown hair and a stubby beard—the man from the Mercedes. And he had a gun!

"Kevin, in here!" She shoved him into a small grocery. She pulled him through the produce section, then cut right, stopping behind a tall wine shelf.

"What are—"

She cupped his mouth with her hand. "Shhh!"

"Why are you shushing me?" he whispered through her fingers.

"That's the guy from the Mercedes," she whispered frantically. "The guy who's been following me."

"Are you sure?"

"I'll never forget that face. And he has a gun!"

Kevin's eyes darted behind her, then widened in panic.

Amari spun round.

It was him, gun tucked into his belt. He placed his hand on her shoulder. "You need to come with me," he said forcefully.

Her response was immediate. She clenched her fingers and brought her fist to her forearm. She flung her elbow back, then lunged it upward into his chin. His teeth clacked and he fell backward into a shelf full of wine bottles. Glass smashed against the floor sending red liquid exploding outward.

"Let's go!" She grabbed Kevin's hand and pulled him back to the alley.

"Let's cut through that restaurant," he said. "We'll go out the back door and lose him."

"Good idea," she said.

They ran across the alley and in through the door. A clatter of Italian words and clanking silverware sounded in the room as patrons ate breakfast. Holding a food tray, a waiter pushed backward through swinging double doors, out of the kitchen, and into the dining hall. They rushed into the kitchen. A chef chopped onions on a cutting board. He paused and looked up.

"Porta posterior?" Kevin asked.

He pointed his knife to an unmarked door and then went back to chopping.

They pushed through the door and hit daylight, but soon found themselves trapped in a rectangular prison of stone walls. It was a central courtyard between buildings. Windows with iron balcony railing looked down. TV antennas littered the roofline. Several cars were parked up against the walls. An arched, truck sized entrance led back out into the street.

"This way," she said. "It takes us back out, the next street over. Look for the park and we find the cathedral."

Kevin stopped her advance. "Hold on a second, shouldn't we call the police?"

"Have you seen any? Do you see a phone?"

"We can find one, back in the restaurant."

"Kevin, what is the most secure building in Turin?"

"The police station?"

"And where is this police station?"

"Heck if I know."

"The *cathedral*. Security there is super tight because of the Shroud." She looked behind her to make sure they weren't being followed. "Besides, we have an appointment, remember?" She moved toward the arched exit.

"I think they might understand," he said, chasing after her. "We almost got blown up!"

"So we need to get there, where it's safe."

"I am kind of hungry," he said as they reached the arched exit. "Father Jacob said they'd have breakfast."

"You want breakfast, at a time like this?"

"I had pasta for dinner" he whined. "It's not very filling."

"Kevin, this is no time for jokes."

A motor scooter buzzed by as they reached the sidewalk.

"Can you see the park? It's right behind the cathedral," she said, checking behind her again to make sure they weren't being trailed by the man in the Mercedes.

"I think it's this way," he said and pointed. "I can see the hedge."

They jogged toward the park. Passersby on the sidewalk cast odd looks at the two tourists running down the sidewalk in church clothes. They reached the park. It was bordered with equally spaced red brick pedestals, hedge bushes in between.

"I see the dome," she said. "This way."

They ran through the park entrance, under the spotty shade of leafless trees in winter, and followed a sidewalk toward the cathedral. She looked behind her again. The coast seemed clear. Almost there. They rounded a circular water fountain and cut down a path between two lawns. They followed the path under a small entrance that lead to the cathedral grounds. A large piazza opened before them, surrounded by imposing building walls on three sides. An ornate iron fence blocked the main entrance. A man swept garbage into a dust pan, but other than him, there wasn't a soul around so early in the morning. Up ahead, three arched doorways revealed a tunnel-like passage through the building, leading to the front of the cathedral.

They jogged into the arched underpass and stopped under a hanging light fixture to get their bearings. On the other side of the tunnel, they noticed a priest getting off a scooter.

"We'll ask this priest," Kevin said and waited for him to approach.

The priest wore a black overcoat and a beard hung down to his chest. His eyes were hidden behind dark sunglasses. He ambled into the tunnel and met them in the dark shadow from the building overhead.

"Father," Amari said and stopped to catch her breath. "Please, we need your help. We have a meeting with the cardinal. Can you help us?"

The priest stared back through his dark glasses. He gave no response.

"I'll talk Italian to him," Kevin said. "Ci può aiutare per favore. Or something like that. Capire?"

Though his face was obscured by sunglasses and beard, there was something vaguely familiar about him—the curve of his cheeks, his short stature, his posture.

"I would be glad to help you," the priest said in English. That voice, so familiar. "Let me take this beard off first. It really itches." The priest snatched a fake beard off his face and let it fall. He then tossed his glasses onto paver stone.

"Jeremy!" Kevin said. "What are you doing here? You ain't no priest."

"You always were the smart one, Dr. Brenner."

Chapter 45

"Oh, the irony," Jeremy uttered. "Don't you see, Kevin, I'm Father Jeremy. Father is the one who started all this. And now Father Jeremy is going to finish it."

Amari moved to Kevin's side. "Jeremy, what are you talking about?"

Jeremy snatched a silver .38-revolver from his inside coat pocket. He moved several steps back. "You keep your distance, Amari. I've seen what you can do with those pretty little hands of yours."

She tensed when she saw the gun, her heart hammering. She had to disarm him, or at least stall him until help came. "Jeremy, why?"

Jeremy's ice blue eyes flashed with livid fury. "You think I wanted this? I'm doing this for the good of the world. It's the least of evils."

"Jeremy," she pleaded and took a step forward. Just a little closer. She'd practiced the disarming move. Maybe Kevin could distract him. It was their only chance. "This is crazy. Put the gun down."

Jeremy stepped farther away. "I told you to back off about the Shroud. I warned you, but you wouldn't listen."

"You warned me about Rahal. You said *he* was dangerous."

"You brought this on yourself!"

"But you hate Rahal. My fight was against him. Why are you doing this to *me*?"

"Religion is a virus, Amari. Can't you see that? It infects the minds of the weak. Powerful men use this to their advantage. War after war have been fought over it. The Spanish Inquisition? The

Salem Witch Trials? Terrorists?" Jeremy's face reddened and his head trembled with rage. "And my father!"

"Jeremy," she said. "I don't know what your father did to you."

"*Step*father," he snapped back.

"Okay, stepfather. But what he and some other people do are the exception, not the rule. There's another side to the coin."

"She's right," Kevin said. "When there's good, there's evil, when there is God, there's the devil. What you're describing is evil, not the good preached by Christ."

"He's right," Amari said. "Evil isn't the Bible's fault. The Bible just warns us it's there. For most people religion is a wonderful thing. It offers hope."

"For you!" Jeremy spat. "Not for everyone."

"And how are you changing that?" she asked. "By killing people and burning down churches?"

"It's like a line of dominos. All I've got to do is knock the first few down."

"Jerry, I know you're trying to start a holy war," Kevin said. "Maybe you think Christians and Muslims will finish each other off. But that's never going to happen. Not because of what you're doing. You're acting crazy."

"Crazy? You think I'm crazy? It took just one bullet to start World War I—the assassination of Franz Ferdinand. I've already killed four. Five if you count my stepfather. The two of you make seven. That gives me seven times the odds. Besides, it's already started. Have you seen the news in Tucson? All it takes is a spark to cause a fire. And it was going so well, until you two came along."

"Because of what we're doing with the Shroud?" she asked.

"Of course, because of the Shroud. If somehow you're right," Jeremy said and pointed to the cathedral. "If you somehow prove that old rag came from Jesus, how many more people will convert to Christianity? You'll tip the scale. It won't be a fair fight anymore. Those people I killed would have died in vain. It would be cruel to let that happen. Un-Christian, don't you think?"

"Jeremy, listen. I'm not that smart," she pleaded. "If I figured this out, somebody else will. It's just a matter of time. Killing us only turns us into martyrs. It will only bring the world's attention to the Shroud. Just like the Christian martyrs helped spread Christianity."

"You don't think I thought of that?" Jeremy said. "You think I came all this way just to kill you? If I tried a little harder, I could have done that in Tucson." He reached into his coat pocket and pulled out a cylinder shaped can with a curved handle. He displayed it proudly in his hand. "This is a military incendiary grenade. This thing will burn a hole in an army tank. After I kill the two of you, I'm going to kill the Shroud. I'll finish what that fire started in 1532," he said and slid the grenade back into his pocket.

"Jeremy, you're delusional," she said. "They have armed guards in there."

"I've got a gun too. Besides, I'm a priest, remember? They're not going to shoot me. They'll be dead before they know what hit them."

A man rushed toward them from the plaza—the man in the Mercedes. He aimed his gun and yelled, "Drop it, or I'll shoot!"

In a flash, Jeremy spun around and shot. A bullet pelted the man's chest. He fell backward, his gun skittering across the stone floor, inches from Amari's foot. She eyed the gun, calculating her chances. Jeremy rushed forward and kicked the gun out of reach.

"Nobody invited you to this party," he said to the man who laid on the ground, clutching his chest. "Don't make me waste any more of my bullets on you."

"Leave them alone," the Mercedes man pleaded, his voice strained because of the pain. "The police are on their way. If you leave now, you might escape."

A rush of realization. Those men in the Mercedes. They weren't stalking her. They were *protecting* her.

"Then I'd better hurry and finish this," Jeremy said, keeping his eyes fixed on her and Kevin.

Jeremy cocked the revolver. Amari braced herself. *Oh, God, please . . .*

A gun cracked. Jeremy jerked his arm back and his gun toppled to the ground.

Kevin quickly stooped down and grabbed the gun. He brought Jeremy into the sites. "Don't move, Jerry!"

Suddenly, Father Jacob ran into the underpass with his own gun drawn.

Jeremy steadied his wrist with the other hand. Red arterial blood gushed from the bullet hole in his wrist. "Ahhhhhoowww!" Jeremy wailed, his cry a haunting echo in the building-walled piazza.

"You're not the only one pretending to be a priest," Father Jacob declared, keeping his gun pointed at Jeremy.

"That really hurts!" Jeremy howled, trembling with pain. The tears in his eyes seemed to magnify their ruthless blue hue. The horror in his eyes morphed into hateful resolve. With his good hand, he pulled the grenade from his coat pocket, pulled the pin with his teeth, and cocked his arm to throw.

Chapter 46

A shot rang from Father Jacob's gun. The bullet pierced Jeremy's side. He hunched over from the pain and dropped to his knees. With his fist tightly around the grenade, he reflexively brought the hand down and applied pressure to his wound, his fingers still tight around the handle. Once he released the handle, the grenade would ignite within seconds.

"You . . . you ruined everything," Jeremy uttered. His black shirt glistened wet as blood spread from his wound. His face grew pale. He drew in a long breath and exhaled. His eyes seemed to lose focus and his tense face relaxed. He fell forward with a thud, atop the grenade.

"Amari, get back," Kevin said and pulled her behind a support pillar.

There was no blast. Just a spitting sound. She peered around the column. Smoke billowed from under Jeremy's corpse, white sparks shooting out the sides. He pulled her back around the column and drew her face to his chest so she couldn't see the blazing carnage. "It's over now. For real this time. Everything's going to be okay."

She pulled free and chanced another glimpse of the terrifying scene. Flame erupted from Jeremy. The grenade hissed and sparked under his flaming torso. Two Italian police officers ran forward but kept a careful distance.

"Let's go," he said and ushered her around to the front steps of the church.

They stood in front of the church as more police rushed in, one carrying a fire extinguisher. Amari was stunned, staring into the square in front of St. John the Baptist Cathedral as she sorted what had just happened. Her eyes drifted heavenward and she mouthed the words *thank you.*

A moment later, Father Jacob and the man from the Mercedes joined them at the steps. Father Jacob had a bloodied gash on the left side of his forehead.

Amari rushed to the Mercedes man. "Are you okay?"

"I'll be sore tomorrow," he said and pulled back his shirt to reveal a bullet proof vest. "Knocked the breath out of me, but I'm okay. What about you?"

"I am now," she said. "Father Jacob? Were you the other man in the Mercedes? The driver? I got a look at him, but I never saw *your* face."

"That was me," he said.

"Why didn't you guys tell us you were on our side?" Kevin asked.

"Our boss ordered us not to," Father Jacob said.

"And who exactly is your boss?" Kevin asked.

"After you meet with the cardinal, I'll introduce you to him. As for me, my name is Jacob Bonelli. My parents are Italian, but I was born in Fresno, California. Obviously, I'm no priest, but I did consider becoming one until I was drafted for the Vietnam War. My partner here is Mitch Parker. We served together in Special Forces over there."

Mitch rubbed at his stubby beard. "I think you might have cracked a tooth," he said to Amari. "We could have used someone like you back in Nam."

"Sorry about that," she said. "You should have said something. You shouldn't have been sneaking around, following me."

"We actually divided our time between the two of you," Jacob said to her. "At first our mission was to investigate you, to find out everything we could about you and report back to our boss. He saw you on television and wanted to know if your claims were credible. We interviewed some of your neighbors. We know about your father, about how you learned the craft of weaving from your mother, and also about your mother's death from breast cancer.

After you were assaulted in the library, our mission was to protect you. It wasn't an easy task. I regret we couldn't always do it, but you should know there were two other occasions, not including this last one, that we were able to help. One attempt on Dr. Brenner's life was thwarted, and one on yours, Amari. He came up behind you on his motorcycle one night, but he broke his pursuit when he saw us following. We tried to catch him but lost him in the desert. Our car was no match for his bike. Something similar happened with Dr. Brenner in the parking lot of his apartment."

"Why didn't you say something?" she asked. "You could have told my dad and you could work together."

"Like I said, our boss ordered us not to. He wanted us to investigate your activities and protect you if we felt you were in danger. Nothing more."

"So who is your boss?" she asked.

"We'll discuss that later. Right now, you have a meeting with the cardinal. He leaves the country soon, so we must hurry."

"Dang it!" Kevin said. "I left my briefcase in your car."

"I'll get your briefcase, Dr. Brenner. You go inside and I will meet you there."

"You saved the Shroud, Jacob," she said. "He was going to destroy it."

"I doubt that," Jacob said. "The Shroud is in a thick vault underneath the church. He wouldn't have gotten close."

"Then why would he even try?"

"Because he's insane," Kevin answered. "*Was* insane anyway."

Chapter 47

Amari used the church office phone to call her dad and ensured him she was fine. She couldn't talk long, though, because the cardinal was waiting. She learned that her dad had called to warn the local police. Unfortunately, because the room was registered under Jacob's name, the police had no way to locate them.

Later that morning, Amari, Kevin, Cardinal Ragazzi, Professor Luigi Messina, and Father Como sat in front of crumb littered breakfast plates. The last few drops of coffee in fine china mugs and juice in crystal glasses sat on a table inside an ornate ballroom. Cardinal Ragazzi wore an ankle-length cassock with red buttons down the front. A red sash wrapped his stomach, and he wore a matching red cap over his silver hair. A gold cross hung from a chain around his neck. He sat nodding with interest as Amari and Kevin made their individual cases, flipping through papers and showing pictures. It was slow going because, even though Cardinal Ragazzi and Professor Messina spoke a little English, Father Como had to translate, especially when it came to Kevin's technical jargon.

When Kevin had wrapped up his presentation, the cardinal asked that Amari and Kevin wait in the hall while he spoke with his science advisor. Jacob waited for them in the hallway, the cut on his head now cleaned and bandaged.

A few minutes later, Professor Messina came out. He took Kevin's hand and cupped it within his own as he shook, and then he moved to Amari and shook her hand. "Thanks a so much. I, uh, very impressed. Now, I have class to teach. Arrivederci," he said and walked down the hall.

Father Como came out next and asked them to come back inside. Jacob waited for them in the hallway. When she and Kevin sat, Cardinal Ragazzi smiled pleasantly and nodded as Father Como did all the talking.

"First of all," Father Como said, "Cardinal Ragazzi would like to thank you for your hard work and remarkable dedication to the truth concerning the Shroud. He heard about what happened outside and has been made aware of the attempts against your life as a way of preventing you from delivering this information. He appreciates your bravery and will most certainly keep both of you in his prayers. As for your research, he and Professor Messina are most intrigued. However, he does not have the authority to allow access to the Shroud. The permission must come from Pope John Paul. And unfortunately, protocols for getting approval to study the Shroud are long and tedious. There is no guarantee a further sampling of the Shroud will be allowed. However, Dr. Brenner, Cardinal Ragazzi wants you to continue developing your tests. Once you have perfected your techniques, then perhaps the Vatican will allow another sampling."

"So what you're saying is maybe," Amari said.

"Yes, maybe. Maybe in a few months, maybe a few years, but I think eventually more study will be allowed. In the meantime, all your research will be forwarded to the Vatican. You have done an outstanding job," Father Como said. "You should be very proud."

"Okay, well, thanks," Kevin said and stood. "That French crepe was awesome."

"Before you go, there's one more thing the cardinal would like to add. Something that might give you solace, perhaps a way to view things differently as you wait for Papal approval."

"We're all ears," Kevin said and sat back down.

"Cardinal Ragazzi wants you to realize that God desires people to have free will. If absolute proof was offered, then people would worship and obey out of fear, which is no worship at all. It would make them slaves to that fear. God wants people to come to him out of love, not fear. If someone chooses by his own will to reject God, he must be given that option. This person will believe the carbon date. But if someone chooses to believe, most of the evidence supports that belief."

"More than ninety-nine percent of the evidence says the Shroud came from Jesus," Kevin said.

"And for those who wish to deny that evidence, they may cling to the carbon date. 'Seek and you shall find, knock and the door shall be opened.' Cardinal Ragazzi encourages you to publish your findings. Publicize them. Make them known to the world. That way, when people do seek, you can make it easier for them to find. And, of course, we will also, with your permission, make your findings public knowledge."

Amari and Kevin looked at each other and nodded. "You have our permission," she said. "Just, would you mind keeping our names out of this? Just in case there's someone else that might, you know, want to kill us over it."

"I think we can do that. Our public records will state the research, without revealing your names."

"Thank you," she said. "That would be great."

The cardinal rose and offered his blessings, then disappeared behind a gold painted door. Father Como escorted her and Kevin back to the hall where they found Jacob waiting.

"So how did it go?" Jacob asked.

"It went well," she said. "I'd say we achieved our goals, wouldn't you, Kevin?"

"Absolutely. Now I just gotta get down to work and develop more tests so the Pope will have more to go on. It might take years, but this is the first step. Next, I gotta find the money."

"You never know what might happen," Jacob said. "Follow me. My boss wants to meet you."

He led them down a long hall with a high molded ceiling. Antique oil paintings lined the walls of the hall. Jacob spoke as they meandered their way toward a staircase. "If it seems like I have the run of this place, it's because my boss is friends with Cardinal Ragazzi. He gives the church millions every year. That kind of charity buys a lot of loyalty."

"Your boss is a rich dude," Kevin said.

"Rich not only in money but in spirit. His name is Ernesto Galliano. His parents are from Italy, from the region of Perugia, north of Rome. When they immigrated to the United States after World War II, Ernesto's father started a car part manufacturing plant in Fresno. He supplied parts for GM, Chrysler, and Ford. The company grew and opened several factories across the United States and Mexico."

"Amari's car might need a few parts," Kevin said.

"Funny," she said.

Jacob grinned and continued his talk. "As I was saying, they had Ernesto in 1952, but it was a complicated pregnancy, and they couldn't give birth again. Ernesto is an only child. Ernesto was drawn to God at an early age and wanted badly to be a priest. His mother encouraged his desire, but his father wouldn't have it. Instead, he groomed Ernesto to manage his business. In 1970, Ernesto went off to Berkeley and, unfortunately, his parents divorced. His mother moved to a mountain estate in Chivasso, just east of Turin. Ernesto remains very close to his mother and often stays with her in her estate. He divides his time between here and Fresno."

"So you follow him out here?" she asked.

"Yes, we are part of his private security." They reached a flight of stairs. "This way. Ernesto was praying in the cathedral, but he should be finished now."

As they descended the stairs, Jacob finished his story. "In 1974, Ernesto's father died and left a billion-dollar company to his 22-year old son. However, Ernesto sold the company and dedicated himself to serving God. He works closely with Catholic Charities. He founded the Rossi Foundation—his mother's maiden name—and he turned his father's estate in California into an orphanage for abused children."

"Wow," she said. "What an inspiring story. But what does that have to do with us?"

"His fascination with the Shroud that lies beneath this church. When he became aware of The Shroud of Turin Research Project, he was captivated by the possibility that the Shroud was the true burial cloth of Christ. When the carbon date came out, he was very skeptical because every other shred of evidence suggested the Shroud was genuine."

When they reached the foot of the stairs, Amari noticed Professor Messina speaking to another man. They said their goodbyes and the professor proceeded down the hall, toward the exit.

Jacob walked over to the man the professor was speaking with. He was young, mid-thirties maybe. He had black, wavy hair and a beard that looked like it could have belonged to Jesus. He even had scars on his forehead that looked like they could have come from a crown of thorns. He wore no jewelry and even his simple wardrobe, a beige tunic-like shirt and blue jeans, seemed to be something Jesus would wear if he came to minister in 1989.

"Amari, Dr. Brenner, I want you to meet my boss. This is Ernesto Galliano."

Ernesto bowed his head respectfully. "I'm so glad to finally meet you. I apologize for not coming forward sooner, but if your attacker saw you associating with my men, then he may have targeted them first, and then come after you. They are like brothers to me, so I couldn't put them in that sort of danger. It was better that they hid in the shadows. That way, they would have the element of surprise and perhaps stop this monster." Ernesto gripped Jacob by the ball of his shoulder. "Which they did, I understand."

"Where's Mitch?" Amari asked.

"They're just checking him out at the hospital," Jacob said. "I think the bullet may have cracked a rib. The first two times he was shot, he wasn't wearing a vest. This is nothing for him."

"Why don't you stay at my mother's estate tonight?" Ernesto asked. "She owns a mountain top palace. You can see for miles. Mitch and Jacob will be there. We can get to know each other better. Stay with us tonight, and I will personally fly the two of you back home tomorrow in my private jet. No layovers. First class all the way."

"You got your own plane?" Kevin asked. "Man, you must be loaded."

"Yes, my father left me a fortune. But I don't enjoy flaunting my wealth. It's a badge of shame rather than honor. When I was younger, I wanted to be a priest, to live in poverty. But I realized that if I used my wealth properly, I could affect far more positive change in the world. And that's why I would like to make a proposal, for the both of you. Full-time jobs, if you accept. To affect positive change in the world."

"Hey, I'm unemployed," Kevin said. "I'm listening."

"Professor Messina told me about your theories. He was very impressed. But you need money to develop your tests, don't you? Work for me and I'll fund everything. Anything you need, you let me know. You develop the tests to prove the Shroud came from Jesus, and I will pull strings to get Vatican approval for the retest."

"You can do that?" Amari asked.

"Maybe. I can't say for sure, but until we have the science to back up our request, we don't stand a chance. They won't let us sample the Shroud again until the technology is perfected, and Dr. Brenner is the perfect man to do it. So what do you say? Are you in?"

"I can't believe this is happening," Kevin said. "It's like a dream."

"So is that a yes?"

"Heck, yeah, I'm in."

"Excellent. Now for you, Amari. Have you ever watched the television show, *The Equalizer*?"

"Sometimes."

"Jacob and Mitch—that is sort of what they do. We look for people who need help and then help them in Jesus' name. I would like to expand my operation and hire two more people, possibly more. Why don't you and your father come to work for me? I could use your detective skills. Jacob and Mitch can help with the muscle."

"You mean just quit everything and go work for you? And my dad too?"

"And Dr. Brenner too, if he's looking for a little adventure. You don't want to be stuck in a lab all the time, do you, Dr. Brenner?"

"Where Amari goes, I go," Kevin said.

"Good," Ernesto said. "I wouldn't want to break up such an amazing team. Amari, finish your degree first, then both of you come work for me."

Amari sat on a bench in the hallway as Ernesto's proposal settled in her mind. She had seen how sometimes the future could hinge on one moment, like the moment when Jenny mentioned the Shroud of Turin. She glanced up at Ernesto's eager eyes and knew she should consider his offer. It was like God had answered two prayers at once. She would work as a detective and help people in the name of Jesus at the same time. It seemed to be a no-brainer, but she wasn't sure she was up to the task.

"So what do you say?" Ernesto asked.

"I don't know if I'm qualified."

"Then your father will be your mentor."

"How do you know he'll take the job?"

"When he sees my salary offer, I think he'll accept, especially if it means he can better protect you."

"You're right. He would do anything to keep me safe."

"So is that a yes? If things don't work out, you can always go back to police work."

"I don't know. I need to think about it—and *pray* about it."

"You know God would want this. He didn't bring us together by accident. You know your mother would want this too."

Amari's mind flashed back to the last words her mother spoke to her. *When the time is right, you will know, Shiyazhi. Trust in God,* her mother had told her. *He will show you his purpose.* Was this the fulfillment of her mother's dying prophecy? Was this what God wanted her to do? It sure felt right. She could only imagine what adventures lay ahead. She would travel the world. She'd be a missionary like her brother, only using her own unique gifts. Yes, her mother would want that. A flood of emotion welled within her, a strong sense of joy and purpose. Yes, a very full and rewarding life awaited her.

She stood and locked eyes with Ernesto. "Yes, I'll take the job."

And someday in heaven, she would tell her mother all about it.

The End

If you enjoyed this novel and think other people would benefit from reading it, please leave a review. You can easily search for it on Amazon.com and leave the review there.

To see some "behind the scenes" information, go to www.rawilliams.us

Please contact me through my website if you have any questions, comments, or suggestions. I'd love to hear from you!

Look for volume 2 of the Amari Johnston series in 2018!

Carbon-14: The Shroud of Turin

Made in the USA
Lexington, KY
09 May 2019